GEARS OF FATE

FORGOTTEN GODS BOOK 1

WILBERT STANTON

Immortal Works LLC
1505 Glenrose Drive
Salt Lake City, Utah 84104
Tel: (385) 202-0116
www.immortal-works.com

© 2017-2020 **Wilbert Stanton**

http://www.wilbertstanton.com/

AISN B08M3Q9STW (Kindle Edition)
ISBN 978-1-953491-07-7 (paperback)

PROLOGUE

Chaos filled the halls of Olympus. Bad enough he had to entertain such undignified company as the one-eyed Norse God, but Zeus couldn't stand listening to everyone squabble. As king of the Olympian Gods, he'd fought countless wars. It would seem he'd been fighting from the moment his mother, Rhea, spat him out. Chronos, king of the Titan Gods, his father, would have killed him at birth had his mother not been clever enough to save him. After spending his life in hiding, preparing, and learning all Rhea had to teach, Zeus conquered his father's kingdom, destroyed Chronos and his army, and banished those who survived to Tartarus where they would rot for eternity. Except Atlas—he suffered a special kind of punishment. Zeus' cleverness when it came to concocting punishments always made him smile.

Zeus sat upon his ivory throne, towering over all the other Olympians and his visiting Norse cousin. He couldn't even tell who argued with whom anymore. Nor did he care. The boredom of it all was enough to put him to sleep. His eyes sparkled with wildfire, a penetrating gaze that took on the visitor with contempt.

His Aegis sat ready for war at his side. The Titan lords forged the shield in lightning and hellfire, creating a thing of immense beauty, and bestowed it with the secrets of godhood. He may have been able to wield lightning with the flick of his wrist, but the Aegis held his true power and remained a mystery to all. Yet there he sat, listening to his great halls echo with the voices of uncertainty.

Odin begged an alliance. *What a ridiculous idea.* How could Odin expect Zeus and his royal blood to cower in fear over some unknown enemy? Zeus feared no man or beast, and Odin wanting help to fend off this invading army only proved him too weak a god to be called cousin. To make matters worse, the other Olympians were starting to believe Odin's nonsense.

This, Zeus could not allow.

He focused on his son, the sensible one.

"Father, we should hear him out," Apollo said. His golden armor gleamed with magic light. Apollo the great general, smart and cunning, with his twin sister Artemis at his side, could face any danger. So why would Apollo choose to humor Odin? "We know nothing of this Fey threat. Perhaps it would be wise to at least take heed of his warning."

Hera sighed and crossed her arms. While Zeus may have feared no man or beast, Hera was a different matter. His wife was beautiful in all regards, but she had the temper and jealously to match even his pride. "Really, child? These barbarians walk into Olympus spouting tales of fancy, and you shiver in your boots. How is it you lead our armies and not Ares?"

"I've been asking you that for an eternity now!" Ares slammed his mighty fist on the table before him, knocking over a goblet of ambrosia. "Honestly, I can rarely tell which one is the bigger girl, him or his sister—"

The petite Artemis would have jumped over the table had Apollo not held her back. "How about I rip your eyes out, since they seem to be of no use to you?"

Ares waved her off with a laugh. "As I was saying. I could handle this threat on my own."

Odin rubbed his calloused hand over his one good eye. He seemed old and dusty, a wanderer who had travelled the world looking for something he could not find, his hair graying like the fading life of an abandoned cobweb. Unlike Zeus whose old features made him look strong and dignified, he looked worn and weary. "Zeus, you sit there in silence while your children bicker. Can you not look me in the eyes?"

Ares snorted with laughter.

Odin cleared his throat and continued. "Can you not tell me why you refuse an alliance? More so why you refuse to take this seriously?"

Zeus could barely look at the gathering without shaking his head "When you've lived as long as I have, when you've fought as many wars, loved, and hated as I, you will understand. I do not fear death because death knows its place where I'm concerned. These invaders you speak of have yet to witness the might of Zeus, and I will not be introduced as someone who cannot stand on his own. Let this threat come, let them fall before me and beg to kiss my feet."

"A grave mistake and foolish," Odin whispered.

Before Zeus could rage over his cousin's insult, a shift in the air stayed his temper. A rush of wind, a blur of motion, warned him of his messenger's approach. Hermes almost seemed to flicker into existence. He knelt with his head held low. The boy always showed the proper respect in front of an audience, usually to mask something of a mischievous nature.

"Grandfather, you have a visitor." Hermes looked upon the king with fear-filled eyes. "I would not turn her away."

"Can't you see I'm at council?" Zeus clenched his fists and seethed. The clouds darkened behind him and lightning ripped across the sky.

Hermes disappeared only to reappear halfway across the court a safe distance away from Zeus. "I understand that grandfather... however, when I said I would not turn her away, I meant... I feared turning her away. Her eyes nearly froze my heart with fear. There is something not right about this woman; she is not quite man nor god."

"Odin, I swear your foolish wives' tales have turned all my Olympians into cowards!"

Concern crossed Odin's face. He looked hard unto Hermes. "Her name, boy!"

"Something strange, perhaps—"

The courtroom doors burst open. A cold wind followed, and a sense of dread permeated the air. A woman came forward, walking with a confidence that bordered between pride and insanity. Her long sinewy arms firmly crossed before a frail body cloaked in leather, leaves, and feathers. Her pale face bore cracks like a centuries-old porcelain doll, upon which sat a cancerous smile that dripped with venom. She came into the court alone and yet had the presence of someone with an army at her side.

"So this is where the children of mighty Chronos hide as my army even now takes back the land." She tapped a long spider like finger at her chin. "Packaged up all nice in one place. If I weren't of a mind for war, I could end this all right now."

Zeus leaned forward, curiosity sparking in his bored eyes. "Who are you to barge into my court?"

She slowly licked her lips, delighted in the desire she saw in his eyes. "I am Queen Mob."

"I know of no Queen Mob, and for what nation do you rule?"

She looked around at the others with a mild curiosity. Almost as if a second thought, she muttered, "Earth."

Zeus laughed wholeheartedly. "You claim rule of Earth?"

With a casual grace, Queen Mob picked up a goblet from the table and drank deeply. The Gods watched dumbfounded, shocked by the creature's brazen nature. "I do."

To Odin, Zeus said, "This is the Fey threat you spoke of?"

Odin inched away from the presence of Queen Mob. "Aye."

"Well then." Zeus stood and stretched his arms. "You hold no claim here, witch. It was a grave miscalculation on your part coming here. I shall end this—"

"The Earth has grown tired of the rule of man. The blood of Atlas runs deep through her veins. His blood has given her enlightenment. The blood you call ambrosia and drink with no regard to its power. Did you know she is alive? This land you so callously abuse. She begs for a savior, someone to set right the wrongs of men and gods."

"What dare you speak of Atlas, the Titan I banished into the depths of Earth for his betrayal?"

"Where he bled and awoke the planet."

"Nonsense."

"What affronts me is how both you and mankind abuse and mistreat her. She gave you life and cared for you as a mother should, even when she is rewarded with nothing but abuse. You gods and man take from her with no thought of her well-being. You are a cancer upon this land that if left unchecked will eventually bring about her last breath. The Fey were born in her aid. We will cure her of this disease, and she will flourish once more."

Zeus sat back on his throne. "Apollo, dispatch this menace."

Apollo stood; he, unlike his father, cautiously sized up Queen Mob. He drew a glimmering gold blade and approached. "We have no quarrel with your kind. Know that you brought this upon yourself."

Even as he stepped forward, Mob couldn't be bothered to pay him any attention. Instead, she looked around the court, inspecting every inch. "This castle may be fit for Oberon, but I have no desire to reside in something so… bright." She passingly waved a hand at Apollo and he fell to his knees. His sword clattered to the ground next to him. His eye bulged and his golden skin turned red.

Artemis didn't miss a beat, her bow and arrow drawn and trained on Mob. "What are you doing to my brother?"

"Oh, you might have made a perfect mate for Puck. But it wouldn't do letting anyone think they can draw a weapon on me, now would it?" Mob waved another hand and Artemis' head turned violently with a crack and her body crashed out the window as if an invisible hand swatted her away. Apollo fell flat on the ground. His last breath escaped his perfect lips in a whimper.

To Zeus, Mob said, "I hope to see you on the fields of battle? I could finish it here. But the Earth deserves to be bathed in the blood of man and god."

Mob disappeared in a flash of smoke and leaves. Zeus breathed heavy with anger while the others screamed and argued.

For the first time he could recall, Zeus felt fear.

1

Midday at the docks, a crowd of boys fought to catch the Job Master's eye. I pushed through the press of bodies with ease. Once they saw my face, they backed off. They knew my name and if they didn't, they knew my faded crew cut, tanned skin, and rank ink tattooed on my neck. Most importantly, they all knew they would be going home with empty pockets.

I heard the Job Master's shout even before I got to the front. "All right, we had one work assignment, only one, and it's been filled."

My lip curled at the sight of him, his fancy dress boasted of finery. He probably never worked a hard day of labor in his life.

"Come back tomorrow and we'll see if we need any of you then," he said.

Mason stood next to him, chest puffed out full of pride. He's the biggest Fringe Rat you'd ever meet. Oil stained clothes and greased up hands from the many jobs he juggled made him look rough. He wore the second best rank tats to mine behind his ear with pride. He caught my scrutinizing gaze and gave me an arrogant smile. I didn't like it; I wanted to wipe it off his face.

"Sure," I yelled. "If you want to waste stacks!"

Mason rolled his eyes and made a show of laughter, no doubt trying to keep the Job Master's attention on him.

"Mason's work is rust at best!" I continued. All the boys quieted down. "So yeah, you got the right guy for the job, if you prefer to pay double the going price and then have to call him back in a couple of months to fix all the patches he left leaking this time around."

"Hop off, Zak!" Mason waved a dismissive hand in my direction. The Job Master looked back and forth between the two of us.

"What? Everyone knows you fix the job so you get a guaranteed comeback. I think it's rust the way you take advantage of the Job Master's generous nature."

"Explain, kid." The Job Master sounded bored.

"It's the oldest scam. You come here offering fifty stacks for a fixer up. His rank tats will impress the big boys with all the cash, so he'll ask for double. Why not? He got plenty skill, no lie. He'll fix you up good. But he'll make sure to set some things off, so you'll be calling him back for a follow up. Double up on the original and now you're out two hundred stacks. Me though, if you know anything, you'll know my name, I got rank. I'll get you all patched up in no time."

"Walker isn't it?" The Job Master asked. "Your John's boy?"

"Yeah. I learned it all from him, and now my work puts his to shame."

The Job Master laughed. "That's not such a hard task, now is it? Rumor has it, your mom came back from a yearlong scavenge pregnant. He took to the bottle after that. Pretty sure he was put to shame a long time ago, kid."

My jagged nails bit into my palms; my blood boiled, and I wanted to lunge. But I'm smart enough to know my place. "Yeah he's a sad sack now, don't mean nothing on his skills, and my skills are just as good—if not better."

He smiled with knowing in his eyes. "Walker's kid, huh? It wouldn't be bad having you on the pipe. What are you, sixteen?"

"Yes, sir and I'm the best here. They'll all attest to that." I spread my arms wide, while the murmurs of agreement rose around me. "So, what do you say? You want the best or you want a hack?"

The muscle alongside Mason's jaw flexed. He didn't bother to wait for the Job Master to say the word; he jumped off the stage and got in my face. "You're a piece of rust!"

Mason's a big guy and truth be told, he put me in the Doc's office one too many times for running my mouth. Regardless, I didn't back down; Zak Walker never backs down. I took a deep breath and let my chest swell. Looking up into his unwavering blue eyes, I waited for the slightest flinch that would warn me of a punch.

"Ease off Mason, you wouldn't want your pride hurt twice in one day." I was always a fan of bluffs.

"I should edge you."

"You could try."

He stared me down for another moment before shoving me aside. He pushed his way past the crowd of boys, off to nurse his shattered dignity.

"Well that was an interesting display of bravado. Come up here, Walker. Let me get a good look at you." The Job Master reached out a hand. I ignored the gesture and jumped up onto the stage. He looked me up and down. "Yeah, I can see it. You got the same shifty eyes as your dad. He was always thinking of a way out, trying to outsmart people he had no business trying to outsmart. You aren't going to give us trouble like that are you?"

"No, sir. I got skill and I earn what I'm worth, that's all there is."

He nodded. "Okay, that's good to hear. The going rate for this job is fifty stacks."

"Except seeing as how I got skill, I'm going to charge double. A hundred sounds about right—Come to think of it, two hundred."

"Two hundred! Why the hell would we pay you two hundred?"

"Because I'll get the job done, there's no going back to Mason now that his pride's hurt. To be honest, I'll probably need the extra to cover my hospital bills after he roughs me up a bit for stepping in on his piece."

"That's absurd! I could just take any one of these other Fringe Rats." He pointed out into the crowd, but they all looked down and started walking away. Rats got pride, but they also got loyalty. "Where are you all going? Don't you want work?"

"The job's mine, they won't turn on me. It's two hundred or none."

He looked over the crowd one last time, trying to find someone that would never step up. "Fine… one fifty."

He gave in way too easy. I didn't expect anything over a hundred. I wasn't going to push my luck. "That's a generous offer."

———

THE JOB MASTER strapped a heavy pack across my back, but I loved it. Something about the tense anticipation got my blood going and made it the best part of the job. It looked like an old model, with frayed straps and the iron plating rusted, but that didn't matter. It was an old build, but a dependable one. I tested the thrusters and a spurt of ambrosia-filled steam shot out, lifting me off my feet for a couple of seconds, strong enough. I buttoned my jacket to the top, slipped on my gloves, and put on my goggles. I looked over the dock edge, an ocean of puffy clouds drifted far below. I caught glimpses of the Earth, specks of blue, green, and brown. Like a painting in a museum: meant to be looked at, but as much as I wanted, I couldn't touch it.

"Don't get any ideas." The Job Master jabbed his finger into my chest. "You know what happens if you try and fly off with our gear?"

"Fuel runs out, I go splat…" I clapped my hands in front of his face for effect.

"My boss said to tell you, if you finish in under an hour, we'll add an extra twenty."

I raised an eyebrow in his direction. "Whoa, not like the boss man to go throwing around money."

"It's like you said. You come with high ranks and he wants this all done quickly."

"Sure, two hundred stacks. I can do that."

"What? We agreed on—"

I ran to the edge of the dock and jumped. The weightless sensation always made me feel free. With my arms spread, I let the sky take me in its comforting embrace. For those couple of moments, I didn't think of myself as a Fringe Rat who begged for rust jobs or lived on the outskirts of a rich city. I felt free as a bird, and the possibilities seemed endless. And like always, I thought about not turning the thrusters on. I could just fall and let the bomb or the elements have me. I would never have pushed the ignition switch if it weren't for Alice.

My little sister depended on me coming home at the end of every day. I hit the button and the thrusters burst to life, slamming me upward with a jolt. I'd fallen far below the depths of Olympus. I soared back up toward my home, and the vast underbelly of the city. Networks of piping, engines, steam, and propellers worked in synchronicity to keep the city afloat. A complex machine of Hephaestus' creation. I saw only beauty and magic.

I let my thrusters carry me into the web of mechanics. It took my eyes a moment to adjust and find the leak of ambrosia spraying into the ether. Minor fixes like this could become devastating if left unattended, due to the volatile nature of ambrosia. I never really knew how it all worked; they kept us in the dark about things like that. Knowing the steam that kept us afloat depended on the ambrosia was all that mattered. Most importantly, I knew the rich mechs and tinkers couldn't be put at risk coming down here, while I could easily be replaced at a moment's notice. The closer I pulled in to the piping system, I realized how serious of a fixer it was going to be. Luckily, there was no smoke, which would've been a clear warning of overheating. I didn't have to worry about burning my skin.

I flew over to the leaking pipe, hooked my line on, and cut off the pack's engine. I hung upside down; blood rushed to my head. It could take a bit to get used to the orientation, but I loved it. From my tool belt, I took out a sheet of flexible copper plating, the material we used to seal leaks. It didn't seem like much but it always did the trick. While I worked at covering up the hole, I had to focus on ignoring the warm, melty sensation going on in my head, a side effect of exposure to ambrosia fumes. I'd once seen a Fringe Rat let the ambrosia take over his head; he felt godlike and unstrapped himself, fully expecting to fly to the heavens. He bought himself a one-way ticket to Hades instead. The stuff didn't mess with me too bad, one of the reasons I outranked so many. I always kept a clear head and my thoughts focused on my task no matter how cogged it got.

I sprayed the edges of the copper plating with my adhesive gun and finished the job. As a precaution, I checked around for other potential problems, things that needed tightening, and holes that needed patching. It was an easy job, a simple fix here and there, nothing too rough.

If you asked me, we needed a complete overhaul badly. These rush jobs wouldn't cut it much longer, but no one ever talked about that. The Job Masters and Money Men didn't give a rust about the underbelly of the outer city, the Fringe. They spent all their resources on making sure the underbelly of the inner city, Empyrean, stayed up to code. If things ever got worse, they could just jettison the Fringe, and Empyrean would be safe and sound. I turned my thrusters back on, unhooked my line, and flew over to one of the hatches leading into Empyrean space. I wanted to bug up some of their gears for a call-back. In the end, it wouldn't matter. Empyrean had their own tinkers who came down to take care of their gears. Instead, I took a wrench to one of the nearby pipelines and knocked it around a couple of times until the nut loosened enough to come undone in a couple of days.

By the time I got back topside, the pack's fuel gauge read critical. Those cog brains didn't even give me a full pack. If I hadn't spidered around most of the job, I would've been taking a dive down to Earth. I found the Job Master leaning his chair back against the side of the guardhouse, dozing off like he had nothing better to do. I kicked the chair leg out from under him and watched with pleasure as he crumbled to the ground.

He shot up to his feet in a flurry. "What the Hades!"

"Just got here," I said. "Looks like you were leaning too far back."

"Never mind!" He straightened out his long ruffled sleeves. "Is the job done? I should be getting home for dinner."

"Yeah it's all brass. You guys should really think about refitting, though. It's really starting to look like rust down there."

"How about you let the Money Men worry about things out of your league, and you worry about getting repairs done in a timely manner."

I nodded, biting my tongue so hard I thought it would sever.

"Right, then. So good job. I'll be heading on home. You should too." He practically ripped the gear from my back and packed it away along with his other materials. Once he finished packing, he handed me the coveted envelope filled with stacks. "Count it if you want, but I'm not sticking around The Fringe any longer than I have to."

"It's brass. Take it easy." I hoped he'd take a long walk off the edge.

The stars came up bright; that's the one thing I appreciated about Olympus, being so close to the stars, I felt like I could touch them. I strolled down the Fringe, staring up at them, trying my best to lose myself in their light. Getting shoved caught me off guard. I stumbled back and fought to keep my balance. Mason stood there grinning like an idiot.

"What the Hades," I said. "No need to be rough."

"I could have been even rougher back there, you know? You're lucky I didn't knock your teeth out." He cracked his knuckles in an obnoxious manner. "I really thought about it."

I took out the stacks, counted out seventy-five, and tossed him his cut. "Why would you do that?"

He caught the wad. "I figured if I knocked your teeth out, the Job Master would be more sympathetic to your bargain."

"Hmm, not a bad idea. Maybe next time." We touched knuckles and started walking together.

"Where you headed, Walker?"

"Home… I guess."

"She'll be fine. Come to the Crow's Nest. Your dad's been at it with Gunnar all day. I have a feeling they'll be hatching it out in a drinking contest."

I had to take a deep slow breath. "How long's he been there?"

"Since the afternoon."

"Which means Alice has been alone all day. Sorry mate, I got to check on her. You know how she gets with her imagination."

He patted me on the back. "She still having those fits?"

"Yeah, screamed her head off most of last night. She thought there were creatures crawling around her room. I checked under the bed and everything, even had to sleep with her. But she wouldn't let up. I really have to check on her."

"Worry none. I'll catch you tomorrow? I got another thing planned for the Money Men."

"Brass."

Mason and I turned down the corner and headed for the bar. The music and laughter begged me to come join in, but my mood was already rust. I wanted to get home to my sister and get some rest. Exposure to ambrosia also left you feeling tired, depressed, and restless. Like a side effect of coming off a drug. Most of my night would be spent tossing and turning, while my brain tried to hold afloat in a sea of depressing thoughts. I looked at the wad of stacks in my hand. All for a measly seventy-five. At least Alice would be eating for the rest of the week.

Mason went inside, and I continued home.

2

I would have to get a handle on my mood before I walked in the
door. I couldn't let Alice see me this way. She needed me to be her
rock. I'd had to be the strong one for as long as I could remember.
This was where my life began and would probably end: a depressing
cabin at the edge of the Fringe where I had to grow up way before my
time.

The broken cabin was a sad dwelling made up of scavenged wood
and rusted nails. A garden of overgrown weeds and grass conquered a
dirt road. We had two bedrooms, a living room, and a kitchen. A
graying picket fence guarded the front, only the front, because the
cabin perched right at edge of the outer ring of Olympus, our home at
the end of the world.

We called it the Fringe, where the poor lived, a shanty town made
up of hastily thrown together homes, shops, and bars. Our cabin,
however, sat far apart from even them, as if we weren't even good
enough for the downtrodden. Clouds and birds as far as the eye could
see. On those clear days or nights, if you had the cogs to peek out over
the edge, you'd find the Earth waiting far below. I approached the
cabin, sat on the rotting steps, and gathered myself, still bombarded

by the memories of the past. They flipped from heartbreak to heartbreak.

———

On a rainy Tuesday morning, I sat on the porch watching the airships drift by the horizon. Airmen ran about their daily chores, swabbing decks and rolling heavy cargo back and forth, while others manned the ropes that kept the massive air balloons under control. I knew this was my future. Dad's breath may have always stunk of whiskey, but he pulled some strings and got me a spot on the Gibson, an exploration vessel that spent months away at a time.

My heart shattered when he told me.

His hard-callused hands squeezed my shoulders a little too tight, and his lost eyes reflected the hopelessness of a man who'd wasted his life. "You won't get anywhere being a Fringe Rat. They'll take all your best years, suck you dry, and leave you a nobody."

His intentions were good. But, I had no desire to be a deck swabber.

Mom would have never had it, not after spending countless nights reading me stories of the world below, and teaching me the history of Olympus, our great city built on motors, balloons, and steam, forever lost in the sea of clouds. Most of all, she taught this silly idea that even though we lived in The Fringe, I could be something more. That all changed when she walked out and never looked back.

"You're the man of the house now, Zak," she said. "Protect your sister."

I tried not to cry. I told myself it would be selfish. My mother's story couldn't end in this city. No matter how much it broke my heart, our last chapter together would end in goodbyes. I squared my shoulders and smiled. She left me at ten, responsible for a two-year-old sister, a hopeless father, and a life I had no control over. Six years later, I still wondered about her, what sort of life did she lead and did it make her happy? Mostly I wondered when she reached that final chapter, would she remember me.

———

AN UNUSUALLY LOUD thump jolted me back to reality. A strange girl lay some feet away as if she'd fallen from the sky. Old goggles with red and blue colored lenses covered her eyes, framed by skin of the faintest brown; her hair, tousled blonde in one of those pixie cuts, wavered in a light breeze. She had an assortment of mismatched clothes, fingerless gloves, an incredibly long scarf that fluttered behind her, a leather waistcoat, black tights, and unbuckled boots.

Her sudden presence made me catch my breath, my heart pounded in my ears, and time stood still. I ran to her side, wondering what to do. She stared at me, the goggles making her eyes seem enormous, and quite surprised. Words caught in her raspy throat.

I leaned in close enough to feel warm breath against my ear.

The stranger shot up, wrapping her arms around my neck with the strength of a metal vice.

Her lips brushed the skin of my ear. "Save me from the things that move at the corner of sight, the shadows that crawl when there is no light, the baby snatchers that trade in promises and build contracts of lies. The Unseelie—they are about and after me."

"What?" I tried to pull her loose, but she only tightened her grip, cutting off my supply of air. She had to be mental; of course, I'd die at the hands of a cogged girl.

"Do you have any bread?" She released me and sat on the ground cross-legged, a crooked smile on her lips.

Her sudden change in attitude took me aback. "What are you on about? Have you lost it?"

"Bread, we need bread!"

"I think we have, but what for?"

"Please, it's my only hope. She collapsed once again, her labored breathing became slow and methodic. Almost as if someone else controlled me, I picked her up in my arms, surprised by the lightness of her body. I didn't even break a sweat jogging with her back to the cabin. She weighed no more than a small child. I kicked open the door and swung it shut once inside. As soon as we reached the living room, I laid her on the worn out couch next to a fireplace that burned cold and held too many memories. The cushions couldn't even be bothered to sink under her miniscule weight. She smiled and curled up into a fetal position, mumbling again for some bread.

In the kitchen, greasy tools and bits of a small steam engine I was working on cluttered the dining room table; empty cups and unwashed dishes covered the counter. I nearly tore the door to the ice chest off its hinges. The sound of glass clattered and a whiff of old milk attacked my senses. A moldy loaf of bread waited in the back, behind other things that no one bothered to throw out. I took my prize back to the front room and found her laid out on her side, knees curled up to her chest, hugging them tightly.

"I got the bread; it might not be that fresh, though."

"Make the crumbs as tiny as possible and line the windows and doors with it!" She waved me off like I annoyed her.

As I unwound the package, I couldn't help thinking how foolish it sounded. She had to be pulling my leg for a laugh. I started to walk back to the kitchen, but whirled to my left, facing the door as a strange wind blew it open, howling. A caress of frigid, spectral fingers ran over me in the breeze. The girl curled up into a small ball, while the breeze no doubt draped her body with the same eerie feeling that made my skin crawl.

Outside, the soundless rain fell on our porch. It seemed like the world grew silent, leaving the soft thump in my chest, a slow tap of the drums growing into a marching beat. In one horrifying instant, the rain outlined an invisible shape, a huge hunched-over thing approaching the house. I looked away, rubbing at my eyes. When I looked back, it was gone.

After slamming the door shut, I broke off pieces of bread and placed them at the base of the door and all the windows, two in the front facing the porch and one in the back kitchen. By the time I finished, my little sister, Alice, stood at our bedroom door staring at me in confusion. She rubbed at sleepy eyes, with her trusty stuffed bear hanging limp at her side. She gave me a questioning look that could only be answered with a shrug.

"I did it," I said, leaning over the strange woman. "I did what you said. This better not be a prank."

"Good," she mumbled, sounding half-asleep. "Now give me a day or two to regain my strength. End of story."

Once she fell asleep, no amount of shaking or prodding could wake her up. I removed the goggles from her face and stared at the long lashes that decorated her eyes. I almost couldn't understand the complexity of her beauty. Something about her screamed at me for obedience and complete devotion. My stomach ached from my desire to touch her. I pulled the comforter up from the back of the couch and tucked it over her tiny body in a protective shell. I watched her for a couple of seconds more, only to be broken from my hypnotic gaze by Alice shuffling up next to me. She stared at the girl for a bit, and to my surprise, shoved her bear under the comforter. The girl's arms seemed to instinctively latch onto it, squeezing it tight.

Alice looked at me. I'd grown so used to her silence I could read her facial expressions just as good as any verbal cue. It was an excited, wanting look.

"Leave her be." I rumpled my sister's unkempt hair. She pulled back. "I need you to watch over her while I go get the doctor."

Alice looked around, then back to me. She wanted to know where dad went off to now.

"Where else?" I said. Alice sighed. I laced up my boots. "I promise I'll be right back. And umm… don't move the bread."

———

I SLOSHED through mud and rain as I marched across the Fringe. Pulling my collar up, holding my coat tight, I looked past the makeshift cabins and homes at the looming lights of the Empyrean, the inner city. The rain and fog could barely conceal the glimpses of the vibrant life I would never have. I jumped at the sudden spray of water from a passing motorbike.

"You rust bucket!" I yelled as the bike sped off into the night.

I cleaned myself the best I could while wondering where the girl curled up on my couch came from. Shouldn't sulk about, I had to get back. I ran the maze of streets; the quicker I got to the doctor's, the faster I could return to her side. But why was I so drawn to her?

Luckily, the doctor set up shop in The Fringe, so I didn't have to waste what little I had on a trolley fare.

I ran into the office yelling. "Doc, it's Zak!" The waiting room always looked simple, a couple of chairs spread out evenly around a long wood table with newspaper clippings. Abby must have been in the back, so I banged on the unattended countertop. "Doc! Abby! I need help."

"By the gods, Zak! I'm not deaf you know." She walked in from a back room. The smell of lavender consumed me. Her hair must have been freshly washed. Her short red dress, with a low cut neckline caught me off guard. I'd known Abby since we were kids. It was hard to forget the plain, fair-skinned girl I grew up with. She usually wore her charcoal hair up under a hat, and her furious black eyes always had something to prove. But somewhere between then and now an unexpected change happened. My feelings for her always got in the way of our friendship.

I held back an uncomfortable cough when I realized I'd been staring. She set her hands on her hips and had that knowing look. It must have been annoying for her; all the boys she grew up with who once treated her like a runt now admired her like some sort of goddess, and yet rather than scornful glares, she gave us looks of gentle pride.

"Abby…" I stumbled with words. "I need to see your dad. It's an emergency. Is he here?"

Her expression changed from playful to concerned; she ran out from behind the counter and put her hand on my arm. "Are you okay?"

"Yeah, yeah, I'm fine. It's not for me."

"Oh gods! Is Alice having another fit? She came by earlier. I practically had to drag her back home."

I sighed. "I didn't know that. Thanks. She's fine now. We just… there's this girl, and I think she might be ill."

"A girl? What girl?"

"She just showed up and collapsed. Is your dad here?"

"No, he's out of town—where's she from?"

I shrugged. "Might be from Empyrean. Can you help?"

Abby's face lit up. She had been apprenticing under her dad for some time now. It came easy to her. She prided herself on the wealth of knowledge she acquired while reading all her dad's books and manuals while the rest of us barely learned to tie our shoes. Unfortunately, the men of Olympus, who felt threatened by her smarts and age, always questioned her talents. Most felt her father wasted his time taking her on as an apprentice.

"Of course I can. Just give me a second." She ran into the back room. A great rumble followed shortly after, as if she rearranged the very foundations of our world. She came lumbering out in a black waistcoat, yellow rain slickers, and an unbecoming yellow rain hat. A satchel of medical supplies hung from one arm, an umbrella under the other.

"Let's go," she shouted.

We walked side by side. She insisted I get under her small umbrella no matter how much I protested. Our arms rubbed up against each other with each passing step, sending waves of current through my body. I worried over our friendship. I could never figure out how she saw me. Was I just a silly boy who crawled around The Fringe acting like a big man to her, while I thought she was amazing and completely out of my league? At times, I mourned for the little girl who would hunt bugs with me behind her house. But I would never have traded her for the charming, beautiful, smart young woman she'd become. To put it simply, she made me feel like an idiot. I never wanted our friendship to change, but I felt like *I* had to change in order to keep up with her.

"So, looks like it's raining hard…" Sometimes I wondered why I never kept my mouth shut.

She giggled. "You don't say? I hadn't noticed."

"Yeah, clearly."

"How come you didn't come by yesterday? I had a great lesson planned out. Something that *you* would have even enjoyed."

"Sorry, Dad was having one of his episodes. Didn't want to leave Alice taking care of him on her own."

"Sorry, I know it has to be rough." She took my hand in hers. "I mean, that sounds so superficial. Clearly, I can't know how it is. But I care—we care, my dad and I. That's why we have you and Alice over as much as we can. That's why I think it's important you keep up with your studies."

"It's just… Sometimes I feel like you're wasting your time. My dad already signed me for ship duty…"

"And you hate the thought of it! My dad already said he would talk to one of his colleagues about getting you into school with me. You just have to do your part."

"Yeah, because those Empyreans would be so accepting of a Fringe Rat." My hand started to sweat in hers. I wanted to pull away, but at the same time, I loved the soft velvety feeling of her fingers intertwined with mine.

"Hey, I grew up out here just like you did, and they accept me."

"Yeah, but you're smart… and beautiful."

She smiled and looked away, her cheeks heating up with a soft shade of red.

I wanted to change the subject but found no words, my brain too preoccupied. So instead, I jumped into a puddle, splashing us both… because that's what mature men do.

"Hey!" she shouted.

It only encouraged me on, and I jumped harder into another puddle.

"I'm going to kill you!" She grabbed at my arm, but I backed away just out of reach. She resorted to using her umbrella as a weapon, swiping at the back of my legs. I skipped out of the way and ran off toward home with her chasing close behind. I enjoyed those moments, when we shared the comfortable friendship we used to have without the awkwardness or feelings, just her and I playing about in the rain.

The carriage nearly ran me over when I turned the corner. I was lucky to have skidded to a stop before it hit me. My boots slipped on the wet ground making me stumble backward. Abby swooped in trying to catch me, but my weight only brought her down with me. We stared up as the iron horse-drawn carriage careened out from the cobblestone street.

The two horses looked exactly like the real thing, only made of iron and brass. Steam sprouted from their large nostrils, and their stomachs glowed a dull orange from the fires inside that powered the legs like an engine. I rarely saw anything like it in the Fringe. The ornate carriage they towed had four large wheels that flung a wall of water over us both as it passed. A well-dressed man sat near the window, tinted goggles covered his eyes, and a top hat sat upon his head, his face filled with elaborately decorated facial hair. He leaned his head out.

"Watch where you step!" he said. "And mind that girl, boy. Before I show you what real men do!"

Blood boiling, I shot to my feet, ready to fight. "Get cranked you piece of rust!"

His laughter only heated me more. I stood there glaring as the carriage continued on; I wanted to chase it down badly, and noted it took the road leading to Empyrean. What business did he have in the Fringe?

"He's a jerk," Abby said. "Don't stress it." She attempted to clean the dirt off her coat and straightened out her rain hat.

I helped her to her feet and rested my hands on either side of her shoulders. "Are you okay?"

She rolled her eyes. "Obviously."

Something in the way her eyes glinted caught my attention; it made it so hard to look away. I let my hands fall from her shoulders to her arms, and down to her hands. She smiled. Taking a step closer, she looked up at me. Her mouth parted with a silent smile. I moved forward until our bodies pressed together under her umbrella. The rain tapped at the umbrella's skin in time with the beating of my heart, drumming wildly in my head. I could run cons on the Money Men and hang from the bottom of the city thousands of feet above ground. But one look from Abby and I turned to rust.

"Come on," I said. "We better get back to my place." I turned away and headed down the block, doing my best to catch my breath and steady my nerves.

We ran the rest of the way home. By the time we reached my front door, the rain had let up, and I could feel the dampness of the air begin to warm. I opened the door and let Abby in with a court bow. She giggled and curtsied before stepping in. To our surprise, we found Alice and the girl both sitting crossed legged on the floor before a burning fireplace. Alice had a look of excitement on her face while she listened to the girl's animated story.

"So the beautiful princess," she said, "was being forced by her horrible father to marry Prince Puck of the Unseelie, because he thought it was the only way to unite both the Seelie and Unseelie Courts. Of course, she didn't want to do it. I mean Puck was just horrible!"

Alice nodded, hanging on every word. Why didn't she react that way when I told her stories?

"So she did the only thing she could." The girl went on, waving her hands about. "She threw a fit! A tantrum of epic proportions—at the ceremonial feast no less—where the two courts were to meet and greet, planning out the rest of her life. She threw a fork at Puck and said his suit looked like dandelion vomit."

Alice smirked.

"As punishment, her father stripped her of her wings. Can you believe it! What's a fairy with no wings? A loser that's what! So she locked herself in her room and refused to come out for two fort-nights. They had no idea of her clever plan. Her parents may have thought they had her contained, but she used magic to escape. She conjured a certain spell that could turn any door into a portal, which she used to get outside the Ivory Castle. She'd hunt in the Wild Woods, shop at the Goblin Market, and ride steel-toed unicorns in the Marshes of the Free Fey. Pretty cool, huh?"

Alice gasped in excitement.

I gave my sister an annoyed look, about ready to interrupt, but Abby's quieting hand hushed me.

"Only one night, she came home and found her father waiting. His anger shook the walls! That's when they took away the last bits of her magic. As if her wings weren't enough, magic is to fairies what blood is to men. It's what makes a fairy a fairy. So, she finally had enough and planned her final escape. She feigned defeat and went along with her parents on all their wedding plans. She waited; the patience of a fairy is something to be told. As weeks passed, and her parents' defenses faltered, she made her move. Sneaking away into the Wild Woods, she sought a place to escape. Defenseless without her wings or magic, alone and scared, still she marched on. After endless nights in the forest, she became incredibly lost, hungry, and weak. She collapsed and would never have woken up again if it weren't for the Scavengers who found her!"

Alice clapped, practically ready to jump out of her skin. She loved stories about the Scavengers. The crews of fearless men and women who sailed the clouds and tempted their luck on Earth's surface. Scavenger stories always made her smile.

"The Highwinds," the girl crooned.

Alice nodded with knowing appreciation. She had a special place in her heart for the Highwind Scavengers. Captain Alana Highwind became something of personal hero to her over the years. She collected newspaper clippings and often sat at the docks for hours on end hoping to catch a glimpse of her ship. She even once attempted to dye her hair red like Alana. I'd spent days trying to scrub away the mess she left all over the bathroom.

"Alana Highwind, Gharis O'Brian, Wilhem the Blind, Sticky Fingers McGee, and all the rest. Even without her wings, they recognized the princess for who she was and took her, expecting to collect a hefty ransom. But who could resist her beauty, charm, and infectious sense of humor? They all became friends, and she stayed on as part of the crew for a time. They had all sorts of adventures, too many to tell, but in the end, they brought her to Olympus." The girl looked at Abby and me and gasped in mock surprise. She jumped to her feet and ran over, throwing her hands around my neck and kissing me deeply on the mouth. "Oh Chris, you came back!"

"What? My name isn't—" I had no time to react. Her lips against mine would have been much more exciting if I didn't sense Abby staring hot razors at us. I looked over at her with my best confused face while the girl buried her face in the nape of my neck.

"When I woke, I worried I'd never see you again," she said. "First boy who saved my life."

"Umm, excuse me." Abby stepped forward. "I thought you didn't know who she was?"

"I don't!" I pleaded.

"Of course not, silly." The girl pulled away, kissing me once again.

I didn't close my eyes this time, the red of Abby's face in clear view.

"We only just met, but he saved my life," the girl said.

"I really didn't do anything," I said.

"Oh, ever the modest one." She playfully hit my arm. "What strong muscles you have."

"Okay, how about you tell us your name?" Abby interrupted.

"My name—" The girl stopped and looked at Abby as if noticing her for the first time. "Did you really wear that outside?"

"What?" Abby moaned.

"That ensemble." She pointed an accusing finger at Abby's clothes.

"Well, what?" Abby asked. "It's raining, it's not like I wear this every day."

"I should hope not," the girl said.

"What does this have… well look at what you're wearing!" Abby shouted.

She patted Abby's shoulder. "Now come, come, there is no need to be catty. It's unbecoming."

"What?" Abby's eyes blazed with the fury I remembered seeing in her before her fist ended an argument.

"My name is Seneca." She turned back to me. "And you are James—"

"Zak," I corrected.

"And the cute little one, who takes after her brother's good looks, is Alice. That leaves you." Seneca looked Abby up and down. "Who are you?"

"Abby, but this isn't about me this is—"

"Pleased to meet you." Seneca held out her hand, and with a defeated sigh, Abby cautiously shook it. "Now, was there really need for all that sass?"

———

THE FOUR OF us sat around the kitchen table, struggling with great patience as we tried to get a straight answer out of Seneca. In the half hour we spoke to her, we managed to find out someone chased her. She had gone days without sleeping or eating, stuck in a constant game of cat and mouse. The last of her flight found her at my doorstep, where she felt comforted in my protection and let the exhaustion take over. She must have been starving, but she didn't ask for anything. I gave her some warm tea and used the last of the bread, the parts free of mold, to make sandwiches.

"So what was the deal with the bread crumbs?" I asked.

"What bread crumbs?" Abby glared at Seneca who pretty much ate her whole sandwich in one bite.

"Oh, that," Seneca said, between swallowing and letting crumbs fly from her mouth. "That's a superstition. Where I'm from, it keeps the bad spirits out. I'm surprised you actually did it."

"I don't know why either," I said. "But you made it seem so important."

She smiled at me and slowly reached for Abby's plate.

"Excuse me!" Abby shouted, smacking Seneca's hand away.

"Sorry." Seneca rubbed at her hand like a wounded puppy. "I didn't think you were going to eat that. Plus, you should probably lay off the pounds…"

Everything went completely silent. I could swear smoke began to shoot from Abby's ears. Her eyes raged, and every muscle in her body seemed to go rigid. Alice thankfully broke the silence by sliding her untouched sandwich in front of Seneca, who attacked it with renewed ferocity.

"Are you going to drink that?" Seneca asked Abby. I pushed my cup over to her.

"So," I began. "What do you plan on doing? Why is this person chasing you?"

"Puck."

"What?"

"His name is Puck."

"Why is Puck chasing you?"

"Because he wants me to marry him, even though I think he'd rather kill me, but that's a whole other story. Don't worry, Zak. I'm not going to marry him. I refuse to go through with it."

"Right, like in your story?" Abby crossed her arms and rolled her eyes.

Seneca nodded her approval.

"So you ran away from home?" I asked.

"Basically. I'm not going back. There's nothing anyone can do to make me. It's horrible there. Don't make me go back, Zak!" Seneca said with a whiney pout.

"I get that. My dad's making me do something big, something I don't want to do either. I hate feeling powerless. Maybe I can help you."

"Great! But we got to mind this one." Seneca obviously tried to nonchalantly nod toward a still frozen Abby.

"We—" I shifted my gaze to Abby, Alice, and back to Seneca "—all want to help you. I understand why you are running away. They can't force you to marry someone you don't want to. But where will you go?"

She got up and walked over to the ice chest. Abby shot me an angry look. Seneca opened the door and shuffled through the sad contents. She came back with a half-empty bottle of spoiled milk and an uncooked chicken. "You guys going to eat this?"

"It's raw!" I said.

"You win some, you lose some." She bit into the pink flesh and chased it down with milk. "I have to find a bar called the Crow's Nest. The owner can help me. I need to talk to him. It's supposed to be around here. That's why I was in the area. But I can't find it. You'd definitely know the owner if you saw him, he has only one eye."

"Yeah, I know old Gunnar. The Crow's Nest is not too far from here. My dad practically lives there. What can he do?"

"Ah! It's like fate brought us together." She threw the cleaned bones onto her plate and finished off the milk. "Can you take me to him?"

"Yeah, but I don't get what he can do to help."

"Connections, it's all about connections. He has the connections that will connect the dots!" She got up and ruffled Alice's hair before giving her stuffed bear a big kiss on the ear. She pulled down her goggles and walked over to the window. Cautiously, she pulled open the curtain and peeked outside. Abby kicked my foot under the table. I shrugged and offered her a weak smile. She did not return the favor.

"Zak, can I speak to you for a moment?" Abby pulled me out of my chair and out into the living room. She looked toward Seneca, sighed, and decided to pull me out onto the front porch.

"I know what you're going to say." I sat on the steps and took a deep breath. "You want me to tell her to go edge herself. Forget she ever existed."

She sat next to me, leaning in close while she rubbed warmth into her arms. It seemed like she wanted to be close to me. So I took it as an okay to put my arm around her. I dreaded that she would be able to feel my heart racing. Instead, she rested her head in the crook between my shoulder and body.

"I was thinking more along the lines of we should edge her ourselves," she said.

I laughed but it wasn't sincere. Abby may have had her reservations, but Seneca interested me like nothing else had in a while. I didn't know if it was her insane stories or just the opportunity for something different to happen. Whatever the case, I knew sticking around would be entertaining.

"I know you want out of here," Abby said. "But can't you just try and enjoy life for a bit?"

"I'm a Fringe Rat that makes money by risking his life for people that see me as less than vermin. My mom's gone, my dad might as well be, and my sister has an imagination that has her so frightened she stopped talking. My dad's also planning to ship me off as an air boy. My life's been out of my hands for as long as I can remember. There's not much to enjoy."

"Not even me, I guess," she whispered.

I almost choked. I hugged her closer. "You're about the only good thing left. If it weren't for you and Alice, I would have pulled a one-way Earth dive long ago."

She hit me really hard. "Don't say that!"

"It was a compliment!"

"I see it in your eyes, you know." She pulled away and looked at me with sadness in her face. "You have this look. You're never fully there. You just go through the motions, doing what you have to do, because it's what's expected of you. I just want you to be happy." Her hand found my cheek and warmed my cold flesh. "Maybe with me?"

"I… of course, I—"

The front door burst open and Seneca walked out with her goggles still on. She looked around the front lawn as if scanning for intruders. She took a step between me and Abby, forcing us to pull apart.

"Okay kids," Seneca said. "Shall we start an adventure?"

We set out to the Crow's Nest after clearing the dinner table. Abby opted to go home; she clearly distrusted Seneca, and urged me to be careful in my dealings with her. She told Alice she had to prepare a snack for her father and left with nothing more than a nod to Seneca. Of course, Seneca didn't seem to notice, being glued to my arm and prattling on about the injustice of having to walk so far by foot, with perfectly good iron horse-drawn carriages about.

The Crow's Nest was a well-known bar situated near the border of The Fringe and Empyrean. It was one of the fancier establishments. The outside was always freshly painted, while the windows were squeaky clean, as well as the welcoming brass door that glimmered in the moonlight. The three-story building had a bar and diner on the first floor and rooms for rent on the top two. People from The Fringe spent what little they had finding escape in cheap drink, while the better-off patrons of Empyrean found the confidentiality a great way to carry out secret meetings.

We reached the bar a little later that evening, welcomed by the sounds of laughter and cheer. Alice held onto my coat sleeve while searching the crowd for signs for our missing dad. Seneca hovered close behind, admiring with wide eyes and a slack jaw.

"Zak!" Mason yelled from across the bar. He came lumbering over, his steps unsteady and his cheeks with a pink flush. He hugged me before I could think to fight him off. "Hey buddy, you made it. I was just about to—" Once he caught sight of Seneca, I lost all his attention. "Who is that?" he whispered loud enough for her to hear.

"Mason, this is Seneca," I offered. "Seneca, this is my friend, Mason."

He pushed past me and took Seneca's hand, shook it clumsily, and practically drooled all over himself. "I've never seen you around before, and I know pretty much all the beautiful women in town."

"I'm not from these parts," Seneca said. "Maybe you can give me a tour sometime?"

Mason's eyes lit up. "Definitely, it'll be brass. You'd have a better time seeing the city with me than Walker; he's a bit of a cog head." A sharp elbow to my side accompanied his laugh. "Besides, if you ask me, Abby keeps him on a short leash."

"Hop off!" I tried pushing Mason aside, but his bigger frame refused to move. "Pick your jaw up, rust bucket."

Seneca cut in and approached Mason. "How about you find us a quiet booth, and you can tell me about the city a little more?"

"No sweat," he said, excitement drawn all over his face. "Follow me!"

He pushed through the crowd and headed straight for the back. Seneca shook her head and sat on an open stool at the bar. Alice pulled on my sleeve once before she took off. It only took me a moment to find Dad. He sat slouched over a deck of cards and empty mugs at a corner table. A dark-eyed mysterious man sat across from him, wearing the same top hat he had when he'd yelled at me from his carriage hours earlier. Dad's back faced us, but his tophat wearing companion caught my eye and tipped his brim in my direction. Alice ran over to his side before I had time to catch her.

Seneca grabbed my arm and pulled me over to the bar, her attention drawn to the pair of gold wings hanging on the far wall. Gunnar always kept the old rocket pack on display, just begging for a test drive. Instead of using your body to maneuver, the mechanical wings did most of the work for you.

"Barkeep!" she yelled. "Your finest whiskey for me and my companion. Money of course, is no matter." To me she whispered. "How much money do you have?"

"None!" I shouted.

"Money of course," she yelled, "is a slight problem, but we will gladly pay in favors!"

Fray came out from the kitchen behind the bar, annoyed as ever. I could never figure out her age. Something always struck me odd about the way she carried herself, as if she came from a regal background. Fray had slight lines of age at the corner of her eyes, black hair streaked with gray and silver, always kept in a neat bun. Yet, her black pants and red bodice with black trimmings made her look like some of the wealthy girls around Empyrean. When it came to The Crow's Nest, Fray was the law, and today seemed no exception. Her fists rested on her hips.

"Zak, good to see you," she said. "Should I set a plate for Alice? Has she eaten dinner?"

Before I could answer, Seneca interrupted. "We had sandwiches, and raw chicken. It was yummy." She smiled deeply, leaning over to rest her head on my shoulder. Fray noticed her and seemed slightly taken aback. She crossed her arms and held Seneca's gaze for longer than I thought necessary.

"No, we are fine," I said, wishing to break the tension, although the grumbling of my stomach tried it's best to contradict my words. "How long has he been at it?"

As if it took a great will of strength, Fray broke her staring match with Seneca and addressed me. "Some time now. I put a stop to his orders a while back. But that other fella showed up, and he started buying. Never been in me to refuse an Empyrean." She nodded toward another man with my father, wearing a white shirt and suspenders. Light seemed to reflect off his bald head. He had a refined look, but not nearly as elegant as the top hatted fellow.

"And what about the guy with the hat?" I asked.

"He showed up a little ago, must be friends with the Empyrean. Just sat with them. If I were a betting girl, I'd say he's Empyrean too. Seems to enjoy taking your dad's money a little too much, so who's to tell?" She turned back to Seneca. "And this is?"

"Seneca Rose," Seneca piped in before I had a chance to respond. She rested her elbow on the bar and leaned closer to Fray, continuing in a voice part growl. "It's been a while since I've seen the likes of your kind."

"What business do you have here?" Fray's demeanor turned dark. The usually emotionless woman surprised me.

"I need some information," Seneca said.

"And what makes you think you'll find it here?"

"A little crow told me," she said, and they both returned to their staring match. I felt awkward and about to intervene, but I caught a struggle out of the corner of my eye.

Alice grabbed at Dad's sleeve. Our old man swayed back and forth, nodding the way he did when he pretended to care, while Alice pointed wildly back at Seneca. My dad's companions stared with delight and hungry eyes. My dad, on the other hand, seemed to have had enough; he effortlessly pushed Alice away. I tensed up, ready to jump to my sister's side. She didn't take the hint and clung to Dad's arm still.

Seneca banged a fist on the bar, drawing my attention back to them still stuck in a silent duel. "I need to see the old one-eyed goat, and I need to see him now!"

"I told you he isn't here!" Fray took a deep breath and rolled her eyes.

"Alice!" Dad yelled over the crowd, the girl still pulling at his arm. "Can't you see I'm in the middle of something? After I win this hand, we can play."

"I know he's here," said Seneca. "I can smell the lie before it even leaves your lips."

I wanted to apologize to Fray for bringing her here and starting trouble.

Fray leaned in, putting her face mere inches from Seneca's. "Can you hear this?" She brought up a balled fist, poised to strike.

I pulled Seneca back when Gunnar came lumbering out from the kitchen.

"You two, calm it, now." He didn't yell, but his voice oozed with authority. Gunnar kept to himself and had an air of mystery about him. He may have been the owner of the Crow's Nest, but for all intents and purposes, Fray ran the place. No one knew where Gunnar came from or how he lost his eye. His good eye always shined bright blue and had a weariness about it, as if he had seen too much and grown too tired. His dirty blond beard hung down to his chest and hid his mouth; matching hair also hung low in a ponytail. He didn't bother with me or Fray, instead his blue eye found Seneca and attempted to bore a hole into her. "What are you doing here?"

"I... I... I'm sorry to intrude. I just need your help," Seneca said, fumbling for words.

"Gods be damned, girl!" Dad yelled. "You made me lose the hand!"

I already knew I was too late; Dad had already shoved Alice to the floor. He wobbled upright on unsteady feet, towering over my sister's tiny body like a monster awakened. The man with the top hat shoveled all the bills and coins toward himself, smiling madly. I sprung from my stool, knocking it down behind me, and ran over to my sister's defense. Before my dad could even think to raise his hand, I shoved him back, knocking over the table, and stood guard over Alice.

"Don't you dare touch her!" I yelled. The bar quieted down, all eyes shifted to me.

"Oh, you did it now!" He found his balance and made his way back to his feet.

His wild eyes glared at me. He hadn't shaven in weeks and looked like a wild man. The familiar smell of alcohol radiated from his pasty skin. As frail and unhealthy as he appeared, his punch still felt like a cement block. One minute he got to his feet, the next I saw a flash of light, and a blow that knocked me on my butt next to a hysterical Alice.

He readied his fist for another strike. Running on pure instinct, I threw my arms around Alice, meaning to shield her from any blows that would come. Her body struggled under me. I waited. Fray appeared at our side; she caught Dad's hand and pulled him into a flip over her back, slamming him on the floor. He tried to get up, but she knocked him back down with a swift kick to the chest and held him in place with her foot on his neck.

"Holy rust! Did you see that?" Mason yelled from somewhere in the background.

"Now," Fray said conversationally. "I won't be having any of that in my place of business. You understand, John?"

"Come now, Fray, that's no way to treat—" He coughed and gagged, trying to force words out under the weight of her foot. "A loyal customer... This is merely a case of a father disciplining his boy."

"Customers pay. I'll have you out on the street soon enough."

"Point taken," he said, with a strained shrug. Just like that, he forgot us.

I surveyed the bar and found my dad's companions taking notice of Alice. I looked for Seneca and Gunnar, but they must have left during the scuffle. Everyone else went back to their drinks. It shamed me that this was normal to them.

"Are you okay?" I asked Alice. She stared hard at Dad. "Alice?" Her muscles tensed under my grip. She shoved me off and ran out of the bar. I took off after her.

4

Alice knew all the best hiding places in The Fringe. I had to make sure to keep her in my sight as she turned corners and ducked into alleys. We raced through a maze of derelict homes and vendors that held all kinds of dangers in the dark of night. I found myself out in the open, nearing the south Empyrean entrance. She had to be heading to the nearest ship docks where she loved to go watch the crews stock their boats and launch off into the clouds.

Four bridges separated The Fringe from Empyrean, positioned at the west, north, east, and south. We lived closest to the south bridge, and as I ran across, I nodded to the familiar guards on duty. They stood near the massive portcullis that opened at eight in the morning and closed a little after midnight.

The looming arch led me into a new world. A place of beauty and wealth meant for spoiled rust buckets. While Empyreans could come and go as they pleased, Fringers had to have special permission. The experience of lavish parks, theaters, shops, and ship ports were a privilege we weren't good enough to have. Luckily, my skills had come in handy when a certain night guard needed his great grandfather's watch fixed. It got me and Alice a pass into the city at night, where we would often go to the docks and watch the ships, or go to the pools and swim under the stars during the warm weather.

The clean streets practically sparkled, granite smoothed down to perfection separated by paths of crystal water. Bridges and archways carved with the finest craftsmanship connected streets and over-looked the canals. It all came together, creating a city of the finest art, every square inch of it screamed of the meticulous intricacies of its creator's craft. From the windows to the gold engraved doorknobs, the granite gargoyle who sat at the edge of the watchtower, to the wood benches lined with gold trimmings and white cushion quilts, to the snooty Empyreans with their upturned noses. I hated it all. What use was a beautiful city to people who took it for granted?

I found Alice right under a bronze statue of Hephaestus wielding a large hammer over an iron anvil.

I sat and wondered if she noticed. She had a distant look in her eyes, the one she got whenever she saw her imaginary friends, the ones that seemed to do more harm than good. It made me think of the last night she woke up screaming in terror. Her imagination always got the best of her.

"Is that the Highwind?" I pointed at a docked ship, its balloon growing as it filled with gassed ambrosia while the crew cleared the deck of cargo. "I believe it is, look at all those windows along the hull, must be where the cannons are drawn."

She shook her head with little enthusiasm. I knew it wasn't the Highwind. Scavenger flags were only allowed entry if the Empyrean needed something.

"Oh," I said pretending. "Wouldn't it be something to see it?"

She shrugged, looking down at her hands. My heart felt heavy, she had no interest in her favorite topic. Usually, she would chase me around trying to force it upon me.

A peddler playing from an intricate box of gears came by with a mechanical monkey that danced along to the sound of music. Alice's eyes lit up. This was my chance to cheer her up, and though it meant my pride and possibly my status, it would be worth it to see her smile. I jumped up and started dancing around, mimicking the monkey's every move. Scratching my head with a goofy face, I hopped from foot to foot. The peddler stopped and clapped his hands along with the music. He seemed amused at me making a fool of myself.

When the music stopped, I thought to sit down, but the peddler grabbed me by the arm. He tinkered with his music box before winding it up again. More music played, this time a little slower but with a happy beat. The peddler looked to Alice and urged her up, clapping his hands and skipping around; the mechanical monkey did the same. Alice didn't need much convincing to dance. I took her in my arms and spun her. She laughed and her eyes lit up. If any of the other Rats saw me, they'd be taking digs at me forever. But I didn't give a rust. I let Alice stand on my feet while I danced around the bench. Alice held onto me tightly as she looked up at me with wide, trusting eyes. She gave me a smile worth more than my pride.

As we danced, iron horse-drawn carriages sped by, airships floated away overhead, and the Empyrean trams swooshed by on cables that crossed back and forth through the city boundaries. We seemed to be at the center of endless possibilities, each and every one of them barred from us, a couple of Fringe Rats play acting where we didn't belong. Background figures who suffered a life of monotony while the important people carried on with adventures and excitement somewhere else. I grew depressed having nothing to hope for; worse still, I knew once summer came, Dad would sign me off to apprentice on a ship. I could be gone for months, in some cases years. Alice would be all alone with a father stumbling out of control.

After the peddler stopped playing, he bid us farewell. I hugged Alice and tried to comfort her even if it meant lying. "Alice, Dad loves you very much. It's just, ever since Mom left, he's been having a hard time. You were too young to remember when it happened, but they used to be so close. It destroyed him."

She gave me a questioning look, as to why Mom left.

"She had to leave… because she wanted something more. She had a fire in her heart and it was slowly being snuffed out here. She needed to find that spark to keep the fire alive. It had nothing to do with any of us. It's just the way it is… sometimes. Dad's sadder than any of us can tell. One day he'll come around; you just have to give him time."

She watched a ship sail off to where the world below met the sky, under the dull white light of the moon and across the fields of clouds. She seemed thoughtful and smiled.

"Wouldn't it be wonderful to ride one?" asked a nasal voice from behind us.

We both turned to find the two from the bar standing there. The top-hatted man, with his fancy coat, jewel encrusted cane, and tinted goggles bowed before us. A couple of steps behind him stood his leery eyed suspender-wearing companion.

"What a dream it is to sail the clouds." Top hat said. "Since the beginning of time, it has always been man's dream to soar on wings and feel the freedom of birds. A most noble dream indeed. Francis, will you get the carriage?"

Francis nodded and hobbled off.

"I've met the one you call father, but haven't the honor of meeting you two personally. My name is Puck, and you are?"

Alice took a cautious step behind me. Puck was who Seneca had been running from. But how'd he miss her at the Crow's Nest?

"What do you want?" I asked.

"Only to talk. You see, your father has acquired a great debt, one that can easily be expunged if you were willing to help me with a favor."

"My dad's debt is his own; I don't give a rust. Nothing to do with us."

"Surely, when it is the home you lay in that he has lost to me, it becomes business of yours."

Alice gasped. I held no loyalties to Seneca; I barely knew her. But this man, I knew instantly, he could not be trusted. He reminded me of a vicious beast that sought to devour his prey, and like all beasts, you could show no fear. "Like I said, my father's business is his own."

"And what will you and your sister do when you are both out in the street?"

"No different than that piece of rust we live in now. Are we done?"

He leaned in closer and removed his hat, holding it gently under his arm. His hair fell down onto his shoulders and beads of sweat formed across his brow. "It's very hot here; I don't know how you people do it."

"We should get going." I took Alice's arm and stood ready to leave, but Puck blocked our path. I pulled Alice close behind me.

"You haven't even heard me out yet," said Puck.

"I told you we have nothing to do with our dad's dealings."

"But should you happen to have seen a girl, a very strange girl, I would be willing to let bygones be bygones." He licked at his lips and smacked his teeth as if preparing to eat his favorite meal.

"I don't know any strange girl."

"You came into the bar with one."

"If I did, why didn't you speak to her then?"

"Neutral ground." His lips turned up into a sly smirk. "Wouldn't go over well, angering Odin in his place of business. Not to mention the Valkyrie tends to be a stickler for old law."

Alice startled and peeked behind Puck, her eyes alight in surprise. Puck followed her gaze and stared at the empty space for a moment before turning back to us. He inhaled deeply as if trying to catch the scent of something faint. "How delightful! I've heard rumors... but I didn't dare think they were true. How convenient Seneca led us right to... you." His gaze fell on Alice.

This guy was cogged. "I'm sorry. We really have to go." I pushed past him.

"Of course; of course. I have no desire to keep you." He removed his leather glove, and placed his pale hand on Alice's head. "Sorry if I frightened you."

She nodded and I pulled her on. "It's okay, but we really have to go." I continued past him, feeling a cold tension, and knew his gaze followed us as we ran off.

———

"Well if it isn't the traitors." Seneca sat on the porch swing, her arms folded behind her head and booted feet resting on the railing. "Back from cavorting with the enemy. How could you? I'm heartbroken!" She stuck her tongue out at me.

Alice ran over and threw her arms around Seneca's waist. Seneca's face softened and she bent down, gently kissing the crown of Alice's head.

"Who is he?" I asked, once again feeling a bit of jealousy watching my sister show affection to someone else. "And why did he come looking for me, when you were right there in the same bar?"

"The Crow's Nest is neutral; we can't go about starting wars in there. But cat and mouse, now that's a different story. He couldn't make a move until I left, so when you distracted him, I hid behind the bar."

"He said that too, the neutral ground thing, what's that supposed to mean?" I sat next to her, Alice squeezing between us.

"There are certain places where certain things can't be done." She looked off. "There are rules and treaties, stuff like that." Something caught her attention off by the bushes outside our fence; she leaned forward, pulling down her goggles. "We better go inside."

Oddly enough, Alice seemed drawn to the same spot. Her eyes went wide with a terrible fright. She pushed in closer to my side, and a slight shiver ran down her body.

"What's going on?" I asked.

Seneca took off her goggles and handed them to me. "Some things are right in front of you, Zak. But you can't process them right, so your brain doesn't bother. It just fills in the empty space with what it expects should be there." She took Alice by the hand and led her inside.

I looked at the goggles, feeling the cool copper frame between my thumb and index finger. The right lens shined blue and the left red. Something weighed heavy on my shoulders, not physically, but a mental burden. My stomach felt uneasy, and the longer I held the goggles, the sweatier my palms became. I couldn't explain it, but it felt almost as if a choice had to be made, a choice that would change everything. But maybe things needed to change for life to begin. I put on the goggles. The world tinted purple. I closed my left eye and everything turned blue, then I closed my right eye and everything turned red. I opened both, stared at my hand while flexing my fingers, and glanced up at the gate.

A figure watched me from the shadows, but it wasn't a man, it was too big to be. Its hands practically dragged on the ground and its body was tall and slender, cocked at odd angels. It noticed me and took a step forward, the motion causing its entire mass to blur. I jumped back, lost my footing, and landed hard on the ground. The goggles fell from my eyes, sliding down my nose. The world returned to its natural color, and the creature vanished.

The monster, the monster wasn't there.

My heart pounded, and the voice in my head said to put the goggles away, go inside, eat something, and take a nap. But my body had other plans. I pulled the goggles up to my eyes and readjusted them in place.

The creature had come closer, near enough for me to make out its features. It looked like a mix of a tree and person, a grotesque fusion of flesh and nature with long gangly limbs and hair made of moss and leaves. It had fangs and intense eyes that stared me down with challenge and hunger. I took the goggles off and it vanished; I put them back on and it appeared again.

Oddly, as monstrous as this creature seemed, its face looked somehow sad. I got up and thought to walk toward it. I took a step and it hunched forward, baring its teeth, ready to lunge at me. I ran into the house and slammed the door, leaning on it for extra support. Gasping for breath, I slid down to sit on the floor.

"Yeah." Seneca knelt in front of me. "Dryad… has that effect on people."

Alice poked out from behind Seneca and gave me a questioning look.

"What's a dryad?" I asked.

"Dryad's his name, he's from back home," Seneca said. "He's been following me. Probably… Puck's eyes and ears."

Alice ran to the window and peeked outside.

"You can't see him because he's invisible," Seneca said as a matter of fact.

This didn't stop Alice from watching the world outside where an invisible creature waited.

"Don't worry." Seneca pointed at the doorframe. "Breadcrumbs."

———

WE SAT at the dinner table. After the initial freak out, Seneca assured me that Dryad couldn't get in. The breadcrumbs spread across the doors and windows would keep creatures of the Fey out. It didn't make any sense. I wanted to close my eyes and wake up from a dream.

"Hey," Seneca said. "You all right over there?"

I refused to encourage her and all her nonsense. Ever since she showed up on my doorstep, she'd been a complete headache, a ball of chaos wrapped up nicely in a pixie cut hairdo. I needed to see Abby.

"Hey, Zak." She snapped her fingers in front of my face. "Try not to be a spoilsport. It really isn't that bad... well it's only kind of bad. Probably really bad. But not in a direct sort of way. It's more of a world about to be destroyed kind of bad, but not really a personal level bad. You know?"

I gave her a blank look.

"I'll admit a lot of it is my fault. I was always raised to own up to one's responsibility. Me running away to here might have brought on the impending destruction of Olympus... but, there is always a but," she winked at Alice, who giggled in return, "it would have happened anyway. I just might have hastened it a bit. But what's in the semantics, you know?"

I nodded.

"The story I was telling to Alice earlier. You were listening weren't you? Well it's all true, each and every word of it. Well not really, *every word*. But the theme is the same. The thing is, the amazing, beautiful, awesomely awesome princess, is me. The Unseelie have conquered my kingdom. I had to escape. And the thing about it, if I didn't come here, they still would have. That's all the Unseelie Court wants. They can't stand the sight of humans, and Olympus floating around in the sky is just a constant reminder of their failed plan. So while Daddy thought this arranged marriage was a way to unite the Seelie and Unseelie Courts, the Unseelie just wanted a united army so they can finish what they started so long ago... are you listening?"

"If I said no," I looked her straight in the eyes, "would you stop?"

"Stop what?"

"Stop talking, for a minute?"

"No, probably not."

"What do you want from me?"

"Nothing! I don't need anyone's help. I can fix this mess on my own."

"Okay, so?"

"So I just need help with this one thing. The only way to save Olympus is to unite the old gods. The reason you guys lost Earth in the first place was because of the feuds going on between them. The Fey were able to just swoop in while your gods fought amongst themselves."

"Do you realize you sound like your cogs are rusted?"

"Yeah... but... I always sound ridiculous, and if you think that's bad, this is going to sound completely ridiculous. Gunnar is Odin, as in the god Odin. I need his help, him and his bar wench Freya."

"You mean Fray?"

"Yeah, she's a Valkyrie. Her real name is Freya. Yeah I know, she's not that original, is she? Well, she's kind of a big deal. Has the power to bring back the dead: dead gods, demigods, and Fey. Only, Odin won't help me unless I help his cousin Zeus."

I watched her closely as she spoke. Looked for tells, same way I had to scrutinize all the Rats when they were trying to pull a con. She seemed completely legit. Stranger still, I wanted to believe every word of it.

"So what do you want from me?" I asked.

"Zeus, the all father. Big man. He's been imprisoned in the worst kind of way. And we are going to bust him out."

5

We spent the night at my house, Alice and I sharing a bed while Seneca slept in Alice's. I wouldn't say I got much sleep. I was wary of my dad coming home and starting a scene; I also couldn't stop thinking about the thing I saw in the front yard. I tossed and turned most of the night. Luckily, at some point I managed to fall into a fitful sleep while Alice slept comfortably at my side.

When the sun finally rose, it shined bright into our room, warming my skin and promising a brand new day free of nonsense. Everything from the night before had to be an ambrosia-induced dream. I opened my eyes to find Seneca standing over me, a curious look on her face.

"What the hades are you doing?" I jumped up, startled.

"You snore pretty loud," she said.

"No I don't!"

Alice sat up, rubbing sleep from her eyes, and nodded in agreement with Seneca.

"See? The princess agrees. You aren't going to argue with the cutest little girl on Olympus are you?" Seneca playfully squeezed Alice's cheek.

I rolled my eyes and stretched out my arms. "Let's get this over with."

———

Abby's face lit up when I walked into the office. She looked bored standing behind the counter thumbing through a book. An empty doctor's office should technically be a good thing. But the boredom drove her nuts; she still had to watch the front, and I would usually spend whatever free time I had keeping her company, yet another thing that would change when I started my apprenticeship. She walked around the counter to greet me when Seneca pushed in behind me.

"Wow, business is booming, huh?" Seneca said.

Abby's happy expression fell to annoyance.

"I told you to wait outside," I said.

"But what fun would that be?" Seneca walked over to the counter and lifted Abby's book with a smirk. "Snatch!" She sat on one of the waiting chairs.

"Zak," Abby said, way too calm for my liking. "Can I speak to you in the back room?"

"Uh-oh." Seneca peeked over the top of the upside down book.

Abby took my hand and rushed me into the back storage room. "What is she doing here?"

"Sorry. I know she's a bit cogged." I tried not to break eye contact. "It's just, we need a favor, and the quicker we take care of it, the quicker she will be out of my hair."

"Seems that ever since she showed up, you only come around when you need something." Abby crossed her arms with a stern look.

"What?" I put my hands on her shoulders, thought better of it, and took a step back. "That's not true at all; it's just… well it's so rust."

"What? Spit it out then."

I motioned for her to come closer and whispered, "See the thing is, I think she's a bit cogged."

"Oh, really?"

"Well, not like cogged in the way you think. I think she's mental; she's paranoid and delusional. I think the only way to help her, and get rid of her, is to help her see through this whole cogged fantasy she's got going on up here." I tapped my finger to my forehead. I hated lying to her, but Abby would never agree to help if I told her the truth and made her think I was cogged too.

"And what's that got to do with me? If you want to entertain cogged girls and their delusions, I couldn't care less."

"I know, but the thing is we need to get into that retirement home, what was it called? Elysium."

"Do you know what will happen if they catch you sneaking in?"

"That's why we need your help." I tried to give her the smartest smile, the one I used to use when we were kids and I had to talk her into doing something bad. *The one that always got us in trouble.* "You go there to drop off medical supplies for your dad, right? You have access passes. Most of the time they never even check you because it's so common, you said so yourself."

"Yeah, I can get in, that doesn't mean you can." She walked away and straightened out some medication. "I don't want any part of this. For one, I don't trust her, and two, if something happened to you..."

"Something won't happen." I pulled her back toward me. "All we got to do is act like we belong. Seneca and I will carry gear and if anyone asks, we'll say we're apprenticing under your dad."

She played with her hair, twirling it around her finger. "I don't know. It's a bit risky."

"Come on, didn't you say you always wanted do something exciting with me?"

She clenched her jaw and her ears went bright red the way they always did when she got furious. "Yeah, I did! But not to follow some cogged stranger on an adventure. I meant the two of us together. Under different... circumstances."

"And what better circumstance is there than helping a friend?"

She sighed in resignation and pushed past me. "Fine, but when they lock the two of you up, don't expect me to stick around."

I followed her out into the waiting room; Seneca smiled at us and shot me a wink. "So, when's the date?"

"For what?" Abby growled.

"The wedding, of course."

"I'm going to get ready." Abby stormed off to another room.

"Stop teasing her," I said. "If you keep pushing her, she won't help."

"She's not helping me, she's helping you, and she always will."

"What do you mean?"

"I mean, you're dumb like most silly little boys are. And she's too proud for her own good."

Abby returned with two carry bags and placed them on the table to double check their contents. The smaller bag contained familiar tools from past medical visits. A stethoscope, alcohol pads, vials to collect blood and urine samples, and gauze, lots of gauze. Seneca made faces at Abby; thank the gods she didn't notice.

"Okay," Abby said. "Since most of the attendants know me, I won't bother with my badge. Seneca you can wear it, and carry this bag." She pushed over one of the bags and tossed the small medical examiner badge to her. "Zak will carry this." She opened the flap on the larger bag packed with medical books. "It's a lot heavier, but this way it will look like you guys are actually learning on the field, and here." Carefully, she attached the badge to my front breast pocket. "Just to be extra safe put these on." She gave us both red medical armbands.

"What's the plan?" Seneca asked, while adjusting her armband.

Abby looked at her and seemed to be holding back. "There is no plan, we keep it simple. We walk up to the gate and rely on my good looks to get in."

"Uh oh," Seneca moaned.

"What?"

"Well if we have to rely on that—"

"So let's get going!" I jumped between the two girls, regretting taking on this venture.

———

ELYSIUM LOOKED MORE like a massive townhouse than an old folks' home; I bet it could house all the citizens of Empyrean who reached that age where no one had time to care for them anymore. The rich could make poor choices like that and not feel a shred of guilt. The four-story property stood regal within a gated community. Beautiful gardens lay welcoming just beyond the large gate that kept those of little wealth out. We could see residents strolling along, enjoying the day and the beauty of their surroundings. The nurses and groundsmen milled about with their daily activities, either attending to the property or chasing after residents who found driving their wards crazy a more enjoyable pastime than watching grass grow.

The three of us walked toward the guard station; I was nervous, Seneca was fidgety, and Abby looked panicked.

"My dad's going to kill me when he finds out," she whispered, taking hold of my hand and squeezing it for support.

My stomach had a sinking feeling, I couldn't say it was the bad type though. It felt brass. I squeezed back. "Don't worry. They already know you. Really, it would be more trouble for them to check out our story."

"And there's always the alternative," Seneca added. "Run like Hades."

Abby rolled her eyes. "Okay, but don't look so panicked yourself." She smiled, and like a magician managed to release all the tension from my body. "Remember you belong here, this is nothing new for you."

I nodded. Seneca stood up straighter with her hands neatly folded in front of her.

"Hey Abby, these two got IDs?" The guard asked. He wore the Elysium approved uniform; white cap with a bronze badge on the front, a blue vest over white shirt, and matching pants.

I stared at him dumbfounded, unable to find words that would come to our aid. Seneca opened her mouth to speak, which I knew would be a bad idea for everyone. Luckily, Abby cut her off.

"Hey, Steven," Abby said. "I have a problem. Things have been really busy, so we took on two new apprentices. But dad doesn't even have time to show them the ropes. So he has them tagging along with me on a couple of house calls. I was so busy packing them up with books and supplies, I totally forgot to give them their papers."

He looked at Seneca and I thoughtfully; I smiled and Seneca winked at him. "Don't worry Abby, won't be a big deal. Do you guys have your citizens' ID?"

"Well that's the thing," Abby continued. "When I was writing up their papers I needed their IDs to fill in their information, and I left it all on the counter. Daddy's going to kill me when he gets back and finds them. So I'm hoping to rush through these rounds and get back before him. I don't want to get you in any trouble, so if it's a problem, we'll just go back home..."

He thought about it for a while. Seneca blew him a kiss, and his cheeks lightened with a smile. "It's all right, just make sure you're more careful next time. More importantly, congratulations on the doctor letting you run some rounds on your own! Hope it's nothing too hard."

"No," Abby said. "He may be giving me more responsibilities, but he only trusts me with a couple of colds, and if I'm lucky, a sprained ankle."

"My momma always said, patience is the best ride to the top!" he said.

"I'll remember that," Abby said.

They both smiled and nodded at each other. For a brief moment, we all stood awkwardly nodding our heads.

"So, who are you here to see?" he finally asked.

"Oh yeah, Mister Barnabas..." Abby said.

"Barnabas? He didn't look ill. I saw him in the garden out back, not just ten minutes ago."

"Yeah... like I said, daddy isn't giving me anything huge, just here for a checkup. Drop off some medication..."

"Well mind his temper. He can be a bit of a handful when his mind wanders. He's straight to the back, over by the pond." Steven looked down, ran his hand over the switchboard, and the gates swung open.

We walked along the side of the home to the garden. Situated away from prying eyes, more residents sat playing card games or talking on benches, while others had deep conversations with imaginary people. A beautiful woman who looked like she couldn't be older than twenty danced around the courtyard. She spun around us, blonde hair fluttering in the air. A thin silk dress clung to her body, swaying along with her every move.

Watching her made my heart swell with a warm sensation. I had an incredible longing for Abby in my stomach; it felt like a free fall that only she could save me from. I looked to Abby and her eyes gleamed with a strange awe. All her attention was turned toward me. Her lip quivered and she took a slow step forward. I ached to touch her, to feel her skin against mine. I would have kissed her right then and there had Seneca not stepped in and pulled us both away from the dancing lady.

"Might want to steer clear of Aphrodite." She pulled us further and further away from the beautiful dancer.

Soon, my head cleared. I was almost disappointed when the warm feelings left. I looked to Abby and found her cheeks practically glowing red.

"What just happened?" I asked.

Seneca laughed. "Probably best we keep that to ourselves, huh? I think that's him over there." She pointed to an old man sitting under a gazebo made of crisscrossing wood, decorated with flowers. The gazebo offered shade and comfort while overlooking a sparkling pond where ducks bobbed above the water. As we approached, Barnabas appeared to be in the middle of a deep conversation, his arms and hands swinging wildly about, as if he spoke to the ducks or some unseen force.

"He's going to help us?" I asked, not impressed with the hunched over figure, his long shaggy hair, and unkempt beard. He seemed frail and erratic. The way he talked out loud and jerked about made me wonder who was crazier: him, or us for seeking his help.

"I'm pretty sure it is." Seneca put on her goggles. She stared at him for a while before a smile crept across her face. "It's him!"

"Tell me a story old man." Seneca stood in front of Barnabas. "And make it a good one. I've traveled a long way to see you."

He looked up at her with heavy eyes, a dying blue that fell into gray. Tired eyes that seemed older than time. His lips parted as he began to utter words, but thought better of it, as if his tongue would betray him. He smiled with a knowing glimmer in his eyes as he inspected Seneca. She leaned in face to face. I expected him to reveal the great secrets of the universe that very moment.

He moaned. "The storm, did you see the storm?" his voice rasped with little use. He struggled with each word. "Such thunder and lightning! Oh how it would have shaken the Earth, such fierce animalistic power."

"What are you talking about, old man?" Seneca asked.

"So loud! I can still feel it shaking in my bones."

Seneca sat in the grass looking up at him and sighed with frustration. "Yeah, we get it. Thunder, lightning, you like storms. Let's try something easy, do you know who I am?"

He licked his lips. "Anna, are you my Anna?"

Seneca screamed, surprising Abby and me. She fell back into the grass staring up into the sky. "No, no, no, I came so far. I came so far. I came so far!"

"Do something." Abby pushed me toward Seneca.

"Hey." I knelt down next to her and shook her arm. "Hey, let's not make a big scene, what's he supposed to know?"

"I came all this way and he's just a husk, an empty husk of old wrinkly skin, brittle bones, and gray hair. I came all this way. And he's just a pervy old man that likes to stare at young girls inappropriately."

Barnabas practically fell out of his seat trying to get a good look at Abby's legs. *I couldn't blame the old guy.*

"Excuse me?" an attendant said. We hadn't noticed her approach. She wore the same white outfit as all the staff. But with her curly red hair, and poised look, she gave off a regal presence. "Why are you children harassing Barnabas?"

"Oh no," Abby pleaded. "We weren't harassing him. We were just visiting my grandfather… and we saw Barnabas on the way in, he looked so lonely. We just wanted to check—"

"Wasting our time!" Seneca yelled. "Is what we are doing. More so, he is wasting our time." She pointed an accusing figure at Barnabas.

"Again I ask, what you are doing here?" The attendant crossed her arms.

"Can it lady, we are having a mental breakdown here," said Seneca.

The attendant's eyes flashed with anger as she crinkled her nose. "Your blood smells of dirt."

Seneca sat up and noticed the attendant for the first time. "What?"

"Child of Earth, what business do you have here?" the attendant asked.

"Wait… what?" Seneca asked.

"I will not ask again; you have upset my husband enough. What is it you are doing here, so far from home?"

Seneca looked at Barnabas, making his best attempts at pinching Abby's dodging legs, then back to the attendant. She smiled and put on her goggles. After a moment of hesitation, she jumped up to her feet and bowed at the hip. "My apologies, Hera. I didn't recognize you. Your beauty is far more exquisite than legends tell."

———

HERA POURED tea for the three of us. We sat around a table of bronze with intricate designs; our hard chairs forced us to sit up extra straight as we sipped tea from small cups of fancy porcelain. Hera helped her husband sit comfortably in his wheelchair and pushed him over to us; he didn't seem to notice us at all, instead he stared off into the sky.

"Now I ask you again," Hera said, pouring a cup for herself. "What are you doing here, Child of Earth?"

"Sheesh, you make me sound like a tree hugger or something." Seneca dipped her finger in her cup, twirling it around the brown liquid. "I came here looking for him. At least I thought I was."

I felt my patience running thin, Abby's kicks under the table told me she shared the same feeling. "Can someone please explain to us what's going on? Seneca, you have been leading us around town with nothing but half-truths and tidbits of information. You show up on my doorstep and I still have no idea who you are."

"And yet you find that you can't help following her." Hera's intensity held me frozen in place. She glanced at Seneca. "Did you compel him?"

"Compel?" Seneca sat back crossing her arms. "Do I look like the compelling type? Really, so what if my sunny disposition and unbelievable good looks attract boys and make them wait on me hand and foot?"

"Unbelievable good looks? Please," Abby muttered.

"Hey!" I yelled, "I want an answer!"

"It's no wonder she has led you astray. Your companion is a Child of Earth; they live for games of confusion and discord," said Hera.

"What does that mean?" I had to keep my anger in check.

"It means," Seneca bowed in her seat, "that I'm a fairy. Seneca Rose, Princess of the Seelie Court."

"I knew I smelled Oberon's stench about you." Hera drank deeply from her cup.

"Oh cut the rust! You're telling me you're from Earth?" Abby shook her head in indignation.

"Ask your boyfriend. He knows it's true," Seneca said. "Tell her Zak, what did you see in the yard?"

"I don't know what I saw. I was tired and you made me wear those stupid goggles." I wasn't ready to accept all this… yet.

"How about you try them on again?" she asked.

"For what?"

"To prove a point." She removed her goggles and slid them across the table. I picked them up carefully, staring at the lenses in fear.

"Go ahead," she said.

"This is so stupid." I put them on, and watched as the world turned tinted purple. "What am I supposed to be seeing?"

"You must understand," Hera said. "That this will not end well."

I looked at her and struggled to catch my breath. The woman in the attendant's uniform was gone. She turned into so much more. Words couldn't come to me, none that could describe her magnificence. Her hair seemed alive like fire, crackling and swaying in the wind. Her eyes sparkled and her face radiated beauty. She wore a white toga trimmed with gold threading and a gold emblem holding up the corner.

She looked at me, and I heard her words without her lips moving. *This is my true form. Be wary boy of the company you keep. Children of the Earth are known for their trickery.* She nodded over at Barnabas—Zeus.

The golden aura pulsating from his body almost blinded me. His once graying hair and beard appeared perfectly white, and his skin shared the same bronze color as Hera's; he too wore a white toga with gold trimmings. His whole body vibrated with untapped power, and yet, he still looked as lost and confused as he did before. Eyes that held such strength seemed overshadowed with confusion.

"This is the true form of Zeus," Hera whispered. "Under normal circumstances, you would be struck down for not showing proper respect. But alas, this is what he has become since losing the war to *her* people." She pointed an accusing finger at Seneca, who to my surprise also looked different. She glowed a shallow green, her ears were pointed at the top and a faint trace of butterfly wings fluttered behind her, as if a mere ghost of what had once been. She noticed me observing her and winked.

I struggled for words. "I can't believe this. Any of this, this isn't real!" I ripped the goggles from my face and threw them on the table. I wanted to leave, but curiosity kept me in my seat, every nerve in my body piqued with interest.

Abby grabbed the goggles and put them on. "Oh, whoa. This is interesting..."

Her face contorted in confusion, which somehow managed to make her look even more beautiful.

"How is this happening?" She stared longingly at Hera.

"Isn't it obvious?" Seneca waved at Abby for attention. "They're enchanted. There's a lot more to this world than you two know. There are many worlds actually, as well as beings. Some are Children of the

Earth like me, and others are of the old blood like them." She nodded toward Hera and Zeus. "Some things are kept hidden from the human eye or those without magic. Once I was stripped of my magic, I couldn't see the things hidden behind the curtain of this reality. I had a favor to cash in and got those. It's for my own safety, really." She held out her hand toward Abby.

"Stripped of your power?" Hera's eyebrow arched.

"Yup, it's a short story, but I'll make it long for the kiddies."

Abby handed the goggles back. We both watched with fascination.

"A long time ago, the old blood and mankind ruled the Earth. They grew and spread at an alarming rate; they consumed and destroyed, leaving trails of colonization in their wake. Mankind was prosperous under the rule of the old blood. But like a cancer, they withered the Earth from which they fed. So the Earth created the Fey to destroy the old blood and drive away the sickness of mankind. A war waged. The old blood had great power as gods, true, but their arrogance left plenty of discord between them to exploit."

Hera nodded along with the tale. "As Fey amassed their numbers, our cousin Odin warned Zeus of the danger, begging that they put aside their differences and join forces against the Fey threat. Zeus, that arrogant fool, wouldn't have any of it. He and the Olympians would crush the threat on their own and never would he dream of taking help. Grave mistake, indeed. It took us losing half our ranks to that demon, Queen Mob, before Zeus agreed to combine his power with Odin. But still we could not maintain order amongst themselves."

"With all their inner troubles," Seneca continued. "The king—my father—with the help of certain mutineers, was able to defeat Zeus and most fell with him."

"My son, Ares, turned on his family and aided the Fey." Hera didn't look sad. The sickness of a pain centuries old covered her face.

"My father, having won his victory, took pity on mankind and said, 'leave this land and we shall spare you. Stay, and you are dead,' another Fey trick. Really, where could they go?"

"Hephaestus, my lowly son, stepped up. May he ever forgive me, for all his life I favored Ares. In the end, Hephaestus dreamed up this city of steam, iron, brass, and chrome. Hephaestus gave us salvation and a way to live in exile." Hera looked sorrowful. "I hope to one day find him again."

"How long ago was that?" I asked, my imagination wild with wonder.

"Long enough for men to have forgotten the gods that walk amongst them." Hera lost herself in thought.

"Wait," said Abby. "Seneca, you said there were two courts of Fey?"

"Yeah. I am of The Seelie, those who live under the rule of my parents, King Oberon and Queen Titanya Rose. We follow order and rules; we live for the protection of the Earth and advancement of our people. My parents stood for justice and peace. After the war, they even sought to rebuild relations with mankind. There have been peace talks with your people." She looked at Hera, who nodded. "And then there are the Unseelie, everything we are not, the chaos to our order. Granted, it is in the nature of the Fey to live a life of mischief, but the Unseelie believe that mischief and Chaos go hand in hand. They were ruled by Queen Mob before she fell to Zeus and Odin, but her spoiled rotten son, Puck, sits on her throne now, with an advisor who has been at his side since the war."

"Ares!" Hera's voice betrayed the emotion she tried to hide.

"Yup, and now they march against my people. The truce between Seelie and Unseelie has been broken. They have taken our lands and killed all who pay tribute to my father's banner."

"Why?" I asked.

"Because whereas my father wanted a truce between Fey and man, Puck wants them completely destroyed. He would not wait for the truce to be signed and risk being the minority. They marched the day after father and Hephaestus agreed to terms. It was a long battle." Seneca looked off, away from the table, hugging herself against the cool breeze. "They made it right into the castle… into my home. You see, you can believe in justice all you want." She looked away and took a moment before she continued. "You can have a heart made of all the bits that make someone good. But when it comes to war, those things don't matter. Well no, I'm lying. They do matter; they matter to the enemy. Because believe me when I tell you, those who follow chaos have no issue doing what's wrong."

"What... what happened to your parents?" Abby asked.

I didn't want to hear the answer, because a part of me already knew.

"They died trying to protect me. They died forcing me onto a human airship, forcing me to escape, leaving my people behind."

Abby and I both looked down, unable to think of comforting words.

Hera spoke first. "I'm sorry for your loss, child. I will not pretend I have any love for those who have conquered my own. However, I do know what it is like to lose those who are close to you. Still, I am curious, you have not answered how you lost your wings or your magic."

With a sigh, Seneca leaned back in her seat and played with her nails. "Before they stormed our castle, there was talk of a truce. Puck and I were to be wed to ensure the alliance. Puck declared there would be peace. My father believed him. It was foolish to believe him. He just wanted us united so he could bring Mob back."

"How?" I asked.

Seneca looked to Hera. "Mob was weakened, but not destroyed. My father feared her power. He didn't trust what she would do after the war ended. So he used blood magic to lock her away deep within the depths of the Ivory Castle. The lifeblood of a Rose is the only thing that can free her. Puck and Ares knew if we were wed they could force our hand."

Hera listened with tight lips.

"They tried to force me to marry him. So I ran away. I got caught and had my wings taken and held captive until I lied and agreed to marry him. During the ceremony, I might have sneezed a handful of fairy dust into Puck's face. I might have burned one of their flags. I might have incited a fight between the goblin groomsmen, and I might have worn all black as if I were going to a funeral. Oh, and I might have said Puck has an unhealthy obsession with his dead mom. Who would have thought that would be the thing to do it? They called off the wedding, and we were at war the next week. This has all been my fault, and I want to fix it… I need to fix it!"

"You have cost you and your people their freedom. What does that have to do with us?" Hera showed no sign of sympathy.

"You don't understand… I still have people loyal to my name. As far as the numbers go, the Unseelie rule all of Earth. Fortunately, my escape prevented them from freeing Mob. I gave you time. Puck is determined and will still march. He plans on wiping out all of Olympus, the remaining gods, and all mankind. I came here to warn you… and to ask a favor."

"What good is warning us?" I asked. "If we couldn't win against the Fey when we had all the gods, what makes you think we can win now?"

"Unlike before," Seneca said, "Zeus will heed the warning. Odin and Zeus will be united." She looked to Hera. "I spoke to Odin already. He said he would stand with Zeus for a price."

"And what would that price be?" Hera asked.

"Zeus has to free Loki from his imprisonment. Once Zeus frees him, the Valkyrie will raise the dead. Loki will man his ship of bones and lead everyone to war. Just like the prophecies of Ragnarok," Seneca said.

"What prophecies?" I asked.

Seneca frowned. "A bunch of end of the world things. You know how gods are."

"So Odin and the Valkyrie are here?" Hera asked.

"Yeah, they run a bar over in the Fringe," said Seneca.

"So it's true," I asked. "Freya can raise the dead?"

Hera's face lit up, filled with so many possibilities. "She is the Queen of the Valkyries. Odin's royal guard indeed has the power. She could raise all my children."

"She can and will, as well as all your favorite demigod warriors too!" Seneca added.

"The Olympians could once again stand in their former glory." Hera nodded her approval.

"You're forgetting something." Abby pointed at a now snoring

Zeus. "He doesn't look like he can use the bathroom on his own, let alone lead a war or free Loki."

Seneca sighed. "Yeah, about that. What happened to Zeus?"

"It was all too much for him. Losing the war was one thing, but watching his children perish was something else altogether. We are immortals; we do not watch our own die. It is unheard of. It is something we are not used to, and to watch as they all fell weighed heavy on his heart. Ultimately, the betrayal of our most beloved son Ares pushed him over the edge. When Ares turned his back on us, he also took with him the Aegis, the symbol of Zeus, his strength, his power, and his ability to wield lightning. With it went my husband's heart... and mind."

"So what do we do?" Seneca asked.

"The Aegis is the key," Hera continued. "If you can return it to him, it will restore his mind and his power."

"The same Aegis which Ares presented to Queen Mob as a sign of loyalty that now hangs over Puck's throne? That Aegis?" Seneca frowned.

"You made it all the way here," Hera took Seneca's hand with pleading in her eyes, "now I ask that you return to your world and find it. It is our only hope."

Seneca looked at me and Abby. "Sure. Let's do it. You guys in?"

"Why are you doing this?" I asked. "Why do you care so much about what happens to us?"

"Because I am just a shiny beacon of hope and virtue," she said. "And because Odin will owe me a favor. His Valkyrie can raise the dead. They can bring them back, so as far as I'm concerned, my parents aren't dead yet. Not with the possibility of Odin owing me a favor."

6

W hile Abby and I strayed in the background, Seneca led the way back to my house. She took on a more serious attitude after we left Hera and Zeus. Abby and I had a lot to think about as well. It felt like a part of us didn't want to speak about tea time with gods out loud, because that would make it all real. A strange truth too hard to accept.

"What are you going to do?" Abby grabbed my arm to hold my step.

"I don't know. It all seems so crazy. But at the same time, it's so brass! There had to be more to my life. I knew it, I always have. I wasn't destined to sit around wasting my teenage years in The Fringe and spend my adult years cleaning the deck of some ship. I have to believe all this is true."

"What's to believe? We saw the proof; it's all real. And it's something we shouldn't get involved in."

"How can we not?"

"Easy," she said. "Let Seneca go do what she has to do. We helped her enough. If she's going down to Earth, let her. However she plans on getting there or what she plans to do is no business of ours."

"But Abby, this could be the adventure of a lifetime!"

"Zak, listen to yourself. What are you going to do, pack it up and go with her? Are you really going to walk out on Alice and your father for some stupid promise of excitement, the same way your mother did?"

Her words stung like daggers to the heart; it surprised me more than anything else. I couldn't believe Abby had the capacity to hurt me.

"...I-I'm sorry. I didn't mean it like that."

"I know what you meant."

I wouldn't meet her eyes. I looked down the street, at the same cobblestone road that led me day in and day out back to my pathetic shack and life in The Fringe. Something about that street felt different. Seneca waited at the corner, watching me thoughtfully.

"Maybe she's right, Zak," Seneca said. "Maybe you should just sit home and pretend you never met me, pretend I don't even exist. Everything you learned, forget it. Surely you wouldn't want to be like your mother." Seneca shot Abby a look of disgust. "I understand what that's like, losing the people who you trust and count on the most. Some people, they just don't get it."

"Hop off!" Abby's face turned hot red. "You don't know us. You know nothing about us. Don't even act like you can relate to him better than me."

"You're the one who compared me to my mother..." I whispered, still not meeting her eyes.

"Zak, I said I didn't mean it like that—"

"Maybe you should go home," Seneca said. "Maybe we don't need you holding us back."

"I said stay the hades out of our business!"

"No, Abby. Maybe she's right. Besides, your dad would kill me if I put you in danger. Something I don't need on my head."

I couldn't look up from the ground. The silence hurt. I could feel Abby staring at me, waiting for me to come to my senses. I didn't want to be mad at her, but something in me refused to back down. Seneca put her hand on my shoulder, and I looked up at her, nodding that we should go.

"Fine…" Abby's voice cracked, on the verge of tears. My heart nearly broke, but when I looked up to confront her, she had already taken off running. I thought to chase her, but Seneca's lithe hand held me firm.

"Listen, if you don't want to help me, that's fine," Seneca said. "But let it be because *you* don't want to help me, not because of some girl who's too busy wrestling with her feelings."

"What feelings?"

"The ones written all over her face. So are you going to help me or not? Adventure of a lifetime and all, or this." She indicated the slums that waited. Even with the sun at its highest peak, a shadow always seemed to loom over The Fringe, and I would always be a Fringe Rat. I knew that, and yet something pulled at me, begging me not to leave.

"I don't know; this is cogged. How do you plan on getting off Olympus?"

"Airship."

"How will you get one?"

"Stealing, bartering, stowing away, something will stick."

"And won't it be hard?"

"Hard? Harder than you can imagine. Earth isn't the world your ancestors left behind. The Fey keep it glamoured so humans can't see them when they leave Earth. Once you reach the surface and the veil is lifted, you won't need special goggles to see all the magic and amazing creatures that lie right beneath your nose. Forest covers every inch, pillars of your past lay abandoned and broken. Fey, both good and bad, bicker and quarrel. There's a war going on; dark elves, trolls, goblins, and evil fairies occupy valleys once beautifully lined with rainbows, flowers, and creatures your wildest imagination could not have ever dreamed. The courts of Puck are spreading their darkness like the shadow of the moon engulfing the Earth. It may be in chaos, but it's still overflowing with such fascination and wonder your heart would swell at the sights. So yes, it will be hard, but the rewards would be well worth it."

"Why, why do you want me to come?"

"Because I promised someone you would," she mumbled.

"What?"

"Let's go already!" She shoved me and took off running toward my cabin.

———

Seneca maneuvered through the streets like she ran with the local Rats. I spent most of the trip home chasing her around corners. She finally stopped running when she reached my front yard. Her demeanor turned stiff and weary. I walked up to her side. She seemed confused and pointed at the porch steps where Alice sat waiting. I waved, and she offered me a slow mechanical wave in return. Seneca put her goggles on, scanned the yard, and lingered on Alice. She looked at me contemplatively for a second then sighed. "I guess we should get inside?"

"What's wrong?" I asked.

"Same old, you know, trying to save the world and all." She marched up to my house, and stopped a foot or two before Alice, who surprisingly sat unflinching. I came up behind her and noticed for the first time a distant look on Alice's face.

"Are you okay?" I asked.

She took her time looking up at me and forced her mouth into a tight smile. Her eyes seemed lost in uncertainty; my nerves began to rattle.

I grabbed her by the arms. "What's wrong?"

"Dad's home," she said.

"False. She doesn't talk." Seneca said.

"Dad's home and he hit me." Alice's voice sounded like grated iron. But my temper was already burning like wild fire.

"Zak!" Seneca continued, but I ignored her. "We should talk."

The drumming of my heart rose, cold sweat trickled down my back. "What do you mean he hit you?" I growled.

"He hit me, here." She put her small hand on the side of her face, and for the first time I noticed the bruise. "But it didn't hurt. It didn't hurt me, at least."

I knelt down and grabbed her by the shoulders, pulling her close into a tight hug. "I won't let this happen again. I won't let him or anybody ever hurt you. I'll edge him."

"Zak!" Seneca tried pulling me away. "I really would like to talk to you."

"What?" I yelled back, feeling the need to strike out at someone, even if it was a fairy princess from Earth.

"We need to go inside," she said, already walking up the steps and carefully pushing the door open.

"You're right! This gets sorted out now." I hugged Alice one last time before barging past Seneca into the house.

She followed at my side, scanning the inside, and put her goggles back on. I didn't have time to think. A sound came from the kitchen. Seneca's small fingers tried to find my hand and stop me, but I wouldn't have it. I yanked my arm away and stormed into the kitchen. I found blood everywhere. Crimson splats smeared the walls, windows, and tabletop. A trail along the floor led underneath the table. I kneeled and pulled up the stained tablecloth.

Dad screamed and nearly took off my head with a knife. His shaky hands clung to the wooden hilt like his life depended on it. He crab-crawled away from me, out from under the table until he cornered himself up against the ice chest. His nose bled and angled wrong, scratches covered his face, and he looked like he had just taken a dip in a pool of blood. *This much couldn't have come from those wounds.* I looked more closely, and I noticed a couple of his fingers missing and a good chunk of his forearm ripped out like a starved animal just got done with him.

"Get away! Get it away from me!" he yelled, his once strong voice replaced by a pathetic cry. "That thing; that's not my daughter!"

"Dad, snap out of it." I tried to get closer, but he waved the knife around in a panic.

"Zak," Seneca said behind me.

"Hold on a second," I said, still trying to get closer to my dad.

"Zak!"

"What?" I turned around to see her looking out of the kitchen; I followed her gaze to Alice who stood by the entrance, her head cocked to one side, staring at the grisly scene with a smile on her face.

"No—no, no, no, keep it away!" Dad cried.

"Shut up!" I yelled, making him recoil into himself, whimpering like a child.

"Alice?" I started.

"That's not Alice," Seneca casually said. "We better kill it."

"What? What the Hades is wrong with you?"

"From this point on," she said with a calmness that frustrated me, "you need to learn to trust everything I say. We have to kill it."

"Shut up!" I walked toward my sister, holding out my hands to her. *My sweet little sister, I should have protected you.* Before I could reach her, a fierce growl escaped her throat, and quicker than I could ever register, she attacked. Clawing, scratching, biting, and most frightening of all—laughing.

We fell to the floor in a knot of flesh. I tried to rip her off, but she clung with a fierce strength impossible for her size. Her teeth clacked together as she tried to bite at my face; I struggled to keep her at bay.

"What the Hades are you doing?" I managed to yell through my struggles.

"Hold still!" Seneca yelled from somewhere I couldn't see. My eyes were too busy trying to make sense of the insanity in Alice's eyes.

"I can't hold—"

A loud whack cut me off. Alice's small body flew off me, striking the wall hard. Seneca stood over me, holding the kitchen chair by its back. *What did you do?* I wanted to yell at her for hurting Alice. She was still my sister, but the primal sounds coming out of her distracted me. Alice rolled around on the floor as if she'd forgotten how to use her legs. I sat up trying to catch my breath; Seneca pulled me up by my shoulder. We both stared at Alice.

"What the hell happened to her?"

"I don't know what happened to your sister," Seneca whispered. "But that's not her."

"Look at her!"

"Yeah, look at her." She held out her goggles with one hand while balancing the chair in her other. Before I could take them, Alice jumped to her feet, snapping her neck back and forth, and tackled me into the kitchen table. The table gave out under me as the legs splintered and we crashed atop shattered wood. Her small hands swung wildly, trying with a twisted desperation to rip the skin from my face.

"What, what have I done? This is my fault," Dad mumbled behind us. "I'm so sorry, I'm so sorry," he kept repeating to himself like a prayer that would find no answers. Alice's head jerked up, her eyes following the voice of our pleading father. I felt the muscles in her legs tense. She wanted easier prey. I held her arms firm, locking her in place. She screamed and spat, struggling to get herself free. I looked back at Dad, he leapt up into a running sprint, nearly knocking Seneca over on his way out the door, screaming at the top of his lungs.

I didn't have time to care about his cowardly move, because Seneca rushed us with a table leg cocked over her head. I couldn't stop her; she brought her makeshift club down on Alice's head with a loud *crack*. My sister howled in pain, but seemed barely hurt. If anything, she looked slightly frazzled. Before she could get her bearings, Seneca rounded the leg over her shoulder and swung it like a bat. Alice's head whipped to the side; I was sure her neck broke, her body crumpled on top of me.

"Oh my gods, what did you do?" I struggled to get out from under her body and onto my unsteady legs.

"I told you, it's not your sister," Seneca said, matter of fact, while grabbing my dad's abandoned butcher knife.

"What are you—"

"Kill first, talk later." She turned toward Alice.

For a second I didn't think to stop her. *Snap out of it!* I grabbed her arm and pulled her close to me.

Seneca gave me a sour look. "Oh come on Zak, stop messing around—"

A blur of movement preceded Alice crashing into Seneca's back. The hit knocked her over the counter and onto the floor. She straddled Seneca, scratching at her face and biting at her shoulder. The knife rattled on the floor next to me. I bent down to pick it up, but my uncertain fingers found the goggles instead. I put them on. My stomach turned at what I saw.

Seneca struggled on her stomach, pinned down by a creature who wore my sister's skin like a cheap costume. Without the goggles, she looked like Alice, cogged if anything, but still Alice. With the goggles, her skin sagged and had rips all over, exposing a scaly fishlike texture underneath. Behind one of her missing human eyes, a huge black pupil swelled. Through another tear in her back, a boney wing jutted out where her left shoulder should be, like the skeleton of a long dead bird. I wanted to throw up.

"Zak," Seneca said, still trying to fight off Alice. "It's not your sister!"

"I—"

"Need to stab it. Repeatedly. Preferably now!" she managed, as Alice banged her head against the floor.

I had no time to think, only act. *But what happened to Alice, was this her skin?*

"Gods help me," Seneca shouted. "If I lose a tooth!"

I picked up the knife, ran over, and sank the blade into the small of the Alice thing's back. She let loose a violent scream. I dropped the knife and fell to the floor, holding my hands over my ears. Seneca rammed her elbow into the Alice thing's chest and knocked it aside before grasping the stove to pull herself up. She leaned on it for support.

"Looks like we'll be eating changeling tonight." Seneca turned the oven on. The thing howled at her, struggling to back away. She opened the oven door with a monstrous smile. "Here kitty, kitty, kitty."

"Seneca, what are you doing?"

"The only way to kill a changeling is to roast it." She grabbed the thing up in her arms, it struggled and fought, but its strength bled away; great globs of slime leaked out of its wound.

"Rust, it's wearing Alice's..."

"No, this isn't Alice's skin. It's just cheap prop skin, it'll come right off." She shoved the changeling into the oven, struggling to get the small hands and feet inside. After a brief battle with the spitting, hissing, monster, she gave one final push to stuff it inside, and slammed the door. She turned the knob all the way, igniting the coal beneath with a hearty fire, and sat back on the floor, leaning against the oven door to barricade it.

She sighed. "Well I bet that's something you don't see every day, huh?"

"What was that?" I asked.

"What was up with your dad? He just ran out on us. You think he pissed himself?"

"That was a…?"

"Changeling. They suck. Some fairies, they love stealing human babies, it's a fact of life. When they do, they replace them with one of their own. This is new though, Alice is nowhere near being a baby. Never seen them pull a switcheroo with an older child. I bet the Lillies are behind this, those baby bandits have no class or appreciation for rules."

"I…"

"Yeah, you probably want to faint now. It's fine, I'll clean up."

All the oxygen seemed to have left my brain, and with it, my chest decided to close up. I fell to my back, and then it all went dark.

7

I woke from a nightmare of an annoying fairy princess, gods in nursing homes, and a thing wearing Alice like an old coat. I struggled to untangle myself from covers, feeling gross by the cold sweat that covered my body and the cheap fabric of my shirt clinging to my skin. I shivered, rubbing at the bruises on my arms and back. *I must have been thrashing about pretty bad.*

I got up and stretched, peeking over at Alice's bed. Even though it was practically morning, Alice's bed hadn't been slept in. Ignoring the dull ache in my body, I walked out to the bathroom. I knocked twice; no answer, I turned the knob slowly, giving her a chance to warn me off. Nothing. I lifted up the toilet seat and had an uneasy feeling tickle the back of my neck as I relieved myself. *Something wasn't right.*

The bathroom door burst open, causing me to jump, accidentally making a mess on the sides of the toilet and floor.

"What the Hades?!" I screamed, trying to make sure I had everything securely in place.

"Hey, big guy." Seneca had a mischievous smile on her face; that and the wink made me double check my fly. "Are you ready to go? You've been out cold all evening."

"Go where?"

"Rescue your sister, reclaim Zeus's power, free Loki, create a hasty, somewhat fragile alliance with a bunch of old arrogant gods, save the world, and stuff."

"No, no, no… I was dreaming!"

"Would you rather we just collapse on the couch in a heap of glory—"

"Wait, where is she?" I shoved past her, running to the living room, then into the kitchen. I found a mess, the chairs broken and blood-stains everywhere. The smell of cooked meat attacked my nose; it drew me toward the stove, toward the lazy black smoke streaming out from the sides. I felt lightheaded again.

Seneca walked in behind me. "I thought we went over this. They took her. They replaced her with the changeling, remember?"

"Who took her?"

She walked off into the living room; I followed close behind. "I'm betting it was the Lillies. They are the only ones I know who make a business of snatching children and leaving those sick copies in their place. You know they are really annoying little pixies. I have no idea how they've managed to even make it this far in baby stealing, that's so archaic. Everyone knows if you want to steal a child, you need to make ill-advised contracts with unsuspecting parents—"

"Can you slow down and try making sense," I yelled. "We need to find her!"

"Isn't that what we were talking about?" She shook her head while gathering up a bag and tossing it to me. "I didn't want to waste time, so I took the liberty of packing you some essential things for our trip. Change of clothes and provisions for the road."

I looked in the bag as she went down a laundry list of items she clearly just grabbed and threw in. "If you're serious about this and she's down below, how are we going to get there?"

"Hmm, maybe you should change your clothes?"

"But how are we going to get there?" I grabbed her arm and dragged her back into my bedroom. "This is cogged, you know that?"

"Cogged? Please, this is just another Tuesday."

I took off my sweaty undershirt and threw it on the floor. After digging through my drawer, I pulled out a somewhat clean black shirt. I decided to stick with the pants I had on. I looked at Seneca for approval.

"Don't forget your coat." She adjusted her goggles, zipped up her coat, exaggeratedly swung her scarf around her neck, and headed for the door. "Meet you out front, and make sure you've done everything that has to be done."

I stared at the door, wondering what else there could have been for me to do. I looked around the old run down cabin, the cabin that held me prisoner for all my life, drove Mom away, and my family apart. I'd be damned if I ever came back to this cabin at the end of the world.

I slung my bag across my back and decided to leave Dad a letter; I didn't know what I was going to write at first. "I'm going to Earth with a fairy Princess to save Alice from a fairy Prince and unite the old gods against the Fey" would sound cogged. But the moment I put lead to paper, something else came out entirely, I wrote away as if the pencil were a magic wand weaving the most intricate of spells. For as long as I could remember, I felt a poison run through my veins, a poison slowly claiming my life, day by day. As I wrote, I somehow managed to bleed it all out. By the time I signed my name I was in tears.

Seneca waited outside looking up at the sky, still dotted with the few last stars before morning, each one shining a promise of other worlds so far away. *At least that's what Mom used to say.* I wondered what the sky looked like from Earth. I wondered if I would ever be so close to it again.

"So this thing—" Seneca pulled out something that looked like a small gun from her bag "—should signal my friends, and they'll take us to the goblin market."

"Who are your friends?" I asked, watching her aim the gun up at the stars. She stuck a finger from her free hand in her ear. The gun seemed to almost explode; a comet erupted from its tip, rocketing toward the heavens, leaving a red tail in its wake. Just as it reached its peak and gravity began to reassert itself, the small fireball of light exploded in a grand mass of red stars, all spreading out across the sky.

She nodded in delight and headed off down the road. I took a moment and looked back; they say you're never supposed to look back. But I did, I had to. Shadows wrapped the old cabin, made darker by the blackness in the windows. A faint *squeak-squeak* carried in the air in time with the wind jostling the porch swing. I stared at the door I'd firmly locked, struck by how the place seemed to have fallen asleep.

We stood out front for a while where the road that led to my cabin intersected with the main road. I didn't have much to say, so I watched Seneca with curiosity.

"What's it like?" I asked. "Where you're from?"

"It's… well." She took a deep breath. "It's different. It's hard to explain. I mean, explain to me what your world is like, it's hard to explain things you take for granted. Things you see every day, you become so used to them that they aren't there anymore."

"How do you mean?"

"For instance." She kicked up some dirt. "Would you bother to explain this road to me, if I asked? Wouldn't you think it's so mundane it goes without explanation?"

"It's just a road of dirt." I shrugged.

"A road of dirt miles above the planet. How far can I dig before I reach the plates of steel and iron, and once I reach those, how far before I fall from the other side? This whole city is a marvel. Think how all those years ago Hephaestus made this small island that over time expanded into this."

"Okay, great. My city is amazing. But, I asked about where you come from."

She sighed, giving me a sorry look. "Where I come from, almost everything and anything is possible. There are dangers around every corner, but it doesn't matter because the beauty of my world is so much that you rarely notice it. That's not to say that the danger just disappears. Think of it like a pretty trap, get distracted long enough and you'll die. But why ruin all the surprises?" She nodded behind me.

I turned to the sound of approaching steps, the loud clattering of iron horse hooves. The horse-drawn carriage careened to a violent stop in front of us. A bulky cloaked figure sat behind the reins. He had intense eyes and a square jaw.

"Came soon as I saw the signal, Lady Rose." He swooped out his hand and offered a small bow. "Is this the boy?"

"That it is, Mister O'Brian!" Seneca bowed in return and opened the carriage door.

"Hi?" I looked up at the driver.

"Come along, Zak." Seneca jumped into the carriage and I followed. I barely had time to situate myself before the horse made a metallic whine and thundered off with us in tow. I fell over the velvet seats, landing heavily on my side before sliding onto the floor. I looked up at Seneca sitting comfortably, legs crossed, and face covered in a smirk. "How's the view down there?"

"Very funny." I pulled myself up into the seat finding it far more comfortable than the floor. "Who is he?"

"I made some deals while you were out. Might have used a glamour or two... What? Don't look at me like that. What's wrong with having a crew of devoted Scavengers at your beck and call?"

I watched out the window as the world passed by. The city stood silent. With the unforgiving cold that washed across Olympus at night, people preferred to be tucked away in their homes or local bars. We rode into the shantytowns, and at our speed, they looked like heaps of garbage piled into different shapes. The transition into Empyrean felt so unreal, the change happened without warning. The clatter of the iron horse hooves eased off from the soft clap of dirt to the echoing pounding of iron on granite.

"Nearing the docks!" Mister O'Brian banged on the roof of the carriage to get our attention. I stuck my head out the window for a better view. Flickering street lamps spread about sparingly did little to fight off the darkness; even so, the bulking form of the ship bearing Scavenger flags stood out, waiting just for us. The vessel docked at the far end, across a lane of points where a crew could moor their ship. No other ships were about, as if all captains knew to steer clear of Scavengers. My heart nearly stopped as the shadows cleared and I realized we were approaching the Highwind. An airship with no balloon, powered by ambrosia, steam, and magic. Everyone's heard the stories of Alana Highwind, she was said to be the only one who could steer that ship, a birthright passed down for generations in her family.

Now here I was approaching the legendary ship.

Sparkling brass piping snaked its way in and out of the hull. It looked like a crazy fusion of wood and copper. Puffs of gassed ambrosia sprouted out from nozzles along the sides and back of the ship, making her sway back and forth with each burst. A burly man dangled dangerously from the main mast while securing the sail. The more I watched, the more I took notice of different men running up and down the deck, securing cannons, swabbing decks, and adjusting ropes. They were like a well-oiled machine, working in perfect sync with each other.

The carriage pulled up closer, and the ship continued to get larger… and larger. Never before had I gotten a true sense of its enormity. I'd only ever heard stories of the Highwind, and felt dwarfed beside such brass craftsmanship. It weighed on my heart; I knew Alice would be hysterical with excitement at the sight of her. Once I brought her home, I would take her on any ship she wanted, I swore it. We jerked to a stop, and Seneca all but kicked me out the door. Master O'Brian jumped off the carriage and carefully offered Seneca his hand. She took it with a mock elegance and stepped out.

"Lady Rose," he said. "Kid, The Highwind is at your service."

"Are we ready to go?" Seneca asked.

Master O'Brian seemed to hesitate for a second. "We are fueling up our ambrosia cells. Should be ready any minute."

"Very good."

"Naturally." Master O'Brian walked ahead of us.

I followed him, still in awe. As we approached the boarding deck, I looked up and saw Alana Highwind standing by the top of the ramp. Her confident stance, hands resting on the pistols hanging on either hip, made me recognize her right away. Her dark skin seemed to glisten in the moonlight, and her hair was a wild mess of colors. A trench coat fluttered behind her, completing the picture. Unfortunately, the closer we got, the clearer her frown became.

Mister O'Brian jogged up the deck and nodded to Alana before he disappeared from sight. Seneca and I took a more cautious approach. Alana's eyes clearly wanted to burn a hole into Seneca's skull.

"Seneca Rose," she yelled. "I swore I would be done with you last time we met."

Seneca waved. "And I swore that we would have a number of more adventures. Don't you remember? It was right after you threatened to kill me if you ever saw me again."

Alana shook her head and pushed past Seneca to me. Face to face, she stood a couple of inches taller than me. Her energy was intimidating. "Is this the Walker kid?"

"Yeah," Seneca said, making her way onto the ship and leaving me to face the captain alone.

I stuck my fist out and offered her a friendly pound. "I'm Zak. It's brass to meet you. I would love to take a look at your engine. I got skills you might find—"

"You got your mother's eyes," she said as casually as can be.

I let out a breath of air and felt myself deflate. "You knew my mom?"

She nodded and ushered me onto the ship. "Yeah, good woman, as brave as they come. I'll tell you more about it later. I have to prepare for takeoff." She marched off barking orders to her men without even waiting for me to pick my jaw back up.

The hustle and bustle of her crew had me disoriented. Men ran back and forth. I had to jump out of the way more than once to keep from being toppled over. A couple of huge men pulled the anchor aboard, while another pulled in the boarding plank. The sails were set and the ship lurched away from the dock. It was a bit disorienting. I lived my whole life on a floating city, and yet feeling the ship move under me made my legs weak.

I found Seneca standing at the forward railing dreamily gazing at the sky. The clouds cleared out and the moon seemed to offer a final goodbye. I took a spot next to her as we pulled away from Olympus. I never dreamed this day would come. The invisible leash of the Fringe pulled at my neck. "This is the first time I'm leaving that rust bucket."

"It's hard leaving home," she said. "Especially when you hate it. Because you swear you'll never come back, there's nothing you'll miss, there's nothing here for me. But once you realize how big and cruel the world is, you'll start to appreciate what you took for granted… you end up wanting to go back. Then you feel like a failure who lost at life and had to settle for contentment. It's tragic really."

"Was that supposed to be inspirational?" I asked.

She shook her head and shrugged. "I don't really do inspirational. Did it at least make you feel tingly inside?"

The Highwind picked up speed with ease. She turned away from Olympus and headed into the sea of clouds. Soon, the city lights were far behind us and we were lost to the vast white and gray darkness. Alana stood at the helm on one of the upper decks. I wanted to ask her more about my mom.

"How do you know her?" I asked Seneca, nodding toward our captain.

Seneca didn't take her eyes off the sky. "They brought me here. When I escaped Puck and the Unseelie, the Highwind got me to Olympus."

"She knows my mom."

"Everything happens for a reason. Fate's funny like that."

"I'll catch you later." Without waiting for a reply, I jogged over to the stairs leading up to the captain. Alana clutched the helm, making tiny adjustments to keep the ship on course. An amulet draped on her chest. Its strange design obscured by the intense pale blue light it gave off. Before I could take another step Gharis O'Brian stopped me with a firm hand on the shoulder.

"Sorry," I said. "Just wanted to ask her—"

"She prefers not to be bothered when she's steering the ship. It takes a lot of effort to control the magic that keeps our engine going."

"The stories are true then? The Highwind's engine is made of brass and magic?"

He nodded once then looked at her with admiring eyes.

"Mister—"

"Just call me Gharis," he said.

"Gharis, I want to ask Alana about my mom.

The way he eyed me up and down made me believe he was trying to decide if I was worthy of an answer. Squaring my shoulders and clenching my teeth tight, I tried to make myself look important. He was about to open his mouth when a shout came down from the main mast. Gharis and I both followed the call to the crow's nest. A man flailed his arms about and pointed off far ahead. I barely had time to question what was happening when a shadow swooshed across the lookout. He barely had time to scream before he fell toward the deck. The wet crunch his body made when he landed could only mean death.

Gharis and I ran to the man's mangled body. Already, other crewmembers started piling in over their dead mate. Seneca grabbed me by the arm and pulled me aside.

Her eyes darted back and forth. "We got problems."

Gharis shouted over the yelling men. "Everyone, man your stations!"

"What's going on?" I asked.

Before anyone could answer, I heard a horrible sound like a swarm of insects. It started far off and approached at a speed much too fast for any bee. Everyone scanned the skies for the source. It seemed like the clouds were abuzz. Small shadows came into view, dotting the sky with fast approaching shapes that became men, practically an army. An army of Fey with wings flapping at incredible speeds, carrying their numbers straight for us. They hovered all around the ship, careful to stay out of range, but close enough to aim their wicked looking spears.

"Oh," Seneca moaned. "I guess they found me."

Before I could even make him out, Puck's lackey from the Crow's Nest, landed right in the middle of the deck. The Highwind crew armed themselves with swords and pistols, their faces fearless of the new threat. Francis' wings had a brown shine and looked like those of a bird, except crafted of shiny bronze feathers, gears and cogs. They were attached to a pack that ticked like a clock.

"Seneca Rose." His voice thundered over the din of noise. "You will give yourself up now, or watch your companions fall."

Seneca stepped up beside me. "Maybe you haven't heard, but I'm way too selfish for selfless acts. It's kind of my thing."

"This is my ship and I'm the only one who'll be making demands." Alana stood in front of the helm with two pistols aimed at Francis. "Now I will ask you only once to get off my ship."

Francis held out his hands imploringly. "Is there really a need for violence? All we ask is for the Lady Rose. What need do you have of her?"

"As much as she annoys me…" Alana said.

Seneca shook her head in agreement. "Can't be denied."

"…I would never bust a deal." Alana shot a warning round. The wood near Francis's feet erupted in a tiny explosion. He didn't seem the slightest bit fazed.

Gharis handed me a sword and drew another from his belt. A simple cutlass, but it felt good in my hands. I took a step in front of Seneca and held the blade firm before me.

"Zak," Seneca whispered. "What are you doing? Let the Scavengers fight while we make a hasty, ill thought-out escape."

"If we don't make a stand, he'll never leave us alone." I pointed at Francis.

"Very well." He launched himself into the air.

The others came at the ship like a hurricane of steel and brass. I caught a glimpse of Alana firing off shot after shot into the mass of attackers. Seneca pulled me back as I swung at any Fey close enough to feel my sword. The deck erupted into complete chaos, men and Fey roared their battle cries and came together in a flurry of madness. Alana's crew fanned out and tried to push the threat back, only to find it hopeless when the enemy took to the air and moved as fast as the wind. Scavengers were plucked up from the deck and dropped off the side of the ship. Their numbers quickly dwindled, and for every Fey taken out, two took their place.

Seneca and I had our backs to the railing. She looked over the side and I could see an idea formulating in her wild eyes. "How far do you think the drop is?"

"We'd never make that!" I yelled.

Francis cut a path through the madness and came right for us.

"I got an idea," Seneca said.

I braced myself for the coming attack. "What?"

"They only want me. If we escape, they'll leave the Highwind alone."

"How?"

Francis was nearly on me when Seneca rushed out in front of me, holding her arms as if she meant to shield me from certain doom.

"Stop!" she yelled. "If I give myself up, will you let everyone go?"

Francis came to a halt and let his sword fall down to his side. A smile spread slowly across his face. "I give my word."

I grabbed Seneca's arm and tried to keep her at my side. "What are you doing?"

"Call them off," Seneca said.

He bent his head back and made a strange ear piercing sound that echoed far and wide. The fighting stopped and the Fey began to retreat, but stayed at a safe distance watching as the scene played out. Seneca looked at me and placed her hand on my chest. Carefully she pushed me back toward the ship railing.

"You can't go with him," I whispered.

She backed up until she bumped into Francis's chest. He wrapped his arm around her neck and watched me with a primal hunger. I took a step forward, but he applied pressure and choked her, keeping me at bay. Alana ran over, joining our showdown, her pistol aimed at Francis's head. He used Seneca as a shield, always keeping her between himself and the captain's sight.

"I called off mine," he said. "Now you call off yours."

"Alana," Seneca said. "Thanks for the ride, but I think it's time Zak and I got going."

The captain gripped her pistol tighter. "You always know how to ruin a perfectly good day."

"It's what I do." Seneca strained a laugh. "So I'm thinking, meet on the border of the Unseelie court?"

"We'll try our best."

"What are you two talking about?" Francis shouted.

Seneca moved so fast it was hard to keep up. She smashed the back of her head into his nose. Her heel came down on his foot and she bent forward. Alana's hand shot up and her pistol fired in one fluid motion. Francis jerked back and his body went limp. He fell to the floor, blood pooling under him.

Seneca pulled the pack off his shoulders as the Fey resumed their attack. A Fey came out of nowhere, grabbing me by the arms and dragging me off the ship.

I watched helplessly as we flew further away. Alana and Gharis, fighting furiously side by side, hadn't noticed me getting snatched. Seneca still struggled with Francis's pack. I had to take matters into my own hands. I struggled under my attacker's iron grip. He had me in a tight bear hug rendering my arms useless. I thrashed about until I broke free. The rust bucket flew away, and for a moment, it felt like I could fly. Gravity had a different plan in mind.

I'm going to die.

Clouds swallowed the world; the white darkness devoured me, the gushing air made my ears pop. I'd never get to kiss Abby; I'd never become a man; Most importantly, I failed to keep Alice safe. *Alice, I'm sorry.*

I closed my eyes and prepared to die. Until I heard laughing. *I'm cogged.* The wild laughter of a maniac got closer, closer, and closer still. Seneca burst through the clouds head first, her body straightened with arms pressed tight at her sides. Goggles covered her eyes, and her smile seemed to go for miles. She caught up and wrapped her arms around me, locking her body against mine.

"Fancy meeting you here!" she shouted over the rush of wind.

"We're cogged!" I managed to get out. "We're going to fall straight to Hades."

"Oh, that! Big deal." She pulled a cord on the strap of her borrowed pack, and the metallic wings shot out. "These are normally only made for one person. Hopefully, I didn't put on extra pounds with all that eating I did at your house."

She pulled the cord again and the wings buzzed to life, a puff of steamed ambrosia shot out from behind her and our fall slowed. We continued to fall, but at a much more reasonable pace. We broke free of the clouds and came out miles above blue sea and sunshine. Earth lay before us, an endless expanse toward both horizons. Further inland, the greenery of trees, and browns and grays of mountainous ranges greeted us. I never realized how beautiful Earth could be.

"Rust!" she shouted.

"What?"

"I think this thing—"

A small popping sound came from her pack and it started to smoke. Her left wing went completely limp. Seneca pulled at the cord over and over again, trying to get the gears going. It was a mess of confusion. I fell wildly and spun through the air. The world turned into a kaleidoscope of colors and shapes. I wanted to throw up.

I would have too had I not hit cold water with such a staggering hard impact it knocked me out.

8

The singing made me realize I was alive. The soft melodic tune of a woman, like a mother singing a soothing song to her child. A magical incantation of peace and harmony. I opened my eyes and saw the cloud dotted sky as I floated on my back. The cool touch of water licked at my skin and soaked my clothes. I didn't care how I got there, because the melody took control of my mind. I followed it and found Abby right there with me.

She floated a couple of feet away, her naked shoulders and arms dipping in and out of the water. Wet hair hung down and covered her chest. Her eyes wide with delight as she casually hummed the tune that woke me from my dreams.

"Abby?" I asked, feeling so confused. Something came over me that refused to acknowledge the logic of the situation. Seeing her was all that mattered. "Abby, what are you doing here?"

Her naturally tanned skin looked a couple of shades lighter, a ghostly complexion that made the black of her eyes stand out more, and her full lips had traces of blue; all signs that she'd been in the cold water for far too long. I wanted to swim over and take her in my arms, but her nakedness kept me put. As much as I wanted her in my arms, my cheeks burned with embarrassment.

She swayed with each passing wave, while her body moved with the rhythm of the melody.

"Abby, what's going on?" I pleaded. "How'd you get here?"

She closed her eyes and tilted her head back, lost in her music. I tried to paddle toward her, but the closer I got, the more waves would push me back. It almost felt like the ocean itself wanted to keep me away.

"Rust! I can't get to you." Water splashed in my mouth. I coughed and sputtered out the salty liquid. "Can you swim to me?"

She looked at me, once again with those haunting eyes. Her smile felt different than the normal smirk I was used to. She wrapped her arms around her body and tried to rub life into it. *She is so beautiful.* The urge to get to her and keep her warm rose up within me, as strong as the urge to breathe. Every part of me wanted only to touch and hold her.

With one last smile, she sunk into the water. I dived after her. I swam as hard as I could, desperately attempting to catch her. But the strong currents pulled me in the wrong direction. Soon, I found myself lost in the endless blue. In a flurry, I fought back the water, begging the gods to let it release me. I couldn't swim; I was sinking, but before I could reach the peak of panic, Abby grabbed onto my arm. I looked at her, expecting to be filled with hope.

Instead, I saw the face of evil.

Abby's smile spread way too wide, her lips curled back revealing inch-long razor like teeth, her whole mouth seemed to overflow with red-stained ivory.

I tried to pull away, struggling to fight her off. Arms grabbed me from behind, locking me in a bear hug. I managed to catch a glimpse of another Abby behind me; her mouth also curled back revealing hungry shark teeth. They both pulled me down deeper into the abyss; the mischievous giggles of little girls replaced their song. I struggled all the way down, but their strength seemed inhuman. I made the mistake of screaming; oxygen fled my lungs and water rushed in. My chest felt as if it would burst. I kicked and punched, but couldn't break free. The deeper we went, the darker it got as my life slipped away.

When the Abby thing turned to me and her jaw opened wide, I found death waiting for me. I clenched my eyes shut, expecting pain.

But it never came; I opened my eyes, the water colored with a smoky red. Abby's body floated away, leaving a trail of red haze running from her chest. The other creature continued pulling me further under. I caught a glimpse of Seneca swimming toward me with a knife in her hand. I had only seconds of fight left in me. I struggled against the other's hold, punching and clawing at her arms. Seneca reached us as my lungs burned for air. She stabbed the monster repeatedly in the side. Her scream filled my ears; she twitched a couple of times before letting me go and sinking to the bottom. Seneca grabbed me and swam upward. I gasped for air as we broke the surface. Once my head stopped spinning, she helped me swim to shore.

I clawed my way onto the beach and collapsed. Hot sand on my face felt strange and alien to me. As much as I tried, I couldn't seem to catch my breath. The hungry waves had tried to claim me, but they would not have my life. Olympus didn't have anything like this. Honest to gods real sand from Earth, hot, grainy, and moist from the foaming tide. I wiped water from my face and regretted it when the fine grains found their way into my eyes.

The shore felt small with lumbering trees standing guard over the rest of what I could see. A path of sand that led deeper into the forest caught Seneca's attention.

"What... were those things?" I coughed and gagged, still out of breath.

She licked her finger and stuck it up in the air. "Sirens. They show you your heart's desire, and drown you while you're preoccupied. Ugh, we are too far south!" She sniffed at the air. "Free Fey territory. It stinks of them."

My legs were practically numb, but I managed to get up and muster as much confidence as I could. Looking around overwhelmed me. The thick forest loomed over me like a hungry monster... endless. I was just a tiny insignificant speck. I picked up a handful of sand and let it fall between my fingers.

"How are we supposed to find her?" I spun around taking it all in. "It'll be impossible, we're so cogged!"

"We have to find the Lillies," she said. "It's our best bet. Even if they didn't take her, they know everything that goes on. Their ears are always to the ground, and their fingers are in every shadow."

"But—"

"We'll find her. It's my fault they took her. I'll make it right."

I nodded and held out my fist. "We're crew. You help me, I'll help you."

She touched her fist to mine and gave me a warm smile. "Remember this isn't Olympus. You may have been top dog there, but here you are prey. This is Free Fey territory. They have no respect for royal blood. The good thing is they equally hate Seelie and Unseelie. Stick close to me and never wander off on your own. Don't trust anybody that isn't me. Don't even trust me while you're at it, and don't trust yourself."

"What?"

"Exactly! Let's go."

She ran into the woods without another word, and I ran after her, feeling the weight of Olympus behind me. The forest opened up into a thin path. Seneca moved like a ghost, jumping over roots and ducking branches with ease. My skills came in handy when it came to keeping up with her. The chaos reminded me of the underbelly of Olympus where wrong moves weren't an option. I imagined the trees and their reaching branches as steel piping, keeping it as something familiar in my head made it easier to maneuver.

Soon, the warm ocean breeze of the beach gave way to an uncomfortable dampness. Sweat built up on my forehead and armpits. My feet sunk deeper into the warm dirt with each step. I don't know how long we ran, or how far before I realized morning shifted into night, and the sounds of the forest that originally greeted us became an unsettling silence. The trees and underbrush grew thinner, further apart, and up ahead, a beam of moonlight shone into a clearing.

Seneca stopped. "We need to rest."

"No way!" I bent over taking time to catch my breath. "We need to find these Lillies as soon as possible."

"If you drop dead, you'll be no use to Alice." She pushed me. I fell back onto my butt, surprised by how weak I was. I was getting tired. But I couldn't bear to think of Alice out there alone and scared.

"We'll start a fire, rest a little, eat, and then keep going. Would you trust me?"

"You said not to trust you."

She looked at me thoughtfully. "Good point." She shrugged. "That's awkward. Don't trust me then, but stay here while I gather some fire wood and food."

Before I could argue, she sprinted off into the forest. Even if I wanted to, I wouldn't have been able to keep up with her. She moved like a ghost in the shadows.

The night air was out to get me. It wanted nothing more than to make my life miserable. I curled up close to the fire, but it did little to warm me. Poor Alice, wherever she was, I hoped she had a blanket to keep her warm. I couldn't fall asleep even if I tried. I couldn't stop thinking about Alice shivering in some cold scary place. Seneca couldn't seem to sleep either. She stared deep into the fire, casually poking at the embers with a branch. Her share of the rabbit she caught and cooked for us still sat by her side.

I leaned up on my elbows. "Tell me about the Lillies. You don't think they'd hurt her do you?"

"Baby Bandits... worst of the worst." She didn't take her eyes off the fire. "The Lillies trade in secrets and promises. They have connections all across the land. What makes them most popular is their ability to snatch kids. Human children are a highly sought after commodity to the Free Fey."

"Why?"

"Because most Free Fey can't have children. Only royal blood can reproduce, that includes the Seelie and Unseelie. Free Fey are born of magic and the Earth. The Lillies use that magic to create changelings to replace the... human children they snatch, like the one we fought at your house."

"So that means most Free Fey are human?"

"Yeah or half-bloods. For some reason, Free Fey can reproduce with humans. It's a whole thing. Nothing to do with Alice. If they took her, it was most likely to draw me out. We'll find them and get her back."

"Where do we look?"

"I don't know..."

9

Alice looks at me with shame in her eyes. She opens her mouth to speak, but words don't come. I run to her, but my feet feel as if they are weighed down, as if I'm trying to run in thigh-deep water. I call out to her. She ignores me and turns away. Soon, she fades into the shadows. I reach out for her, but my legs sink into the earth. I'm trapped. The colors of the world drip away and leave only the darkness. I scream and scream, but Alice is lost to me.

———

I WOKE WITH A START. Cold sweat covered me, and my clothes stuck uncomfortably to my body. Finding myself deep in the woods, lying underneath the moon and stars between swaying trees that breathed with ancient life shook me. A shadow running across the outskirts of the clearing caught my attention. It resembled Alice's small frame and her laughter sang across the space between us. I caught a glimpse of her hair as she ran between trees, as if she were playing a game of hide and seek. With the foggy remnants of the dream still running through my head, I didn't stop to think about what I was doing, I just got up and ran after her, forgetting my boots and Seneca.

I couldn't believe I made such a rookie mistake running in the forest without boots. The sharp twigs and jagged rocks made their presence known with every step. I navigated the thick branches and trees that stood so tall I feared the stars would be trapped. Soon, I'd completely lost sight of Alice, but her laughter lingered. The deeper into the woods I went, the cloudier my head felt. The laughter became a faint wisp to far too hear, soon replaced by the subtle cadence of a violin.

The music reached out to me with a welcoming embrace. I followed blindly as if lost in a dream. The forest fanned out around me, and soon I found myself in the center of a glade bathed in moonlight, where dozens of white stone sculptures stood frozen in time, their bodies in strange contortions as if caught in the middle of a wild dance.

I tried to clear my head and take note of my surroundings. The moist grass chilled the bottom of my feet, a welcome sensation to the harsh forest paths. Comfort and warmth blanketed my frigid body as I approached, mesmerized by the statue garden. Figures great and small, all types of creatures I'd never seen before on Olympus surrounded me. Winged and fanged things, gremlins, fairies, and pixies

Focusing on every detail became hard. The glade faded in and out of existence as if I were trying to grasp the ending of a dream. The enchanting music seemed to emanate from the trees in every direction. I shook the fog from my head and found what I was looking for. There amongst the statues of dancing pixies lay a circle of six stones, within which lurked the shadowy figure of Alice. I took a step closer, the music stopped with the pluck of a violin string. My head cleared while the glade came into focus. Another hesitant step and another pluck of the string, this time a deeper note. I looked over my shoulder and searched the tree line for the musician.

When I reached the circle, the shadow vanished. I anxiously looked around one last time hoping to find the person responsible. The sweet scent of lavender wafted by. It calmed my nerves, made me relax, and reminded me of Abby. A breeze ran across the grass and shook the leaves, carrying a whisper that rattled my nerves: the soft angelic voice of a woman, a voice too enticing to be safe.

"Welcome, wanderer," she said. "Boy who fell from the clouds."

I turned and faced a beautiful fairy, red hair mixed with bits and pieces of twine sprung out at either side of her head in pigtails. She wore a top hat tilted to the side, with a fancy pair of brass goggles perched on the brim. Her clothes were a flurry of colors, black leggings with sizzling white stripes, and an overcoat covered in copper wires. Her wings fluttered behind her, made of gears, cogs, and brass feathers. The violin in her gloved hand impressed me the most, a shimmering copper instrument with gold strings. In her other hand, she twirled the bow around her fingers. Even her pupils took the form of a six-pronged copper gear. Her mischievous smile put me on guard.

"Who are you?" I asked, taking a step back.

"I am the song of the forest," she said, matter of factly.

"What's that supposed to mean?"

"It means it is I who makes the forest dance. Would you like to get started?" She stepped forward with an encouraging nod, readying her violin.

I held up my hands, warding her off. "No thanks, I have something to do…"

"But what if that something is dancing?" she asked.

"Why would I want to dance?"

"Why not?" Her cog-shaped pupils stared at me as if I'd asked the most foolish question imaginable.

"Because I have to find my sister. I thought… I saw her." I walked past her, trying to escape her gaze.

"I can see the struggle in your heart, but wouldn't you rather leave that behind and dance amongst the stone?"

"Look, what don't you understand?" I yelled. She wasn't startled in the least; she nodded and brought the fine violin up to her chin.

"I have a song. One that calls out just for you."

She closed her eyes and began to play a ghostly verse, almost on the verge of silence. She swayed back and forth with each stroke of her bow letting the melody move her. Something about the whisper of sound made me want to stay and listen forever. She opened her eyes and caught my enchanted gaze. A smile filled her lips and she nodded.

Her wings fluttered to life; she jumped back several feet, landing nimbly, far out of reach. I thought to follow, but before I could take a step toward her, she picked up the pace of her tune. The gears of her violin turned as she played with passion and speed. Power and longing gave birth to her music. Soon, the whole glade echoed. She swayed with each beat, bouncing around on lithe feet, never staying in one place for too long. Her body moved as one with the waves of the music itself.

I nodded uncontrollably, moving along with the beat that caressed my body. The music charmed me so much that I didn't care when the statues around me came to life. At first only their arms uncoiled, moving along with the violin. The effect spread over them, and the figures shook off their stone façade as if shedding skin. Color filled in over blank white stone, and their faces radiated life. All the beings of the glade joined in, their laughter and cheers so infectious, it swept me up.

I chased after pixies that danced circles around me; the excitement made me trip over myself, only to land in the arms of a fair-haired fairy. We spun around holding each other tight. I didn't want to let go, nor did she mind. We laughed, dipping and dodging others overcome with the same joy. A goblin cut in and whisked her away, spinning her on her toes. Normally that would have angered me, but instead I clapped and hopped from foot to foot.

The violinist took flight and came to land in front of me, not once breaking from her complicated moves. I tried to keep up with her and not break the rhythm, but no matter how hard I tried, I couldn't. It didn't matter, though. Just being lost to the music meant the world to me. I danced amongst the goblins, gremlins, fairies, and pixies as the moon passed its highest peak and the stars began to fade. *How many hours have gone by?* I couldn't catch my breath; my legs cramped and my arms were tired of flailing about. I felt like I could collapse, and desperately needed water, yet even though I knew I couldn't take much more, my body wouldn't stop. My mind shifted from panic to delight as if a great war raged inside. I looked around at the creatures cavorting around me. They laughed hysterically, eyes that once glowed with glee shimmered with a sick insanity. Madness had taken over!

"What's going on?" I shouted, while spinning around in a circle. "Why can't I stop?"

The violinist continued to play. "Why would you want to stop? This is so much fun."

"Yes—no, no… no!" I tried to force my body still, but had no control. My feet burned with pain, bloodied footprints followed in my wake. "I can't stop, what are you doing to me?"

"You are so weak, silly creature." Her soft smile turned sinister. "Don't think to fight it. You will be one with the forest."

I skipped into a two-step. Past the pain, my anger surged. "I'm not weak!" I fought against her music, trying to ignore it as best I could and force my body still. Every time I felt control, it would easily slip away. *I could just give up, couldn't I?* A cramp shot up my back. *But I would never see Alice again…* at the thought of her, my body switched up dance moves. I held my hands out remembering how she stood on my feet and we danced and laughed.

"I can fight this. I will see Alice again," I shouted over the music. The more I fought and focused on Alice, the more my tense muscles loosened; my fingers gradually became mine again, and then my toes. I was able to plant one leg down as the other bounced back and forth. *I can beat her.*

"Tsk, tsk, tsk," the fairy said. "You cannot beat me. You will be my puppet and I will watch you dance!" She picked up speed on her violin, bowing the strings with renewed passion. The music grew louder, faster, and angrier.

The mindless dancing of the others turned from joyfulness to violent thrashing and pushing. I couldn't stop myself. I banged my head back and forth, wind milling my arms around like a wild thing. Her laugher sang throughout the glade. She watched us all with great pride. But I would not be controlled. I closed my eyes and thought harder of Alice; I focused on her smile, her eyes, and the way she looked up to me. I stopped thrashing my head and slowed my dance once again. I imagined holding her tiny body in my arms, protecting her from all the evil in the world.

"Stop it!" The fairy bowed even faster, the tune becoming a loud whining screech. "You will dance until the end of time," she growled.

I held the memory of Alice's laughter; it broke through the powerful violin, soon I danced to a tune of my own, and no matter how powerful the violinist, I could no longer hear her. I swayed back and forth to the music of my sister's laughter.

"Stop it! Stop it! Stop it!"

Her shout sounded as if it came from far in the distance, followed by the satisfying snap of a violin string.

"You will not, you cannot—" Another snap. The music fell flat, but still the fairy tried. I finally saw her true form, a demon. Her eyes ablaze, the violin almost smoking with the speed she played. The others all collapsed in heaps, rolling around, still trying to dance to the violent tune.

"Nobody calls me weak," I said. I let Alice drift from my imagination and stared the demon down. I bowed and found myself in complete control of my body. She screamed a shrill cry and attacked the last two strings of her violin until they snapped, the music stopped, and the creatures of the glade turned back to stone.

"You will join my garden one way or another." She threw her violin down and ran her hand across the fabric of the bow until it turned razor sharp.

The demon attacked with such speed I tripped over the circle of stones trying to escape. I grabbed a fist-sized rock and rolled out of the way of a downward slash that carved a divot out of the grass. I sprang to my feet and ducked another swing, instinct taking over as I fought for my life.

"I will have you!" she said.

She moved fast, but anger must have clouded her judgement because her strikes were easy to avoid. I dodged and sidestepped, waiting for an opportunity to smash my rock into the demon's skull.

Her furious slashing pushed me back, and I soon found myself pinned up against one of her statues.

It was now or never.

She raised the bow-turned-sword over her head, roaring with rage. I ducked into a roll as the weapon struck the statue behind me, shattering it in a puff of smoke.

The demon cried out in horror as she stood over the pile.

"How could you? How could you destroy one of my children?" She came at me with a renewed anger.

I barely had time to duck.

"You brought this on yourself," I said. "My name is Zak Walker. You should remember that." I ran past her to another statue; rock raised high over my head, and bashed it in the head. The stone crumbled. She screamed after me, but I went on to the next and destroyed that too. She fell to her knees as if weighed down by seeing her stone garden come to an end. I destroyed two more statues before she dropped the bow, her eyes filling with water. I almost felt sorry.

She gave me a pathetic look of sorrow, one that broke my heart. "You destroyed everything… why have you come here?"

"I… came for my sister—you started this. You attacked me first!" The rock, for the first time, felt heavy. I threw it off to the side.

"I meant you no harm; I just wanted you to dance amongst the stones forever," she said.

"Sounds to me like you wanted my life," I said.

"I am a fairy. It is my nature. Get out of here! Leave me be!" She lowered her head and cried into her hands, her wings drooping behind her.

"Tell me where my sister is and I'll leave you alone," I said.

"I don't know where your sister is!" she yelled. "My magic shows you what you want to see… I just wanted my garden to grow."

"The Lillies, do you know who they are?"

She looked up at me with a sick smile. "If the Lillies have her, you'll never see her again."

I leaned in close so she could feel the warmth of my breath on her skin. "Tell me where they are."

"The Lillies make business at the Goblin Market. Head west for two days, nearing the border of the copper desert. Now go!"

When I returned to the glade, I found Seneca still asleep. I shook her awake, wanting to be on our way. She jumped up and swung. I threw myself back, narrowly avoiding her fist.

"I had the strangest dream." She stretched and looked around. "It's practically morning already?"

"I was attacked!" I said. "This cogged fairy tricked me into the forest. She played the violin and made me dance."

She got up and scanned the area. "That sounds like Maeve. I've heard of her. She must have glamoured us into a deep sleep, and you being the mentally weaker of us..."

"I'm not mentally weaker. If anything I'm the stronger one, because I kicked her butt and found out where the Lillies are!"

She patted me on the back. "Sure. Good for you."

"They are at the Goblin Market!"

Seneca glanced over at me with the first spark of genuine interest in her eyes. "It's never in the same place for long. Did she say where it is?"

"Two days west nearing the border of the Copper Desert."

"So what are we waiting for? Let's go!"

We packed up our things and headed back into the forest. During our journey, we had to alter our course to avoid a migrating horde of steel-toed unicorns. I asked why we couldn't just travel through them. Instead of answering, Seneca showed me the bloody remains of an unfortunate tribe of gnomes. Pieces of pale green flesh dangled from the trees, while the grass and dirt ran red with blood. The stench of death and decay almost made me throw up. I had to run off to some fresh air and wallow in my shame.

We ran for most of the day. Occasionally, we would stop to catch our breath and eat a snack while Seneca tried her best to cover up our scent and track the horde. More than once, she would come back running and we would have to quickly gather our things and take off. At night, we set up camp. She assured me that unicorns didn't hunt at night, so we were safe to sleep. Even though I wanted to continue on, I couldn't deny I was drained.

By the second day, Seneca proclaimed the unicorns had veered south. We could finally drop our guard and focus on getting to the market. Finally, I got to experience the warmth and beauty of the planet. Flowers of the brightest reds, purples, and yellows made me think of the smile on Abby's face every time I came to see her. The curious little rabbits that followed in our wake, only to hide when we turned on them made me think of my sister's curiosity. I missed Alice and Abby, and felt so lonely without them.

10

––––––––––

My legs could barely hold me up by the time we reached the market. I thought of a cozy inn room, sitting next to a fireplace while sipping on a warm drink, and laying my head on a soft bed for the night.

The Goblin Market excited me but I had to stay on guard. Tents filled the forest clearing, where tables displayed wares and customers haggled under the shade. Voices of all sorts mingled and sang across the air with a strange mix of highs and lows. I wandered in a daze, staring from place to place, knowing that each sight would be a new discovery. Not only did the sights catch my eyes, the people, or rather the creatures to be exact, made me stop and stare.

Two pixies sat near a keg, they couldn't have been more than five inches tall, but still looked human, with the exception of their tiny butterfly wings. They laughed their heads off while hiccupping and brandishing thimble-sized brown mugs. A bearded dwarf yelled over a table filled with knives at a sickly thin man lost amid the folds of a billowy cloak. A hint of a scaly green cheek showed under his hood. Scars marked his face in strange designs. Every time he spat a price at the dwarf, I caught sight of his sharpened teeth and decided to steer clear. From the look of it, the argument would soon turn into a fistfight.

An explosion and cheers filled the air off to the right. I followed the sound to a rising plume of smoke; small children laughed and ran about as two tiny mechanical dragons chased each other in circles spouting balls of fire.

All the merchants wore similar cloaks decorated with exotic symbols. Aside from their scales, they had forked tongues and catlike eyes. I couldn't stop thinking about the nighttime stories we were told as kids. About the goblins that hid under the bed, waiting to nibble at children's plump feet.

"Don't stare too hard. Goblins can be short tempered." Seneca pulled a hood up over her head, concealing herself in its shadow.

"Are they dangerous?" I asked, not wanting to look away and show fear.

"Not really. Only if you have something they want. If you insult them or their wares, if you disrespect their blood, if you show no manners when conducting business... or if you look appetizing, but other than that, no, not really."

"That's reassuring."

"Are you scared?" she asked, with a curious look.

"Me, scared? Please, I got too much skill to be bothered."

"Hiding behind a wall of arrogance will only make you look dumb. It's all right to admit when you are scared." She walked off shouting over her shoulder. "I'm going to see if I can find anything out. Don't do anything that'll get you turned into a frog."

I let my shoulders droop and decided to explore. Walking amongst the creatures and people of the market made me uncomfortable. Back home I had rank, people knew who I was and knew to show respect when they got in my way. No one looked me in the eye too long, and those that did gave nods of respect. Here they looked at me like supper. Strange creatures poked and pulled at my clothes. I had to shove hands away one too many times, while bigger things laughed and pointed. Still, I held my head high and didn't let the slight shaking of my knees show.

A group of fairies experimenting with a winged pack caught my attention. The long metallic wings spread out wide, flapping back and forth, as a boy pushed on the thrusters, and gushes of steam propelled him through the air. A young girl sat in the grass watching him float back and forth, pointed ears sticking out of her blonde locks.

That's what I need, a winged pack. I meant to make my way over to them when someone knocked me down. I jumped up swinging, but froze in place at the sight of a centaur standing over me.

From the waist up, he had the body of a man in a fancy jacket and buttoned down shirt. The rest of his body resembled a mechanical horse. His hooves kicked at the ground, sending up gusts of dirt, each move of his legs accompanied by a creaking sound of rusted metal. The creature appeared annoyed at me, as if contemplating running me over.

"Heavens," he said. "Sometimes the legs of this metal beast get away from me. Would you mind?" He pointed to his side where gears and pistons worked their magic. Behind him, a spinning hand crank where a tail should be came to a gradual stop. "Terribly, terribly, inconvenient having the crank up my bum, wouldn't you say?" He exploded into a roar of laughter that broke into uncontrollable neighing.

I stepped behind him and experimentally turned the crank.

After a few turns, he sighed in relief as if I had released some great pressure. "Ah, don't be shy; get those elbows working!" I turned the crank faster until I couldn't turn it any more. When I stopped, the crank started rotating in the opposite direction and the gears and cogs worked away. He experimentally lifted his front legs, then the back ones. "That's more like it. You wouldn't believe the trouble I had trying to get one of these ill-cultured ingrates to wind me up."

"I can imagine. It wasn't really smart putting the crank back there was it?"

"Well it wasn't as if I asked to be cursed this way. That despicable witch didn't even have the decency to assemble me properly. Now my legs are all buggered, and my bum always needs winding!"

"What witch did that?"

"The evilest witch of them all, the Witch of the Woods." He neighed and jumped up on his hind legs, shaking a fist at the heavens. "Such a foul creature!"

"Why would she do that to you?"

"When I traveled to the land of the Free Fey, I thought it would be a grand opportunity. Instead, I found myself penniless and without a home. It didn't matter. I could live in the woods, amongst nature, and under the stars. As fortune would have it, I ended up camping in the she-devil's woods and didn't know. I spied a doe my first night, and brought it down with a swift arrow. As I ate supper, the witch approached me, disguised as a beggar. She asked if I was willing to share some of my supper."

"I have a feeling you made the wrong choice."

"Such cruel trickery by that unholy harpy!" His neighing drew the attention of others. "I turned her away, and why not? This land had been hard on me ever since I stepped foot on it. My whole journey filled with misfortune and annoyances. I deserved that delicious, succulent doe for all this land put me through. I would not share it with a lowly beggar!"

"But the beggar turned out to be the witch. She cursed you for not sharing a doe you killed on her property… and that makes her evil? I'd say you got what you deserved."

He looked shocked and hurt. I almost laughed. "Well, I never! You have offended my good nature, sir!"

I held up my hands, trying to calm him down. "Hey, listen. You seem too refined for the Free Fey. I'm guessing they are beneath you. Why did you come here anyway?"

His front hooves beat at the ground. "I shall forgive you for your brash tongue, because you clearly have a keen eye. Alas, most of us are fleeing the Seelie Court. Puck's army has taken hold! That horrible fiend seeks to besmirch our beautiful land. I have faith that one day all will be as it should. Rumors have spread that the princess is still alive!"

Customers started to draw near, listening to the centaur preach about the missing princess. As his audience grew larger, he completely forgot about me, thank the gods. A hand emerged from the crowd and grabbed me. I pulled back, thinking someone was trying to pick my pocket, but found Seneca instead. She gave me a beckoning nod, and I followed her toward an inn off the side of the market.

"Any luck?" I asked.

"Yeah, they're inside." She looked back at the building crowd and shouting centaur. "And let me do the talking."

———

THE INN SMELLED TERRIBLE. I held my breath as long as possible before gasping like an idiot, taking in all the disgusting aromas in one large gulp. It smelled of sweat, smoke, and ale, like my father did most nights, but this smell had a bitter taste. I could barely think over the sounds of laughter and arguments that filled the hall. I took a moment to take in the sights and sounds of the strange creatures surrounding me, while Seneca looked for the Lillies.

An arm wrestling match between a husky dwarf and a creature that looked like a raccoon standing upright with a huge smile on his face caught my attention. Other customers crowded around, waving mugs of ale while shouting to spur the dwarf on, but no matter how hard he tried, the raccoon seemed to hold his own. With an arrogant smile, the raccoon slammed the dwarf's pudgy hand down. He barely raised his arms in victory before the dwarf pulled a wicked looking axe from under the table. People jumped in, holding the two apart while they threw curses back and forth.

I walked on toward the bar, passing singing goblins and a group of pixies taking turns diving into a mug of ale. A horned horse poked his head into a far window near the back of the bar. The copper horn had a spectacular shine. The unicorn bobbed his head in my direction and neighed loudly. Spit dripped from his lips as they snarled back to reveal a mouth full of human teeth. A man so large he remained hunched over in order to keep from bumping his head on the ceiling raised a barrel in one hand. With a hearty laugh, he placed it before the unicorn who nodded in thanks and took to drinking its contents.

Seneca motioned me over to a booth at the far side of the inn. Two pixies fluttered over a large cup, fighting each other over who got to drink from the stem straw next. Seneca sat across from them without waiting for an invitation, and I squeezed in next to her. The pixies didn't even take notice.

"It's my turn!" one yelled, shoving the other to the table. She had purple hair, yellow skin, and a patchwork of leaves for clothing.

The other, who looked much the same except for her bright pink hair, rushed at the first pixie and knocked her into the wall. "You stupid dandelion!"

"Your mother is a dandelion," Purple Hair yelled. At this, they both stopped their bickering and broke down in a chorus of wind chime laughter.

Seneca took the cup and drank it down in one gulp. "That was delicious."

The two pixies stopped laughing and shot her death stares that made me snicker.

"Oh man, you made a huge mistake," Pink Hair said.

"A mistake your whole family will regret." Purple Hair cracked the knuckles of her tiny fingers.

"Calm down ladies," Seneca said. "I'll gladly buy you another round and cover your tab if you answer some questions."

The two gave each other curious looks, then shared a nod.

"What exactly do you want to know?" Purple Hair asked.

Seneca leaned in. "Are you the Lillies?"

"At your service. Name's Lenis Lillie, and this here is my sister Liliana," Purple Hair said.

Liliana pointed a threatening finger at Seneca. "Yeah, and don't you forget it!"

"Where's my sister?" I waved her off. "If you hurt her, I'll stomp all over the two of you."

Seneca held me back. "My friend is jumping to conclusions. Sorry about that. We were just curious to know if you had anything to do with his sister's abduction."

Liliana marched across the table and jabbed her finger into my chest. "Who do you think you are? Coming in her demanding us about. What, you think just because you're a stupid giant you scare us? If I wasn't partial to this establishment, I'd rip off your skin like the stupid dandelion you are."

Lenis bent over at the waist, laughing hysterically. "You dandelions obviously don't know who you are messing with do you? We are the Lillies. We are the scourge of the night, the nightmares that bogeymen fear, shadows flee when they see us coming. Mothers take their children and run when they catch wind of us, and most importantly, we don't scare easy."

Seneca took the empty cup of ale and dropped it over Lenis, trapping her inside. The cup bounced up and down while muffled curses escaped from underneath.

"Oh you did it now!" Lilliana yelled.

I grabbed her by the waist in a tight fist. She struggled to break free, but a quick shake of my hand got her under control. "I asked where my sister is."

"Listen, man. We were just having a laugh," Lilliana said.

I raised her up close to my face. "Do I look like I'm laughing?"

"No," she said. "No, you're right. There's a time and place for everything. My sister and I, we like to joke you know? It's in our nature. You have to laugh when you do the sort of work that we do."

"Stealing children?" Seneca asked.

"I wouldn't necessarily call it stealing—hey would you mind putting me down? No? Okay no problem—anyway, we prefer the term child procurement and relocation services. We take children from bad homes and bring them to loving, needy Fey families. Hey, listen we even leave cute cuddly replacement children in their place."

"Yeah, like the changeling that we cooked up the other day," Seneca said.

Liliana put a thoughtful finger to her lips. "We haven't procured any babies... ohh—weeds!"

"How about I crush her and we question her sister?" I asked.

"Whoa, whoa, hold on a second." Liliana held up her hands. "I can help you guys. Your sister right? She's the quiet one? We snatched her the other day—"

Lenis yelled something we couldn't make out, the cup nearly toppled over, but Seneca placed her hand on it to keep it in place.

"Where is she?" I asked.

"See, that's the thing," Liliana said. "Confidentiality agreements and all. You'd have to offer up something really interesting for us to break the trust we have with our clients. In our line of business confidentiality means everything—"

I shook her around and turned her upside down.

"Puck!" she screamed. "We told him we don't snatch kids over the age of one, but he insisted we take this job. Also, him being the prince of the soon to be ruling party, we couldn't turn him down. Wouldn't have been good business—I'm getting dizzy."

"Why would Puck want her?" I asked.

"Don't know, don't care. We ask no questions, it's our motto."

"He's using her to draw me out." Seneca looked broken. "This is my fault."

I put Liliana down. "Where did Puck take her?"

She straightened out her leaf skirt and cracked her neck before glaring at me. "I'm going to kill you and everyone you love."

"Really?" I swatted her onto her butt. "I'm not in the mood!"

"Okay, okay!" she shouted. "Man, you dandelions are grumpy. We delivered her to the Unseelie court."

"What do we do?" I asked Seneca.

Seneca shook her head. "I'm sorry, Zak. This is all my fault. Everything is my fault. I can't believe this…"

"It doesn't matter. What matters is we get her back. We get her back and stop this war."

"What's the quickest way to the Unseele Court from here?" she asked Liliana.

The pixie struggled, trying to free her sister from under the cup. "Take the Dreadnaught to the crossroads. You'll have to deal with Hecate, though. She's not as pleasant as me. Man this is heavy, can you give me a hand?"

Seneca and I exited the booth. I ran after her as she stormed out of the inn. Outside, I found her pacing back and forth, taking deep breaths as if she couldn't breathe.

"What's wrong with you?" I asked.

"That sweet little girl, she got taken because of me. I mean, I thought maybe the Lillies just took her, out of pure coincidence—it was stupid, I know! But it was directly because of me. I put her in danger. I put all of you in danger. My parents, this war, it's all because of me. Because I refuse to grow up!"

"Hey," I said. "Calm it. If anyone should be upset it's me! You had to do what you had to do. You didn't know what the fallout would be."

She walked toward a nearby road. A sign pointing off into the forest bore the words "Copper Mine Station."

"Zak, they've been trying to mold my life since I was born. They wanted me to be this perfect princess. They expected me to be the queen who unites the Fey and Olympians. Do you know what kind of pressure that is? I became the exact opposite of what they wanted. I didn't care about what that meant for my people. I just cared about myself and my freedom..."

I took her hand and pulled her close to me. "Hey, I know exactly how you feel. That's all my life's ever been. Ever since my mom walked, it's never been my own. I've been stuck in the Fringe, eating rust for a buck, trying to do right by Alice. Meanwhile, my dad plans to ship me off next summer. Abby wants me all nice and proper. No one's ever asked what I want. I don't even know anymore. I just know I deserve more. Me and Alice. So, we are going to get her back, yeah? And then edge Puck and anyone else who tries to control us. Our lives —our own lives start now."

"I like the way you think." She held out a fist. "Crew right?"

"Yeah, crew!" I gave her a pound and we went in search of the Dreadnaught.

11

We walked in silence along the edge of the forest, keeping near but never venturing in. Wheel, hoof, and footprints battered the road. A steady procession of signposts promised we were nearing the station.

"Stop right there!" A familiar tiny voice halted us in our tracks.

I spun around. A few feet behind us, the Lillies hovered, flanked by two goblins brandishing blades and a dwarf who hefted an axe bigger than his body. He held the leashes of two other creatures, a couple of rough-looking beings that resembled men except for their glowing eyes, pointed ears, and caps that dripped with a thick syrupy red liquid. I took a cautious step back.

"Really, you guys again?" Seneca stepped forward.

Liliana spit. "You didn't really think you could mess with us and get away with it did you?"

"Yeah," Lenis shouted. "You don't mess with the Lillies and not get dead!"

"Whoa there, calm down," I said. "No need to cog things up. Everything is sorted."

"Be cautious," Seneca whispered. "Redcaps are born of madness; they aren't to be taken lightly."

I eyed the two up and down. Slight twitches and flinches rocked their bodies, their lips drew back revealing sharp bronze teeth. They pulled at the leashes so hard they wheezed as their collars choked them.

Lenis darted forward with a sword that resembled a toothpick. "You trapped me in my own cup. You drank my ale. Worst of all, you promised us rounds and didn't make due!"

"My apologies," Seneca said. "Where are my manners? We were in a rush—but if you want to go get a couple of drinks, on me of course, we can do that."

The Redcaps dropped down to their hands and knees, straining to charge forward like wolves. The dwarf held tight to their leashes, and eyed me up while gripping the handle of his battle axe a bit tighter. The Redcaps licked their lips and cast their murderous gaze on Seneca. Tempers were high, and the slightest spark would set this bomb off.

"Maybe there's a misunderstanding." I pulled Seneca behind me.

"Misunderstanding?" Liliana cried. "You tried to crush me!"

"And you kidnapped my sister!" I shouted.

"It was business, nothing personal. But when you attacked me, it became personal." She growled.

"I've killed for less," Lenis said.

Liliana held her hand up. "No, I get to kill him."

"No way, they trapped me in a cup!" Lenis pushed her sister out of the way.

"Are you kidding me?" Liliana grabbed her sister and swung her to the ground. "He shook me like a salt shaker!"

Lenis tackled her sister and they both crashed into the grass. "I was trapped in my own cup!"

"You're so unreasonable sometimes!" Liliana pulled at Lenis' hair.

Lenis flipped Liliana to the ground and bent her tiny arm behind her back. "Your mother is a dandelion!"

"Your mother mates with humming birds!" Liliana head butted her sister, and the two broke out into an all-out brawl.

The dwarf looked on in confusion, while the goblins tried to split the two apart.

"Maybe now would be a good time to run?" I whispered to Seneca.

"I kinda want to see how this plays out," Seneca said, barely holding in her laughter.

I grabbed her arm and dragged her off, running down the road. The Lillies continued shouting as their argument raged behind us. Soon the growls and wicked screams of the Redcaps drowned the pixies out. The hairs on the back of my neck stood on end, fear ran through my body and gave my legs that extra boost.

"The train stop is just up ahead." Seneca said.

"Are you kidding me?" Lenis shouted from behind. "They're getting away!"

The Redcaps attacked like a pack of wild dogs. I knew nothing would stop them until they had us in their clutches.

"Where's this train?" I huffed. "I don't see a station."

"You won't see the station," Seneca answered. "Until you see the station."

"That doesn't—"

A growl cut me off. I glanced back at the red blur of the Redcaps running on all fours. The flashing of bronze teeth and wild eyes said they fully intended on ripping us apart. The Lillies and others chased behind them. Ahead of us, the road reached far and wide, no real way of escaping.

"We have to fight!" I yelled.

"Would you stop posturing?" Seneca had a strange look on her face. "And keep running. I can feel the tracks. Just up ahead."

The road went up a rise I couldn't see beyond. I had to trust her.

We reached the top and found nothing except a perfect view of the Redcaps making short order of the distance between us.

"Where's the tracks?" I yelled.

"They're coming." Seneca looked around. "As soon as it shows, jump."

"This is rust! They are going to catch us."

"I hear it." Seneca grabbed my arm and pulled me in her direction. "Look!"

She pointed down the slope, where I didn't see anything worth our time. But she wouldn't let me turn away. I kept looking until the air wavered like the surface of a lake. The thick smell of iron and steel filled my nose. The ground rumbled, and a horn bellowed so loud I fell to my knees and covered my ears, but Seneca pulled me up by my arm and dragged me down the hill. The ground shifted before my eyes, almost as if reality couldn't make a proper decision.

"Are those tracks?" I gasped, seeing them but not believing they could just appear out of nowhere. They cut across the road leading deep into the forest. Seneca stopped right before the tracks, holding me steady as I swayed to the earth-shattering rumble.

She shook me, using her free hand to slap me out of my stupor. "Be ready. When the train passes, we have to grab on."

"Grab on to what?" I shouted over the roar of engines.

"Anything you can!"

A bright light cut across the forest path, followed by the drumming and screeching of wheels as a hulking iron thing, black as a smith's anvil, came forward. A massive chimney along its top spewed gray smoke, polluting the sky as it burrowed through the forest. The engine shot by, leading a precession of cars with such fury I feared I would be sucked under its wheels.

"A freight car is coming up," Seneca said. "This is where we get on. Jump when I say."

I bent at the knees waiting for the signal. Sweat streamed down my back as the Redcap's growls clawed their way after us. I looked to Seneca, expecting her to shout out something, anything. Instead, she stood calm as if waiting for spring to arrive. I glanced back over my shoulder at the Redcaps, who would be on us in seconds.

"Now!" Seneca yelled.

Instinct took over. My body made the decision before my brain was even aware. My legs launched me forward. There was no way we would make it. Gravity insisted I fall under the tracks. I could practically feel the warmth of the Redcaps' breath on my skin. Before panic set in, I hit the wood flooring of the freight car and rolled to a stop next to Seneca. I swung around ready to defend myself. The first creature must have tried to make the jump, his clawed nails dug deep into the edge of the doorframe. The train moved too fast for his foot to get a good purchase, leaving him hanging from the side, trying to claw his way in.

I ran over and stomped his fingers until they came loose. He vanished in a blur, sucked under the wheels. I averted my eyes an instant before the crunch of bones.

Seneca came to my side and peeked outside. "You want to know the first thing I plan to do when I'm on the throne? Easy. Unprofessionally devote all my resources into hunting down the Lillies and trapping them under mugs forever."

The train moved through the forest at such incredible speed it made me nauseous watching the trees and land go by. A blur of motion, the mixed greens, browns, and yellows bled across my vision. Soon, the world exploded into endless sparkling copper brown. As far as I could see, desert surrounded us. The sun burned down on a wide vista that almost seemed like an entirely different world.

"We're slowing down," Seneca said. "Let's find the passenger train."

The smell of roasted chicken, steak, and pork chops saturated the next car. I couldn't help salivating. Silverware clanked and people idly chatted, reminding me of a time when I had to work washing dishes at a dining hall meant for the rich. Now here I was once again walking amongst people of a different station.

Fancy dressed Fey sat at elegant tables enjoying their expensive meals and sipping on drinks. A waiter shooed us out of the way while speeding past with a tray of drinks held high above his head. Had Seneca not dragged me along, I would have grabbed a chicken leg off a pompously dressed woman's plate. She rolled her eyes at me in disgust while I watched her eat with pigeon like nibbles. I blew her a kiss and enjoyed her unpleasant reaction before stepping into the next car.

We entered another car lined with seats all along the wall. There seemed to be a more diverse array of passengers here, but mostly fairies dressed in fine clothes, top hats, and corsets. The well-to-do of the fairy world only traveled by train I presumed. Seneca chose seats for us toward the back. She sat heavily, and I squeezed in next to her.

She looked out the window almost as if she couldn't meet my eyes. "More of the fallout I suppose."

"What do you mean?" I asked.

"These are all Seelie. Why do you think they're so far from home?"

I looked around. "Your people don't seem anything like you."

"Thanks, it's a compliment. But still… they are refugees aren't they?" She sounded as if she asked herself more than me.

"If you ask me, they seem pretty content."

She sighed. "The Seelie always make do. We are taught from a young age to meet great disaster with elegance and a smile."

"Still," I said. "They don't seem all that bothered. They are a lot more well off than I ever was."

She finally looked at me and her eyes burned with sorrow. "Everyone needs a home, Zak. Even if you hate it, at the end of the day, we need to know there is some place to return to." She motioned to the Fey around us. "They have nowhere to go. It's all my fault."

I sat back and thought about The Fringe, Abby, and even my dad. Once we got Alice back, and I helped Seneca stop this war, I'd have to go home. I may have hated it, but she was right. It was nice knowing I had some place to call my own, lay my head down, where I could easily find people I loved. Dad sending me off to work on a ship was a huge blow. Obviously, I didn't want to leave Alice and Abby behind, but being away made me wonder if I had also been scared of leaving.

I looked around at the Fey I was so quick to write off, and paid closer attention. Their smiles never reached their eyes, laughter ended in long sighs and periods of silence, and most of all, they all over indulged in alcohol. These people masked their feelings the same way I always had.

Not knowing what I could say to cheer her up, I decided on the next best choice. "I'm going to see if I can find us some food."

"Just don't drink any pixie ale," she said. "That stuff is brutal!"

I found the next car alive with amazing music. A band played various string and brass instruments on a low stage. Women in refined dresses and elegant masks spun around on high heels and sparkling shoes while men in suits laced with silver and gold danced around them with wanting eyes.

A buffet of food off to the side drew my attention. The spread wafted with lingering smoke, and the scent of yummy things hung in the air. Pointed-ear waiters stood impatiently on the other side of the table, watching me with a bit of distaste. I made sure to offer up my most fringe smile while sticking my fingers in a tray of meat then licked the gravy off my finger. The waiter all but fainted in front of me. I grabbed two plates from one of the disgusted waiters and piled on large amounts of food, most of which I couldn't even begin to identify.

Fey surged into the entertainment train, and the room came to life with graceful dancers. I dodged my way across the floor on nimble feet while trying to balance my plates and avoid being run down. It was time to leave. After a night of endless dancing with Maeve the psycho violinist, I swore to never dance again. I headed back to the passenger train. When I stepped between cars, the warm desert breeze brushed against my face.

I stopped and took in the warmth. *Soon Alice. I'm coming for you.*

Seneca and I ate our dinners in silence. Each bite I took filled my mouth with a new explosion of flavor. No two bites tasted the same. It could easily be the best meal I'd had in as long as I could remember. I was so wrapped up in my food I hadn't noticed Seneca stopped eating. She put down her plate and leaned back, sinking into the seat cushions.

She pulled her hood down lower over her face. "I think someone recognizes me."

I looked up and across the aisle, a man with long blond hair and an arrogant smile stared back at us. He didn't try to pretend he wasn't watching. I sat up straight and leaned forward, letting the muscles in my jaw clench while putting my perfected "hop off" look on display. He nodded, turned to his companion, and whispered something into his ear.

"How bad would it be if someone recognizes you?" I asked.

"Depends. If it's Seelie, I'd be welcomed with open arms. There'd be some crying, it'd be a whole thing. If it were Unseelie, well the reception wouldn't be that grand… then there are the bounty hunters. Puck has a bounty out on me, not sure how much it's for. But the way that guy is looking at me makes me think it's a lot."

The blond and his companion both openly stared at us. His companion, to my surprise, had the body of a man and the head of a hog.

"What should we do?" I asked.

She looked out the window. "I don't know how far we are, but it may be a better idea to continue our journey on foot." She got up and motioned for me to follow. "Let's head back to the freight and hop off this train."

"Stay close to me." I pulled her behind me.

We walked down the aisle toward the door. We would have to pass the man and his companion to get back to where we came in. I hoped he had no intentions of making a scene in front of everyone else on board. If he were a smart bounty hunter, he'd want to keep it quiet and have less competition. He watched us approach with the maddening patience of a true predator. Three more steps and we would be on top of him.

"Good evening," he said, with a singsong voice. "How have your travels been?"

I kept myself between him and Seneca. "Fine, thanks. We were just heading up front."

His friend sniffed at us and grunted under his breath.

"Really?" he said. "But the view here is so much better. All that's up ahead is the engine and some lonely freight cars. Now why would you want to go there?"

"None of your business really," I said, fists clenched and ready for a fight.

He held up his hands. "Sorry, I didn't mean to intrude. I really was just curious." Still holding up his left hand, he held out his right for me to shake. "I am Nolan Wolfe and this unsettling fellow here is my life-long friend and partner, Gorge."

I looked at his hand for a moment before shaking it. We both squeezed harder than necessary. "I'm Zak Walker."

He tried to get another glance at Seneca, but I kept step in front of him. "And who might this be?"

"My friend," I said. "And we have to get going."

I took Seneca's hand and tried to lead her past the two. Nolan had other plans; he put his hand on my chest to stop me, while Gorge crept in behind Seneca and sniffed at her hair.

"Zak," Seneca said. "I think it's time we leave. So maybe a bit of violence will do?"

Nolan's smile spread wide across his face, revealing sparkling white teeth. It was an easy target, so I punched him in the face. I definitely felt something crack under the weight of my knuckles. He did his best at cursing me while trying to keep blood from pouring out his nose. Whatever Seneca did to Gorge worked, because he hunched over, grabbing his crotch, squealing like a pig. We didn't stick around long enough to see what kind of damage we did. I ran for the door at the far end of the train and pulled it open. She ran in and I after her.

We rushed through the dining car pushing surprised Fey out the way as we went. Trying to keep up with Seneca, I accidentally knocked over a waiter. We both fell to the floor, his tray of drinks spilling glasses and liquid all over. Seneca helped me up, and I yelled an apology over my shoulder as we ran to the door to the freight car. The side door was shut and locked up tight.

"Hades!" I shouted.

"Let's keep going." Seneca pointed toward to the next door.

Nolan stormed in, his nose bent at the wrong angle and blood staining his upper lip. He tried to smile, but to my enjoyment, was missing a tooth. Gorge limped in behind him, breathing hard, and let loose a long, angry squeal.

"See the problem with people today," Nolan shouted. "Is that they can't just talk things out. Why did we have to jump straight to fighting? You know I had a whole speech planned out and everything."

Arms of solid muscle grabbed me from behind and lifted me into a bear hug. Hot putrid breath washed down my back and made my skin crawl. Nolan smiled his missing tooth smile as another hog-headed man grabbed Seneca up in his muscled arms. The three hog men squealed along with Nolan's laughter.

Seneca struggled to get loose. "Wait, so you're like king of the hog people? Nolan Wolfe, king of the hogs! Wouldn't it have made more sense if you, I don't know, trained some wolves to be your cronies?"

"Insults won't get you anywhere," Nolan said. "Not when all I hear coming out of your mouth is the sound of my sweet reward."

"How much?" Seneca asked.

"Enough to bring honor back to my name." He ran his hand through her hair.

"Don't touch her!" I yelled.

Nolan nodded to my captor. The hog man flexed his muscles and crushed the air out of my lungs. I gasped, desperate to breathe. My legs flailed uselessly as he swung me back and forth like a broken toy.

"Ease off!" Seneca yelled.

Nolan nodded once again and the hog loosened up his grip. I inhaled deeply and felt the relief of my lungs expanding.

"As I was saying," Nolan said. "This reward is enough to get me a ship, set myself up with a good crew—"

"Maybe train some wolves?" Seneca said. "I get it would really help your image. But the thing is, if you turn me over to Puck, you aren't just turning over the Seelie Princess, you're turning your back on your people. If Puck gets what he wants, he won't stop at the Seelie lines. He'll come for the Free Fey next. He wants the whole land united under his rule, and trust me, it won't be a just rule."

Nolan waved his hand and faked a yawn. "It's all very interesting. Unfortunately for you, I don't care. You see, I'm an outlaw. Regardless of who rules what, I will remain outside the law because that's where I am most comfortable and most profitable."

"So what's all this talk about bringing honor to your name?" I asked.

He leaned in close enough for me to smell the sweat of his hair. "The Wolfes were once well known and feared throughout the land. My father unfortunately made some bad decisions where his finances were concerned and lost his ship and crew."

"Sounds like my dad and your dad should get a drink together," I said.

"He died a coward's death." Nolan shrugged.

"Ouch," Seneca said. "Way to put your foot in your mouth."

"So it's up to me to restore my family's honorable name as the most feared and powerful—"

"Yeah," I moaned. "We get it. You're a loser that should have been edged a long time ago."

Nolan laughed so hard I thought he didn't understand the insult. He bent over and clenched at his stomach while his laughter filled the train. The hog men looked at each other in confusion before cautiously laughing along with him.

"Did you break him?" Seneca asked.

I didn't have time to answer. Nolan's laughter stopped abruptly as he introduced his knuckles to my face.

———

I woke with a start, feeling the dull ache of my jaw. My wrists were bound with rough rope that bit into my skin. I squirmed around on the floor trying to sit up as the train shook and jostled me back down. Seneca leaned against the wall, her arms secured behind her back as well.

"Rise and shine sleepy head." She scooted over to me. "Man, Zak, I would have thought you could handle a punch better. He barely tapped you."

"Shut up for a minute," I said.

She rolled her eyes and hummed a strange tune. We were still in the freight car, one of Nolan's hog men stood guard near the door, his head kept tilting forward as his eyes fought to stay closed. Whenever he opened his eyes, Seneca hummed louder and sleep would seem to overpower him.

"Are you doing that?" I asked.

She nodded. "Hogs love a sweet tune."

"Keep him distracted." I pulled at my bindings, wincing as the rope cut at my skin. I knew a little trick that would get me out of this situation. I just had to brace myself for the pain. I took my left thumb into my right hand and felt around for the bone. If I twisted it just right—snap! I gasped in pain, trying to bury a scream deep down in my throat.

Seneca shot me a look. "What was that?"

I ignored her and went to work. With my thumb dislocated, I could fold my hand in on itself. Still, I had to pull and struggle, my skin burned raw as the rope ripped away layers of flesh. I exhaled a sigh of relief when I felt the noose slip over my hand and around my fingers. I whipped my hand free and jammed my thumb back into place with a faint *snap*. I hugged my hand close to my body and took a moment to get myself together while Seneca watched with an impressed smirk.

I looked over to the hog man who snored peacefully. "Make sure he doesn't wake up."

Seneca turned her back to me and continued humming. I had to use my teeth to help get her tight knots loosened. My thumb felt numb and sore so it wasn't much help. After some frustration, I loosened her bindings enough for her to slip free. She rubbed life back into her hands and thanked me with a nod.

"What do we do?" I whispered.

"Let's try to get to the front of the train. Maybe we can find an emergency pack of wings."

"Wait… You stopped humming."

We were cut short by a squeal. The hog man, now fully awake, came at us at a full run. We ran for the door. I pried it open, let Seneca go first, and followed. She opened the door to the next train only to find Nolan and two other hog men surprised by our being free. She slammed the door.

Seneca looked over the side of the safety railing. "Too risky to jump from here."

"Let's climb." I pointed to the ladder leading to the train roof.

I helped her get on and climbed up behind her. We climbed to the top just as the doors to both cars opened and Nolan and his crew came stumbling out. We took off running toward the front of the train.

The engine spewed black smoke from its rusted chimney three

cars ahead. I couldn't risk looking back, but I knew they were close every time vibration of their heavy steps made the roof shake. When we reached the end of the car, Seneca didn't even bother to stop. She leapt across the space onto the next one, landing in a roll. I was confident I could do the same. Only, I judged the distance wrong and my jump came up short. My foot clipped the lip of the roof, tripping me up and almost making me fall clear off the train. Seneca caught my arm a second before I fell to the desert floor.

"Gods you're heavy!" She struggled to pull me up, but we were only sliding further and further down the side of the train.

"Rust!" I kicked at the air, trying to find something to prop my feet on. "Let me go!"

"What?"

"We'll both fall if you don't!"

We looked down the train. Nolan and his crew were catching up. I scowled at Nolan's arrogant smile. In his mind, he'd already caught Seneca.

"Ah, cog it!" She tightened her grip on my arm and jumped.

13

She pushed off with enough strength to push us clear of the train wheels. Unfortunately, we fell hard. I landed on my back and had the wind knocked out of me. Seneca landed on top of me. I tried to wrap my arms around her and take the brunt of the impact; it was all a chaotic mess of sand, flailing limbs, sky, and pain as we rolled down a hill of scorching hot sand. When we finally came to a stop, the two of us lay under the sun for a while. At that point, I didn't care if Nolan showed up. I just needed to catch my breath.

"That worked out just like I planned." Seneca sat up and brushed sand from her hair.

I took a deep breath. "We could have died. What if we fell under the tracks?"

"Then we'd be dead and wouldn't be having this conversation. But since we are, everything is fine." She got up and scanned the horizon, using her hands to shield her eyes from the sun. "Guess Nolan didn't have the guts to chase after us."

"Or he had the common sense to not jump off a moving train."

"Or he was scared of desert orcs."

I jumped up to my feet and looked around for orcs. "You aren't serious, are you?"

She shrugged, looked around and pointed in a seemingly random direction. "We go that way."

"How do you know which way to go?"

"It doesn't matter. Nobody gets out the copper desert, unless Hecate wants them to. My father and her made a truce that granted the Dreadnaught safe passage as a way of bridging the desert. Unfortunately for us, anyone on foot is fair game."

I had no other choice, so I followed. Seneca walked ahead, tracking the movement of the sun, wind, or bird rust, I didn't know. However, she seemed to be confident in the direction she'd chosen, so I trusted her. I hung back and gave her space, not wanting to disturb her. We both seemed trapped in our heads. I knew she blamed herself for what happened to her parents and people, and I had no idea how that felt, carrying such a weight. I could only imagine what it would be like to have the guilt and hurt felt over losing Alice multiplied by hundreds.

I watched the skies and looked for any sign of Olympus. No matter how lost I got, at least I knew I could easily find home. I may not be able to touch it for now, but I always knew where to find it. Floating off to the north, barely visible beyond a blanket of clouds, glittered the motors and machinery of my city. Thoughts of returning home with Alice at my side, and swearing to work at repairing the relationship we had with our father gave me the strength to keep going.

I couldn't tell how long we walked. Only that my feet eventually hurt so bad I wanted to cry. I refused to complain. Seneca must have noticed because she would make us stop and rest whenever it got too much for me to bear. By nightfall, our throats were so dry our speech came out as horrid scratching. I laid my head on the sand, ready to die. I twisted and turned trying to find sleep, but the rumbling of my stomach kept me awake.

Three days and three nights we walked. A seamless stream of light and dark, rest and go. We didn't speak or look at each other, we both were suffering and only our blind determination on saving the ones we loved kept us going. Worry that Alice thought no one would come for her scared me more than death itself. When I reached my lowest point and wanted to fade away into the endless dunes, I pictured her face waiting for me at the end of my journey, and it gave me the strength to take another step.

"That's… cruel…" Seneca whispered. She stopped in her tracks and stared out into the horizon, swaying back and forth on weak legs.

I put a hand on her back. "Come… on, we have to keep moving."

"But these hallucinations… they are getting really lifelike…" She took an unsteady step forward. She licked at her badly chapped lips. "It looks just… like a real forest."

"What are you talking about?" I asked, checking her eyes for any sign of madness.

She tilted her head to the side and took another step forward. "No… oh no, that's too good." Her cracked lips spread. "That's too good!" She put on her goggles and turned a dial that switched out the tinted lenses for a clear one. "Zak, look!"

She pointed off into the distance where I could barely see a glimmer of green. It wavered in the heat and made my eyes feel tired.

"Is that real?" I asked.

"If it's not," she said. "I give up."

With renewed energy, and a little bit of faith, we ran toward the distant green, and I prayed to the gods we found salvation.

Eventually, the sand gave way to dirt, sprouts of grass, and other vegetation. We practically cried with joy as we found our way out of the desert. Mountains loomed in the distance cutting off what once looked like an endless horizon, finally an end. The road we traveled led deeper north into a thickening forest of greenery. My heart nearly burst when we came upon a stream of water. The crystal clear liquid looked so welcoming I couldn't stop myself from jumping headfirst into its cool embrace. After we filled our bellies with water, I looked around and tried to figure out where to go next.

"Do you know where we're going?" I asked.

Her shoulders dropped while she tried to catch a glimpse of the sky through the canopy of green. "We have to head toward the west, but I can't tell how far off course we are."

"Look!" I yelled.

A flickering orb of light dancing behind her caught my attention. It split into two separate smaller spheres, flashing between reds, blues, and greens. They spun around our hands and feet in a colorful show of brilliance. The lights darted up into the trees, illuminating the night sky. They came forward and forced us to take a step back before shooting off deeper into the darkened path.

"Will o' wisps," Seneca said. "We have to follow them. They'll lead us to the crossroads… to the goddess Hecate. This is her territory, and we entered without permission. So, you know, no getting out of here without her permission."

"Who is this Hecate anyway?" I asked.

"Goddess of the crossroads," Seneca said. "She can see all the roads that men walk; past, present, and future. She can also guide those she deems worthy onto the path they are destined to follow… or send them to their death. Either or."

"Sounds like someone we should meet." I followed the lights.

The path they led us down didn't seem to make any twists or turns. Yet I had a feeling the forest reshaped around us and moved about on its own as we walked a straight line. Magic had to be at play. But still, the orbs didn't abandon us. Whenever we fell far behind, they would wait until we caught up before moving again. Finally, we came to a stop in an area so dense with trees the sun couldn't leak in. Only the glow of the two orbs floating four feet above the ground lit our way. They grew brighter until the darkness melted away into the corners and cracks of the forest. Brilliant white radiance faded to reveal a long table filled with food and drink. Where the will o' wisps once floated now stood a woman who held two torches, one in each hand.

She looked statuesque in all her beauty, with ivory skin, red lips, and hair done in fine golden curls, a tight copper collar and locket bound to the skin around her neck. Her bare shoulders ended at a red bodice, its black strings threading the front tightly closed. A long dress dragged across the grass as she made her way toward us.

"Welcome travelers," she said with joy. "It has been so long since I've had company. Please, please, do sit down and join me. Surely, you are famished from your travels." All kinds of meats, cooked and dry, fruits, vegetables, and drinks filled the table. My stomach growled at the sight. My mouth watered like a starving dog watching for scraps. She placed the torches on the table. "I am glad my light found you and led you to me. Won't you dine with me?"

"Best not be rude," Seneca whispered in my ear. "Turning down the hospitality of a god can be very dangerous. Plus, I'm starving!"

We each took a cushioned seat on one side. The woman walked to the head of the table and sat softly with a huge smile.

"Are you Hecate?" I asked. "The Goddess of the Crossroads?"

"Indeed I am. And you are Zak Walker, the boy who fell from the sky. You have come a long way from the mundane life you lived in Olympus. Has your wanderlust been sated, or is your only goal to rescue your sister?" Her smile lingered on me for a second more before turning to Seneca. "Princess Seneca Rose, you carry such weight, hiding your true fear behind a façade of immaturity, and yet now you fear your mistakes will never be mended."

"Well then. Now that we are all introduced," Seneca said. "You are the one who sees the roads traveled."

Hecate nodded.

"What of your sisters?"

"Perhaps you should enjoy your food before you meet them, yes?" She picked up a fine gold goblet and pressed it to her lips.

Seneca needed no more convincing. She shoveled as much food as she could onto her decorated plate. I poured a full cup of water; the cool liquid flowed down my dried throat and replenished the life that seemed to be fading from my limbs. After my third cup, I helped myself to some chicken. The spices screamed with so much flavor I could barely keep myself from swallowing pieces whole. It almost felt like a dream. The more I ate, the less I worried about anything else.

"Do you know where we have to go?" Seneca asked between mouthfuls of food.

"I can deduce that from the actions of your past, the ones that led you here. But beyond this point I cannot see. Those are curses for my sisters to bear."

Seneca ripped a piece of chicken clean off the bone. "So why don't you introduce us."

"Very well," she said without a hint of emotion.

She lifted her hair over her head and used a ribbon to fasten it in place, exposing her slender neck and milky skin. The keyhole in her locket glimmered in the torchlight. She reached into the top of her bodice and pulled out a silver key, which she placed in the keyhole and turned once to the left. Her neck made a loud snap and the locket ticked like the hands of a clock. With each tick, her head turned to the left until it faced backward. I gasped—the back of her head bore a new face, this one sneering with angry eyes and black lips that curled up in disgust. She let her hair down and as it fell about her shoulders, the golden locks faded into a dark black.

She hunched in her chair, elbows on the table, leaning unceremoniously. "Of course, that sister of mine is always offering food to strangers."

"What just happened?" I asked.

She rolled her eyes at me and spoke in a mocking tone. "'Come, dear travelers, feast on our food. Eat it all,' as if we didn't have enough useless freeloaders wandering around these woods."

"We didn't mean to intrude. I'm sorry if we upset you," I said.

"The future is bleak. Try living every day knowing the exact time and place you are going to die. The horrible agony that lay in wait to snuff out a useless life of servitude spent in these cursed woods waiting the return of a god who long forgot you."

"You can see your death?"

"You can see your death?" she mocked. "Of course I can, why wouldn't I? I can see the future. Have you not been paying attention?" She pointed at me. "Falling, simple enough, huh?" And to Seneca. "In glorious battle. Trying to regain what was taken. Hmm, you don't seem like the battle type. Probably why you die."

"I refuse to believe the future is set in stone," Seneca said. "You may have seen our deaths, but death isn't the end."

"And how to you plan on avoiding it?"

"Me and Zak are going to fix things."

She laughed and laid her eyes on me. "The boy? The boy who dies of a fall? How can you and he do anything?"

"What god?" I asked. "You said you were destined to wait here for a god who has long forgotten you."

"The one true god of course. The one I sacrificed myself for, cursed to this rock of filth so he could flee. Zeus. He never returns..." Her eyes became distant as if she were seeing another time all together. "He promised he would."

"And we have been sent here to restore his glory!" I shouted. "He's been in the rust house because of Ares. He has no power or memory of who he is. We were sent here to steal back his Aegis. When he has regained his power, I'll make sure he keeps his promise. If he still doesn't remember, I will remind him. Just grant us passage through your woods."

"Do you speak the truth? But your death is so clear, so vivid and spectacularly satisfying."

"When Zeus raises Loki from his prison, death won't matter." Seneca said.

"I cannot see what is truly in your heart. You must speak to my sister right away!" She reached for the key still in the keyhole and turned it to the right two full turns. The collar ticked and her head ratcheted to the right. Her hair stayed in place as her head turned a half a turn, revealing the innocent face of a child: freckled skin, button nose, thin wispy lips, and joyful eyes. She tied two pigtails in her hair and shook off the black to a dirty brown. She crossed her legs in her chair and nervously giggled.

"Hi," she said with a squeaky voice.

"Do we have a deal?" Seneca asked.

She looked at me, her eyes burrowing into my soul. "You are so scared. You act like you aren't... but you are. A big old scaredy-cat that hides behind pride and boasting. Oh, don't be scared anymore! You are strong and courageous. It's not a lie... even if you believe it is." She giggled at Seneca. "You are angry. Angry because you let down your family and people. But you can't give up, okay? You don't have to hide it. Anger is what gives you strength."

"I wouldn't say I'm angry," Seneca said. "Maybe a little misguided…"

"You've seen who we are. Do you believe we can change things? Will you let us through?"

The little girl that Hecate wore squealed in excitement. "Yes, yes! That makes sense. I can see it. You both have such strong will, determination, and ambition… you blindly believe you can change things. Even if the gods don't believe you can. You don't need the gods to believe in you, all you need is to believe in yourselves."

"What does that even mean?" I asked.

"It means that they may not believe we can succeed, but they want to see how it'll play out." Seneca stood up, ready to leave.

"I never said *I* didn't believe in you, gosh…" Hecate threw up both her hands and two passages opened up into the forest at her left and right side.

From the left passage, a snake slithered out and came to rest at Hecate's side. From the right passage came a low growl. A wolf walked out and sat licking his paws at her other side.

"There are two paths before you," Hecate said. "One will lead to the Seelie Court." The wolf lifted its head and barked. "And the other leads to the Unseelie." The snake hissed and wrapped around itself. "Which one will you choose? The cute puppy, or the icky, slimy snake?"

"I just thought I should point out," Seneca said. "It's very saying about where we are going when a snake has to lead us there. Just my thoughts, always open for discussion."

"We follow the snake." I said.

The wolf got up and ran back into its forest passage, which closed behind it. The dinner table vanished and with it all the food and aromas that made my stomach happy. Hecate also vanished, leaving only the snake. The serpent waited a moment as we gathered ourselves, before slithering off into its forest entrance.

14

The forest road grew denser the further we traveled. Soon, we had to walk single file in order to keep from getting caught up in all the shrubs and branches that pressed in on us. After a while, we reached an entrance made of mossy stone. The snake coiled up in a circle and dissolved into smoke in front of the doorway.

"That was pleasant," said Seneca.

The huge double doors sparkled with a silver sheen, glinting from a carving of a deer wearing a snake as a crown. The snake's tail vanished into its own mouth, the creature devouring itself.

"What's the symbol mean?" I asked.

"It's the crest of the Unseelie," Seneca answered. "You still want to go in?"

I pushed the heavy doors open, letting musty air escape. Spider webs draped from the corners of the doorframe where dead birds hung trapped in webbed coffins. Seneca brushed them aside and headed in first. I followed down a long corridor that soon forked into many paths.

"It's the Labyrinth." Seneca looked bothered. "Once we get through, we'll be in Unseelie territory."

"That doesn't sound so hard," I said.

"Guardians," Seneca added. "Places like these always have big, bad, ugly guardians."

A ferocious roar echoed down the corridor, unsettling the dust and filling me with dread.

The passage led us down a hedge maze of twists and turns. We walked through narrow halls with walls so high the ceiling appeared to be darkness. Thorny vines snaked in and out of the green hedges, catching bits and pieces of clothing and biting our skin if we walked too close. A light mist clung to the ground, making it impossible to see where our feet landed. The humidity soaked our clothes. Most unsettling however, had to be the continuous howls of pain echoing from deep in the maze, the cries of a man in anguish. I cringed, thinking of the pain that could cause such endless screams.

"It's Loki," Seneca said. "This is where he made his last stand. When Zeus, Odin, and the others fled, Loki sought to stand and fight. He's been imprisoned here ever since. The Labyrinth was built as a prison. If we follow his screams, it will lead us to him."

I stopped in my tracks. "Wait, Loki is here?"

"Yeah… that's what I said."

"Did you know all along we would find him here? Why didn't you tell me?"

She shrugged. "I don't know. I wasn't really thinking about it. We were more concerned about Alice."

"Were you?" I said. "Or was it just convenient?"

She flashed me a surprised look. "Look Zak, I don't know what you are trying to say, but Alice is priority—so is saving my people—our people. We're crew, remember?"

I turned my ear toward another scream. "Just remember, we don't leave until we have Alice."

"Agreed." She walked off without meeting my eyes, and I had no choice but to follow.

I couldn't be sure how far we walked or if we may have even been lost; it all looked the same to me. With the approach of every turn or fork in the road, I hoped it would be the last, only to find another path waiting. Loki's shouts never seemed to get any closer or farther. Gradually, I lost my will to go on. The maze seemed hopeless.

Seneca stopped. "We are being followed."

"Is it Loki?" I asked.

"No. His shouts are coming from ahead. I think we're getting close. But I've picked up on something behind us, a stink the wind has carried our way." The howl of a beast shook the walls with such a ferocity that my heart nearly stopped. "It knows we know."

"Rust." A shiver ran through my body. "Maybe we should be doing more running and less talking?"

Stomping footsteps and snarling approached. We ran, but with every path we took and corner we turned, the heavy breathing and stomping followed. Soon, the stairs carried us to higher levels, where passageways led to gravity-defying upside down corridors.

We pushed on until we went into a passage of darkness devoid of all sound or light. Here, too, a weightless, strange feeling came over me, as if I had no body at all. I couldn't even see my hand in front of my face. I tried to touch my body and felt nothing but air where my chest should have been. I felt for my legs and arms and had no sense of touch. I tried to scream out to Seneca, but made no noise. I struggled to will my body forward, barely grasping the tips of sanity as my mind went full on cogged.

I gasped with relief when we stumbled out into the blinding light of a forest that seemed ten times bigger than us. I felt like an ant running across a grass field, dodging mountainous roots and avoiding the strange chirping sounds of insects no doubt monstrous in size. As we ran, the world shrank, or we grew in a slow, but steady transformation. Once we reached normal size, the path led us back into the hedge maze. Through it all, the beast growled and rumbled at our heels while Loki's cries grew nearer.

The Earth shook with the beast's thunderous roar. The maze angled downhill to the point we had to slow our run and lean back in order to stop from tumbling forward. The further we went, the more awkward our footing became. We practically crab walked down until my leg slipped from under me and I went rolling into Seneca. My weight swept her forward, and we tumbled on, a knot of body and limbs. The tunnel grew steeper and steeper until we plummeted in a straight drop. The world spun around; darkness, stone, and flesh all mixed together at a sickening speed. I braced for an impact that never came. A plunge into icy water shocked me back to my senses. We struggled to untangle ourselves. My foot scuffed stone, and I realized we'd landed in a waist-deep pool. I gathered my legs under me and stood.

Torches hung along the walls, making shadows dance at every corner. The screams became so loud we covered our ears. We waded among the remains of decaying body parts and mauled bones... all human. The pool bottlenecked into a narrow tunnel, forcing us to walk sideways. I could barely breathe, and my nerves were getting the best of me. At one point, Seneca had trouble squeezing through; stuck behind her, dark shadows closed in around my vision.

The screams coming from ahead didn't help my panicking. I needed to be outside with sky easily in view. How had I come so far from home, lost deep beneath the bowels of Earth? I pushed at Seneca, trying to force her ahead. She offered me some appreciative curses before popping out of the other side. I struggled after her; I had to get out before I fainted. In my haste, I turned wrong and wedged my shoulders between the rocky walls. I couldn't breathe!

"Zak," Seneca shouted. "Calm down. Take a deep breath and try to turn sideways."

I gasped for air, but my lungs refused to work. The walls wanted to devour and suffocate me. I fought and pushed, but everything only seemed to get me jammed tighter. At least when I crawled through the small spaces under Olympus, I could enjoy the air or warmth of the sun on my skin and see the sky. But this place, trapped miles underground, was horrifying.

"Relax!" she yelled.

"I can't breathe—get me out of here!"

She grabbed my arm and pulled. My body scraped on the rough stone, but I didn't care. I would gladly have been skinned alive if it meant freedom from this coffin.

"Focus on something, anything. I can't get you out with you panicking like this."

"Get. Me. Out." I needed to focus. Focus on what I was here for… I needed to find my sister. I needed to rescue her. How could I expect her to be brave if I was acting like a coward? I imagined her sitting quietly, waiting for me to come get her. Because she depended on me. No, she trusted me. I had to be brave for her. I closed my eyes and focused on my breathing. *Slow it down. Easy, steady.*

"Exhale; it'll help make you smaller," she whispered.

I emptied my lungs. I turned sideways, and with her pulling and me pushing, broke free. I fell out the other side almost on the verge of tears. If I wasn't waist deep in water, I would have laid down, closed my eyes, and checked out for a bit. We entered a grand cathedral, ivory pillars reached up so high into darkness we couldn't see the ceiling. Carvings of men fighting battles with tiny creatures and monsters alike decorated all the surfaces. Painted pictures on the wall's glistening tiles were rich with detail.

The beauty of the cathedral meant nothing compared to what awaited us in the middle of the room. A man decked out in bronze armor sat upon a beautiful throne of ivory and emeralds. Horns rose from his forehead like wicked antlers and fine black hair hung low over his shoulders. A sword rested at the side of his throne, in a scabbard encased in black jewels and leather. His eyes shone dark like the night itself and stars seemed to sparkle in them, watching us closely. He did not speak. Chains bound his wrists and legs.

Behind him stood a copper statue of a woman, a sculpted immortal look of sadness on her face, and a snake draped around her shoulders. She rose up above the throne and held a bowl over the man's crown, beneath the snake's massive head. Its mouth open wide, drops of golden liquid dripped from its fangs into the copper vessel. With each drop, gray steam billowed from the serpent's nostrils.

The man breathed long, hard, desperate breaths, beads of sweat dripping down the side of his face; his jaw clenched as if he awaited an attack. When we finally came to stand before him, I noticed a faint ticking, barely audible above the swishing of water. It stopped, and a bell chimed so loud that Seneca and I both ducked. The man tensed up.

With each tick, the statue turned; all the while, the snake's head stayed in place. Soon, the bowl no longer hovered over him, and the venom dripped on the man's head. He let out a torturous scream and thrashed wildly at his restraints. His crazed eyes filled with tears as he tried so hard to fight against the pain. Horror and shock kept me frozen in place; I didn't know if Seneca felt the same, but she didn't turn away.

Once the bowl no longer hovered over him, the statue upended it, letting its contents pour into the water. The statue righted itself and continued its slow revolution. All the while, the poor man howled in burning agony. Finally, when I thought I could take his suffering no more, the statue completed its circuit and came to a standstill, once more catching the venom.

The man took a moment to compose himself. Once he relaxed, he looked at us and spoke with a tortured voice. "Have you come to watch my torment?"

"Are you Loki?" I asked.

"There are no other gods on this cursed land but Loki," he said.

Seneca inspected the chains that secured his legs. "How long have you been here?"

"Since the time of the Fey uprising… only you can tell me how long ago it's been."

"Years… many, many years," she whispered.

"I have lost the ability to track time without the passing of day and night in so long. There is only pain and waiting."

"Who would do this to you?" I asked.

"I did this to myself… I sided with the gods and watched as they fled, leaving me to make a last stand. My penance for betrayal."

"They just left you?" I asked.

"I am the one who summoned the Fey to this world. I wanted Odin's throne. I was foolish enough to think I could control them. When I realized the error of my ways, I tried to make amends with my kin. They would not have me… so I made a sacrifice to regain their favor." He chuckled. "A favor that they will not soon give me. For betraying the Fey, Mob built this prison just for me, where I should suffer for eternity."

Seneca pulled on the chains. "If only I had my magic!"

"I thank you for your effort," he said. "But these chains cannot be broken. Not by any—"

"Can Zeus break them?" I asked.

He closed his eyes and seemed to think it over. A moment passed before he spoke. "I believe he can. But he has yet to try. So I have no hope for even his divine intervention."

I stepped forward so he could look at me better. The sorrow in those endless black eyes made me shiver. "Help will come. Zeus has lost his power. Ares stole his Aegis, and with it, his power. The Fey plan to march on the people of Olympus, and you are our only hope."

His laughter rumbled throughout the room for a few seconds before it died down into thankless sobs. "What hope am I? Look at me!"

"Odin sent us," Seneca said. "He promised to side with the Olympians if Zeus freed you from your prison. The only way he can do that is if his power is returned. We've come to restore Zeus and stop the Unseelie."

"Odin has not forsaken me?" Loki asked.

"No, he swore to only help if Zeus freed you," Seneca said.

Loki's eyes filled with water and tears freely fell down his golden cheeks. For the first time, he smiled, a smile that reached his eyes. "Knowing that, I can endure my pain for millennia to come. Go then and continue your quest, know this... when I am freed, I will rain down a vengeance that these cursed Fey will never forget! Behind me, there is a passage that leads to the land of the Unseelie. Take it and be on your way. I will be free of these shackles yet."

"Remember me." Seneca stood up straight. "Seneca Rose and Zak Walker are the ones who saved you... my parents died for me to be here."

"I understand," Loki said. "And it will be done. Free me, and it will be done."

I placed my hand on his. His fingers felt like ice, lifeless. I looked to Seneca next. "We should go."

"Wait," Loki said. "Take my sword. It is called Jotunn and has the power to slay gods. This was a gift given to me by the Fey for betraying my kin, and a way to end Odin's reign. The reason for everything that has happened. Let my redemption begin with this sword. It has the power to end those who seek to destroy us. Be wary though, every use will freeze the soul just a little bit. Mob left it barely within my reach, as a constant reminder that I will never escape."

I picked up the sword, a sharp chill rushed up my hand into my heart. I had to brace myself against the shock to keep from toppling over. I breathed out a gush of mist, as if the room itself froze over. I drew the blade and found it made of ice. Vapor rose from its clear blue sheen, and the room grew colder. Seneca shivered; she cautiously backed away with a fearful look. I sheathed the sword and the temperature returned to normal. I wanted to speak my thanks when the alarm rang out again. The statue started its slow turn.

"Quickly," Loki shouted. "Go now! End this misery!"

"Let's do what the man says." Seneca grabbed my arm and dragged me into the passageway behind the throne.

I didn't want to be in another narrow space, but Loki's screams urged me on. A light far ahead beckoned. *Please let that be sunlight!*

15

We ran straight for it and never looked back. I could almost taste the fresh air. I ran faster and faster with the promise of seeing the outside world again. When we finally reached the lip of the tunnel, I threw myself out onto wet grass and inhaled deeply. I rolled around and found the familiar sky looking down on me. I never realized how much I missed it and how much it reminded me of home. Seneca took a more graceful approach emerging from the cave as she casually stepped over me and sat against a tree.

I questioned her somber mood. "What's the matter? We're finally out of that Hades hole."

The beast's roar came from the darkness. An explosion of dust and rock shook apart the cave opening. Smoke erupted from the entrance and the earth rumbled under out feet. The soot cleared to reveal the cave torn wide open, and standing in the hole was the beast that pursued us.

The head of a bull sat on massive shoulders, with copper horns, and mechanical eyes and snout. Mighty hands shielded its eyes, and it crouched down. Its lower body was a mix of tendons, fur, and steel merged into flesh that led into large hooves. It had a man's torso, arms nearly as big as me, and leathery brown skin bursting with muscles over every inch. It stood to its full height, towering over us, and raised its arms while bellowing out another roar. The trees ruffled and waved as birds fled. The forest cowered in fear before the beast.

"Run," Seneca said.

"We can't. It'll just keep chasing us." I let Jotunn's scabbard fall to the ground. The cold of the blade seeped through my body. The whole forest grew chilly. I shivered but still held the weapon ready to fight. I advanced, staring the beast down. It huffed steam and stomped its metal hooves, kicking up chunks of dirt. Its intimidation was working, but I wouldn't let it show. I took a deep breath and watched the vapor escape my nose. The forest came to a standstill, as if waiting to see what would happen next. I would put on a show. I ran at the beast with the sword held high. When I came within striking distance, I brought it down hard, but not fast enough. It swung its arm, catching me in the side and knocking me clear across the field. My back crashed into a tree, and I fell into a world of hurt.

I looked up as Seneca jumped on its back. She wrapped her arms around its neck and rode him like a wild horse. I got up to one knee, feeling the cold pain in my side, but forcing myself to ignore it. The beast swung Seneca back and forth until she lost her grip and crashed to the ground. I had to get back to my feet. I stuck the blade into the earth and used it to help support my weight. Tendrils of ice ate away at the soil around the blade, spreading like a plague. With the sword almost frozen in place, I struggled to pull it free. Once I snapped it away from the block of ice it created, I readied myself to strike.

Seneca struggled to get back to her feet. The beast must have sensed easy prey. It grabbed her by the throat. She made strange gurgling sounds as it lifted her higher. Its head tilted sideways, curious mechanical eyes widening.

I ran across the field, dragging Jotunn behind me. One foot in front of the other, each passing step brought on an explosion of pain. *Are my ribs broken?* I struggled for every gasp of air; every move tortured my body. Seeing Seneca's face change color, purple spreading from her lips, gave me the boost I needed to fight. I had to stop being a child and fight back the pain. I forced my legs to move faster, forced the adrenaline to pump into my veins. *Let my anger take control.* The beast had its back to me; it didn't see me as a threat. It would soon regret it.

As soon as I was within range, I thrust the sword into its back. It cut flesh and bone with ease. The beast dropped Seneca and howled madly. It spun around and knocked me from my feet once more, yet the sword remained lodged in its back. It tried to grab at the hilt, but it was just out of reach. Every time it turned its back toward me, I caught glimpses of ice spreading across its flesh. The bease fell to its knees, and its monstrous howls turned to whimpers of agony. Soon, its whole back glistened with ice. It coughed twice, fell flat on its face, and the half-frozen beast went still.

Seneca came over and helped me up with a genuine smile. "You should have run."

I approached the frozen beast and pulled the sword free. "Why didn't you?"

"Because I follow orders just as well as you." She patted me hard on the back, sending another wave of pain down my spine. I fell down moaning.

We were both in bad shape, and with night quickly approaching, we decided to set up camp and regain our strength. Seneca made a small fire, and we huddled together trying to keep warm. No matter how close I held my hands to the flame, the cold presence of Jotunn still lingered on my skin.

Seneca had nearly died trying to help me. We were just strangers that circumstance put together and tossed into a whole world of craziness, and yet I still felt a sense of trust in her. Something I hadn't had in a long time. I laid back and looked at the sky; the stars sparkled like a road map leading me home.

"Wake up!" Seneca practically shook my arm loose when I opened my eyes. "Zak, we should get going. We're so close I can practically taste it."

"Any idea how we are going to get into Puck's castle?" I asked.

She gave me one of her legendary shrugs. "You know me. I prefer to not think things through. I'm all about jumping into the fray without being properly prepared. It's part of my charm."

I got up and stretched the kinks out of my back. My body felt broken, but I would not give up. We continued on our journey because there was no other choice. I officially hated walking through forests. The moist air didn't agree with my lungs, it made my clothes stick to my skin, and the tree roots kept tripping me up. I felt like I'd reached the end of my rope. I wanted to be back on Olympus where I ruled over the Fringe. I wanted to be done. I even thought about taking a proper job like my father wanted. As long as I could sleep in my own bed at the end of the day, it surprised me how much I ached to go home.

The forest grew sparse and sickly. The trees—broken, withered things—hung over the trail where the grass turned to a coppery brown and crunched under foot. Rusting pipes jabbed out of the earth here and there among the trees, spewing thick tendrils of black smoke. The pipes grew more numerous the farther we walked, until only a few trees remained in a forest of rusting metal. Stray piping seemed to have merged with trees, creating eerie hybrids of nature and industry. We had to cover our mouths to keep from choking on the filth and soot that filled the air. Black smoke polluted the sky, hiding the sun with a thick coat of filth. *How could people live like this?*

"Where is all the smoke coming from?" I asked.

Seneca tied a scarf around her mouth. "There are factories underground where the Unseelie work day and night forging weapons, armor, and all manner of things. Not to mention the city itself runs on coal and ambrosia."

"It's horrible."

"The creatures that live here don't seem to think so." She pointed toward a gravel road. A mechanical horse pulled a carriage made of splintered wood, splattered paint, and cracked windows, toward us. We stood to the side to let it pass. A woman watched us with bored eyes from within, her hair a mess of black and gray, mixed with cobwebs and dried twigs. Makeup covered her face, with a heavy emphasis on black eye shadow. When I caught her eye, she curled her lip in disgust and pulled the shade down.

We continued on the road, soon met by a wide range of people and creatures traveling away from the city. None seemed to give us a second thought, and those that did look at us reacted as if our existence annoyed them. Goblins fought over carts filled with wares, a centaur hammered away at a broken down mechanical contraption, and fairies wearing dark armor and bronze wings patrolled the road with crude weapons and wary sneers. Soon, the sights and sounds of all the creatures lost their novelty, and I just kept my head down and followed close behind Seneca.

"Where are they going?" I asked.

"Away from here… probably to the Seelie Court. The Unseelie are like cancers, devouring all there is until there is nothing left. Stripping the natural beauty of the earth and leaving all this industrial waste."

"Will the Seelie fight them?"

"My parents are dead, I'm missing as far as they know, and the Rose armies are astray. The Seelie Court is fair game now." She took on a somber tone. "But we can't give up on them."

"The Seelie Court is just a stop. They plan to march on my home too. We all stand to lose if they aren't stopped."

"I hope we'll be enough."

"Why not?" I let my hand find its way to the hilt of Jotunn. "We'll have to be."

She laughed but didn't bother to say more. She stopped and nodded off at the sprawling city before us. This whole time, I expected to find a castle atop a mountain range, or surrounded by a moat with a drawbridge like in the storybooks. What stood before us was a mockery. Massive smoke-spewing chimneys, rickety mills, and crude factories made of glass and rusted bronze all meshed in one horrible sight. The sky looked like a black hole over the highest tower, where the bulk of the smoke and smog congregated into an infinite tunnel of darkness. I could make out the distant images of people climbing up and down towers of ash, and running in and out of the buildings.

"It's horrible," I said.

"It's called Helheim."

"How do we get in?"

"Zak, haven't you realized by now I always have a plan?" Her smile and wink weren't the least bit reassuring.

16

The inn near Helheim reminded me of the Back Alley Den. People sat around lost in drink while selling and buying secrets. Green smoke lingered in the air, and mischievous giggles whispered around every corner. Seneca marched into the midst of it all with an arrogant stride. It impressed me. Clearly, these were the type of people who preyed on weakness, and she knew how to walk the walk. She looked around as if she wanted to find someone specific. It wasn't too long before I heard a familiar voice.

"Kid," Gharis shouted from across the inn. "Over here." He and Alana sat at a table looking on impatiently as Seneca rushed over to join them. I have to admit I was happy to see them alive and well.

Seneca sat near Alana.

"Glad to see you made it here on time." Gharis said.

"On time?" Alana huffed. "We've been waiting on her for days. Not to say I don't mind spending my days here drinking while you run up a tab. I'm still charging you, you know?"

"How'd you guys get here?" I asked.

"Once you two jumped to your doom, the Unseelie lost their will to fight." Gharis took a hefty drink and wiped the froth from his mouth. "Not without losing a large amount of their numbers to my blade."

"Didn't Seneca tell you the plan was to meet here should we get separated?"

I gave Seneca a questioning look. "No… so when you wanted to jump ship, we weren't just abandoning them?"

"I'm not stupid. I knew Puck would have me followed. So you know, being that I'm wildly clever, I had a backup plan."

"Which included us jumping into the ocean in the middle of nowhere?" I growled.

"And everything worked out perfectly." She playfully punched my arm.

"It did take you two a lot longer than we originally planned to get here," Alana said.

Seneca nodded with a huge grin. "It all worked out perfectly!"

"We've had our men watching Helheim closely," Gharis said. "We think we've found a way for you to get in unnoticed."

"I take it you still refuse to come?" Seneca asked Alana.

"I feel like you still don't quite get that I don't like you," Alana said.

Seneca pulled the Scavenger captain into a huge hug. "I know you don't like me, you love me!"

"You may be the Seelie princess, and we may at times find ourselves allies, gods know why. However, with war coming to these lands, we must remain neutral. Picking sides during a war is never good for business." Alana pushed her off with what seemed a great deal of restraint.

"Alana," I said. "I wanted to ask you about my mother."

"Fortune?" A little girl called from across the way. Her curly red hair barely covered tiny horns that poked out from her forehead. She had round black eyes, and her face seemed to be a strange mix of human and deer. I pointed at myself with a questioning look. She nodded and trotted over. She wore a pretty dress decorated with strands of vine and green leaves. The fabric seemed soft and flowed like air over her body. Her steps made an odd clicking noise. I looked down and caught a glimpse of hooved feet peeking out from under her dress.

"You're new around here," she said. "I've never seen you. Want to know your fortune?"

"Sorry," I said. "But I haven't got much money."

She looked at me thoughtfully for a moment and sat near me. "My fortunes are free," she whispered, and the way she shot glances back and forth around the bar made me think her lying.

"Why would you read my fortune for free?"

"Why should I charge you to know your own future?"

"That's a good point," Seneca said.

I shrugged with indifference. "Everyone needs to make a living."

"I live here in the stables. Fenton, he owns the inn and lets me live here for free. All I have to do is tell him his fortune every night before he goes to sleep."

I leaned on the table and got a better look at her. "That seems awfully generous."

She giggled and leaned in closer as well. "A Night Wraith put a death curse on him for hunting stags in a blessed area. He was meant to die a week later. Fenton being the wise businessperson he is, bought me off a slaver after I told him how he was to die. Now death is constantly at his heels, trying to take back what was denied. Every night I tell him how he is to die, and he is able to avoid it and live another day. Today, he's getting run through by a unicorn. He took the day off and locked himself in the basement." She giggled.

"Okay," I said. "Let's see what sort of skill you got."

The Fortune Teller reached into a small purse hanging loosely from her shoulder, shuffling around through various magical trinkets I'm sure. She took out a pair of small dice, numbers etched on each of the six white sides. After blowing on the dice and giving them a good shake, she let the dice fall onto the table. I leaned over so I could get a better look. The numbers four and three stared back at me. I couldn't see how these would be able to tell my future. I startled when she looked up with glazed-over white eyes. Her body went rigid, and her fingers traced invisible lines in the air.

"Oh, why did he have to ask for his fortune?" Alana whispered.

"You've lost something very dear to you," the girl said. "Your heart is gone and you search desperately for it. But you've also lost your soul..."

"That doesn't sound good does it?" Seneca mocked.

"But on your journey, you will find someone who has been lost for so long. A lost memory that has shaped your life, and will restore your faith."

"None of that makes sense," I said. "How about you tell me how I die?"

The Fortune Teller tilted her head as if listening to something far off. "You will fall saving the one you love." Her calm demeanor jumped into a wild scream, clawing at her face and rocking back and forth. "Falling! Falling! An endless fall. Everyone is at war and you fall to your doom, through the clouds from the edge of the world." Finally, she stopped and gasped for air. Shivering still, the white in her eyes cleared like clouds, leaving them black once again.

"That was intense," Seneca said.

"Please don't go near the edge!" The girl got up and ran off into the crowd.

"On that note," Alana said. "We should get going, now that the little fawn has drawn attention to us."

Gharis settled their tab and we all walked out into the night. We traveled with caution, bandits and all types of violent creatures walked the Unseelie streets. Gharis guaranteed if you didn't know your way around, you could easily find yourself in a dark alley with a gang of Redcaps ready to steal the flesh from your bones. Because of this, we stuck close to the Scavengers and let them lead the way. One alleyway led to the next and another. We moved so quickly I could barely keep up with all the twists and turns. When we walked around a corner, a shimmering unicorn with steel hooves and horn casually trotted past us.

"Here we are." Gharis nodded toward an indentation in the wall. "There's a switch right there."

I inspected it and gently pushed the brick in. We all backed up to the sound of gears winding and turning in protest. Seneca and I followed the sound up to a staircase being lowered from a second level.

"Oh, I love secret passageways," Seneca said. "And this leads to the residential area?"

"To the help quarters. But the residential area is just one floor above," Alana said.

"And the throne room, is it guarded?" Seneca asked.

Gharis avoided meeting Seneca's eyes. "Most are marching toward the Seelie court. Those of the castle guards who stayed behind are off drinking or gambling at dice. The throne room is only a couple of rooms over, but you have nothing to fear."

"Okay… so you'll keep your eyes to the sky?" Seneca asked Alana.

The Scavenger captain shook her head. "I'd warn you to be safe, but why bother?"

Seneca walked over to the staircase and stretched out her arm, inviting me to go first. "After you."

I drew Jotunn and took a step onto the stairs. Seneca grabbed my arm and pulled me back. "It's the help quarters. You'll draw more attention if you show up with a magical ice making sword." I sheathed the sword; relieved when the warmth returned to my hand.

The stairs scaled the side of the building in a zigzag. The higher we got, the safer I felt. The pull of gravity always calmed my senses. With the wind blowing at my face, I couldn't help but think of home once again.

Soon this will all be over.

17

The stairs ended at a balcony overlooking the whole city. I eased open the doors that led inside. The sweet smell of honey wafted in my nose and beckoned me in. I walked right into a large room with a steaming bath in the center. White tassels and candles decorated the walls, while all the furniture shined with ivory and plush pillows. Women in loose white bathrobes sat across the couches fanning themselves, while others relaxed in the bath. The talking stopped, and all eyes turned to me.

Seneca pushed past me. "Is it me or does this look like a bath house?" A moment of silence passed before the room erupted into giggles.

A lady with purple hair and pointed ears jumped to her feet and hooked her arm in mine. "Can I offer you a beverage?" She snapped her manicured fingers, and a well-dressed man appeared with a tray of gold cups and a pitcher of purple liquid.

"No thanks."

I tried to wave off the drink, but she shoved an amply filled cup into my hand and led me over to the couch where she pushed me to sit between herself and another well-endowed woman who leaned in experimentally. I thought of Abby's reaction if she could see me and leapt to my feet.

Seneca reached for a cup, but the server walked away.

"We should be going." I said.

Two more women made their way into my circle of admirers, picking at my clothes and touching my face. I stumbled over a cushion, trying to back away. This only made them giggle more. It didn't help that my cheeks felt flush.

"But you've just arrived!" one said.

I laughed uncomfortably. "Thing is, I really have to use the bathroom. Is there one near here?"

The purple haired woman pointed out the door. "Down the hall."

"Okay, we'll be right back." I wrestled the hem of my shirt back from one delicate hand.

I grabbed Seneca by the arm and dragged her out into the hall. The inside of Helheim didn't match the outside. Sparkling white hallways with marble floors and thorny vines decorating the walls made the place look lavish. Paintings of elves and fairies in regal poses hung every couple of feet, separated by stone statues of ferocious creatures. We walked down the hall passing doors at random intervals, none of which seemed promising.

"Maybe we should split up?" I said.

Seneca looked back and forth. "Okay, let's meet back in the bath house if we don't find anything. Try not to get hurt. There's a whole room of women waiting for your safe return."

"Not funny." I walked down one hallway and she the other.

I didn't have time to check all of them, so I hoped the throne room would stand out. The hall ended at two large ruby double doors, with the Unseelie Coat of Arms etched into the marble wall over it.

I pushed open the door and peeked in. A great gloomy amphitheater waited on the other side. What little light existed shone from a lonely torch hanging over a throne of brass and iron. I walked in with confidence, thinking no one around. The room had to be abandoned, its owners making their way to the Seelie Court no doubt. I let the doors close behind me, sending up a billow of dust. Hastily placed black tarps covered the windows, and velvet sheets protected the furnishings, all but the throne. The closer I got, the more detail I could see: sparkling copper, shining steel, and ruby cushions. Silver vines engraved up and down the arms and legs and interlocked along the front of the backrest. Above the throne hung a copper shield that sparkled under the torchlight, revealing the inlaid cogs that decorated the front. All along the outer rim of the shield, diamonds glittered like the stars of the sky. *The Aegis.*

"This room is off limits." The voice came from behind. "But of course you would know that if you weren't a trespasser."

I followed the voice to a darkened corner. It took my eyes a moment to adjust to the shadows. Soon the outline emerged. A man sat back lazily on a chair. He stood in a fluid motion and approached. He had a smooth walk, casual yet determined. He wore a leather trench coat that draped about his legs, zippers and chains decorated his dark clothes. His eyes glowed with a fury that stirred my soul. I stumbled back and fell into the throne. The air in the room seemed to vanish all at once, and my nerves fled with it.

"I, umm… I—" I couldn't find words.

"Yes you are trespassing." He leaned in closer, staring deep into my soul. "You don't even belong on this planet. What are you doing here?"

"I…" *Why couldn't I speak?* I could feel the moisture gathering in my palms, my legs shook with an uncontrollable need to flee. Panic took over, and I couldn't pull myself to look away from his intense eyes.

"An agent of the Seelie, I have no doubt. But what is it you seek?"

I tried to stand, but my body wouldn't listen. I cowered before the monstrous presence.

"No matter. I will dispatch of you quickly." He casually brushed back his coat and revealed a sword at his side. I knew once he pulled his weapon, my life would be over. I had to fight through my fear.

"It was…" I had to force every word out. "Zeus—Zeus sent me!" At that, he stumbled backward as if punched. A bit of the pressure released from my head, and the fear ebbed from my bones. I stood up straight and stepped forward. "Zeus sent me to get back his shield."

"My father?" His eyes lost the fire, and he looked at me with worry and wonder. "He still lives?"

Ares. The God of War stood before me, cowering over a simple name.

"He's alive no thanks to you," I said, feeling my confidence return. "How could you betray your own father?"

"So much happened back then, so many things I had to consider… and I—"

"You were a spoiled brat!"

He held his head down.

"So you turned on your crew, you turned on the people you were supposed to protect. You turned on all of us!" Without the fear running ice cold through my veins, anger surged to the surface. I wanted Ares to know hatred. "You're pathetic."

He laughed as if my words were a joke, and looked up with glowing eyes. I gasped, and the world rocked under my feet.

"You dare speak to me that way?" He stood stronger and taller. "Me, God of War? You should be groveling at my feet!" He placed his hand on my shoulder and squeezed until the bones popped and pushed me down to my knees. "You should beg for my mercy."

I struggled against his power, trying to get back to my feet. No use. His gaze filled me with overwhelming fear, and his strength easily overpowered me. I reached for Jotunn, my fingers barely grazed the handle before Ares smacked the sword away. It clattered across the hall and fell out of reach. He dug his fingers deeper into my shoulder, his eyes blazed fire.

"Excuse me," Seneca called from the entrance. "I was looking for the bathroom. I've been holding it in ever since I left Olympus and—"

Ares spun around in a fit of rage, throwing me to the floor. "Does this look like the bathroom?"

Seneca held up her hands, sparing me a slight glance. "Calm down friend. I must confess I did have a bit too much to drink. Also, people always told me I wasn't right in the head… what is this, the throne room?"

"Father, will I be cursed to walk amongst these wretched lowlifes forever?" Ares yelled. He took two long steps toward Seneca. He practically glided across the polished floor.

She jumped back. Unfortunately, she found herself backed up against the closed doors. I knew she would either flee or be bludgeoned to death at any moment. I needed to use my time wisely. First things first. My shoulder throbbed in pain; I could barely lift my arm. It came out of the socket, so I had to snap it back in place. I struggled up to my knees, held my breath, and bashed it into the throne, biting down hard.

Seneca pointed an accusing finger at Ares. "Don't think just because I am a fool I don't have a plan to defeat you."

I couldn't reach Jotunn, but the Aegis hung right above me.

"For a god, you move as slow as a one-winged pixie!" Seneca ran circles around Ares, dodging his attacks.

I crawled onto the throne, still feeling every nerve, but I had no choice. I hoisted myself up onto the back and leaned all my weight against the wall, reaching for the shield. My fingers barely touched the bottom edge. I used the leverage to pull up my injured arm and grab a hold of it with both hands. I yanked, but it refused to budge. Behind me, Seneca and Ares exchanged cutting insults, but there seemed to be no immediate danger. I pulled harder at the shield, the bottom peeled away from the stone, letting me slip my fingers behind it and get a good hold.

"Uhh… Zak," Seneca shouted. "I do understand you're busy at this point in time. But maybe you could hurry—"

I glanced over my shoulder as Ares picked her up by the neck and slammed her to the floor. All the fight fled from her body. She lay prone under the weight of Ares' hand. I didn't have time to worry. I turned back to the Aegis and yanked.

"What are you doing?" Ares shouted.

The shield pulled free. A moment of weightlessness came over me as the momentum threw me back. I crashed to the floor with the shield clutched in my hands. Ares charged; I rolled onto my side and jumped to my feet to find his fist already flying straight for my face.

I knew he had the ability to knock my head clean off. The savageness in his eyes surprised me so that I barely had time to lift the Aegis. His fist stopped inches from my face. Thunder clapped across the room and the lights burst into heavy flame. Ares flew feet over head across the length of the hall. The Aegis sizzled with energy; tendrils of electricity shimmered over its shell.

Ares stood, shaking his smoldering hand. He growled and came at me again. This time I stood my ground. I held up the shield as his other fist came in for the kill. He made contact only a second before thunder and electricity erupted from the shield and sent him soaring again. Aegis in hand, I reclaimed Jotunn. The left side of my body tingled with electricity and the other chilled to the bone.

The power felt incredible.

Ares got back to his feet and brushed himself off. He removed his coat and carefully folded it before putting it down by his feet. "You've annoyed me. I'll give you credit, though. Not many people have faced my anger and lasted this long. So now I ask you this. What do you expect will happen here?"

I hefted the Aegis and took a step toward Ares. "You let me and her go." I pointed Jotunn at a still unconscious Seneca. "I need to find Puck and get my sister back. Then I'll return this to Zeus, he gets his powers back, and we can stop the Fey army from destroying my city. You can come back if you want… your father will forgive you."

"Your sister?" Ares said.

"Puck took her. She's only a kid. I need to get her back."

Ares looked at me with curiosity. "I can see the resemblance."

"You've seen her?" I stepped forward.

"You're a fool. They aren't here. Puck took her to Oberon's Ivory Castle. You came all the way here for nothing."

My heart sank. "I got Zeus' Aegis. It'll stop the war. That's something. If you help me, Zeus will forgive you."

He laughed. "Do you know my father? He'll never forgive me for what I've done. I am the great shame that stains the Olympian bloodline. There is no redemption for me." He eyed Jotunn.

"So what does that mean for us?" I asked. "Obviously, you've figured out that you can't screw with me now that I have the Aegis."

"Perhaps, perhaps, but will it protect your friend?" Ares moved with such speed, he had Seneca in his arms before he finished speaking, holding a crude looking knife at her throat.

The cold that seeped from Jotunn intensified, making my fingers go numb. A wave of wanting came over me. Jotunn and I hungered for blood. Freezing cold ran up my arm and into my head, clouding my judgment. I stopped thinking and let instinct take over. I ran across the length of the throne room, letting my sword lead. Ares' eyes caught mine. He could have moved or fought back, but didn't. He just stood there and let the blade punch home into his heart. Ice spread across his shirt while his skin turned a pale shade of blue. He fell to the floor. I watched as the life escaped his body on wisps of vapor. His eyes held the flare of rage until the bitter end. Relief replaced the anger.

I ran over to Seneca's side and tapped her cheeks.

"Please tell me it's all been sorted?" she moaned.

I strapped the Aegis across my back and helped her up.

The door opened and a guard stepped in. He looked from us to Ares, took a step back, and let the door close in front of him. Not a second passed before shouts of alarm went up.

"Rust! We have to get out of here." I dragged Seneca to the door. We stepped outside to the echoing thunder of guards storming down the hall.

"We have to get to the roof," Seneca said.

We headed in the opposite direction around a corner and found a stairway that led upward. It would have been best to go down, but we had no choice. Seneca could barely stand on her own, and I had to lend her as much of my strength as I could spare.

When we reached the top, I used my bad shoulder to barrel through the door and almost cried out in pain. The smog-filled sky greeted us with embracing arms. I pushed the door closed and leaned against it. Seneca sat next to me to add her weight. From our position, the whole rooftop lay open and bare to us—we had nowhere to escape.

"We could jump," she said.

"We could, but we'd probably die," I said.

"Most likely."

We both jolted with the force of the guards banging against the door. We used our feet to push us back and barricade it. The guards continued to yell and pound. Luckily, with the stairwell's narrow passage, only a few would be able to push at a time.

"We could fight until a glorious death," Seneca said.

"I do have the Aegis that seems to make me impenetrable."

"And a god killing sword that makes you breathe out cold vapors."

"But we're cogged when it comes to the numbers game."

The door thudded with much more force. They must have brought in a heavy hitter.

"We could fly out of here," she said.

"Sure why not. Why don't we just sprout wings and soar on out of here."

"No, I was thinking of something more stylish. Like that." She pointed toward the sky at an airship bearing familiar Scavenger flags.

"It's the Highwind!" I tried to get up in excitement, but another round of banging kept me put.

The ship came in closer, Alana hanging from a ladder off the side, her arm hooked around the prong while her free hand aimed her pistol at us.

"Get ready to jump!" Alana shouted.

I looked at Seneca. We shared a nod and leapt to our feet, sprinting toward the edge of the tower. The door burst open, but I didn't look behind me. The clamor of guards scrambling through the door behind us drowned in the report of Alana's pistol. The ship came in close and hard, and turned just enough for Seneca and I to jump onto the ladder.

Alana only had to shoot off one more volley before we could breathe easy.

18

As the Highwind soared above the clouds, tension eased off my shoulders. The cool breeze and endless expanse of powder blue sky felt like home to me. I searched the horizon for any sign of Olympus, even though I knew we couldn't see home from this location. But still, I couldn't help but let my eyes wander. Excitement coursed through my veins.

I walked along the deck, watching the wind fill her sails. I knew she didn't need sails, yet they carried us across the sky.

"It saves on ambrosia." Alana came to stand beside me. "If we let the wind propel us. I have a feeling helping Seneca Rose is going to cost us a lot in the long run."

"Yeah," I said. "Thanks for coming after us."

"I didn't intend to leave you guys stranded. She asked us to meet you on the roof. I was thoroughly against it… but I made a promise to your mom."

This time I wouldn't let her get away. "Please, will you tell me about her? How did you know her?"

Alana crossed her arms and smiled with pride. "We met a long time ago. She hired us for an expedition up north. Your mother was well known for her scavenging. She's one of the few Olympians who have seen so much of the Earth. She's someone to be proud of."

"Yeah, someone who would ditch her kids just to keep up with her adventuring."

"It wasn't like that." She sighed. "There's way more to it, and it's not my place to say. But I can tell you that she crewed up with us for a while. She's one of the only people I'd trust with my ship." She put her hand on my shoulder. "She's a good woman Zak, don't forget that. Sometimes a mother has to make the hardest choices just to do right by their kids. It may not seem like it now, but you'll understand someday."

"Sure," I said, without the slightest bit of sympathy. "She's brass."

"I have to go check on the engine." Alana didn't look comfortable. "We'll talk more soon."

I leaned against the railing and stared down at the world slipping by below. Everything seemed so perfect when you looked down on it from high above. No signs of war, hardships, or pain. Just an endless expanse of beauty for as far as I could see. I couldn't believe the people down there wanted to destroy my home. After a while, the ship ascended higher into the sky and a white blanket of clouds hid the world from my prying eyes. Pressure built in my ears and I welcomed the sensation.

All the excitement started to take its toll, my body demanded rest.

———

I LAY on a soft mattress and listened to the soft crackling of wood adjusting and expanding, the ship groaning like a living thing. Still I relaxed. I ran my hand along the smooth wooden paneling against my bed, feeling the gentle vibrations of life running through the ship's body. I wished Alice could share this experience with me. Hopefully after we find her, she and I would be able to ride the Highwind straight home.

The smell of cooking eventually lured me from sleep. The aroma beckoned, leading me from my room, down a narrow hall, and into a cramped kitchen. I found a table overflowing with dirty plates and mugs, with chairs haphazardly thrown about. Along the wall sat a stove and refrigerator. Seneca stood over a boiling pot stirring its contents with a ladle. I picked up one of the turned over chairs and sat near the table, pushing aside some plates to make space for my elbows.

"You're rusting me, right?" I said.

Seneca turned around and gave me a questioning look.

"The mysterious princess, who is to lead her people, is also a master chef?"

She laughed. "I wouldn't say I'm a master chef. It may not even be edible... but yeah." She twirled the ladle around her hand and dropped it. "Nothing like a home-cooked meal before saving the world."

I rolled my eyes. "Sure. What's for dinner?"

She grabbed a bowl from the table, wiped it with her shirt, and ladled what looked like stew into it. The scent nearly made me fall out of my seat. I couldn't remember the last time I had a proper meal. She placed the bowl in front of me and offered me a dirty spoon.

"Careful it's hot—"

I didn't wait, shoveling the food into my mouth. The taste of meat, beans, and rice burned its way down my throat. It wouldn't stop me from devouring the meal. She sat next to me with a bowl of her own, and we both ate in silence. When I finished, I leaned back in my chair and stretched. The top of my mouth felt as if it caught fire, and my belly swelled to bursting ...

"I guess four bowls might've been a bit overboard."

Seneca looked to be deep in thought.

"Are you okay?" I asked.

"I was just thinking that we are so close. We have the Aegis already... it's a big risk taking it to the Seelie court with Puck and the others there."

"Maybe we should hide it on the ship? I don't know—it's our best defense. When I used it against Ares, it felt good. It made me stronger, powerful."

"Humans aren't meant to wield the power of the gods you know."

"Right. But still, I think with the Aegis and Jotunn, getting into the Seelie court and rescuing Alice will be easy."

She nodded, still not meeting my eyes. "It's just a big risk to come all this way and take chances. This war depends on us."

"I get that. So we'll leave it with Alana and Gharis."

She didn't answer, instead picking up our empty dishes and throwing them into the sink. She watched me until it became uncomfortable. More than once, she started to speak, but seemed to think better of it and held her tongue. Finally, she took a deep breath and said. "Listen, I know we have to save Alice, but—"

"Seneca!" Gharis walked into the kitchen. "We're coming up on The Seelie Court. Alana wants you on deck." He looked me over once. "And I guess the kid too."

I rushed to the bow and gazed out over a field of endless white clouds. Straight ahead, a glint flashed among the gauzy shapes. As we neared, shining marble pathways and ivory towers emerged from the haze, pavilions of alabaster and quartz, archways that bridged over sparkling rivers. It made me gasp with wonder. Whereas the Unseelie Court seemed to be sucking the life out of nature, the Seelie Court merged seamlessly with the surrounding forest, and there in the center of it all, stood the grand Ivory Castle.

"Welcome home," Seneca whispered at my side.

"It's amazing," I said.

"But how long will it last?" She pointed off to a line of decay cutting through the forest at the back of the castle, a road heading all the way south toward the Unseelie Court.

We landed the Highwind on the outer edge of the city. Seneca, Gharis, Alana, and I disembarked and took in all the beauty that stood before us. A pain stabbed at my heart knowing that the Unseelie wanted to destroy such beauty, Seneca's home. I swore to myself that I wouldn't let that happen. We left the Aegis below deck, not wanting to chance losing it to Puck. Seneca was right; no matter how much I enjoyed the power, we couldn't risk it. The air smelled like dying rose petals, a mixture of bitter and sweet, delicious and unsettling.

"This is where we leave you," Alana said to me.

"Still don't want to get involved?" I asked.

Alana looked off to the side where Seneca stood looking worried. "She didn't talk to you, did she?"

"Talk to me about what?" I asked.

Seneca took a deep breath and marched over to us. "Zak, listen… I… I don't know how to say this. Okay, we're friends. I've come to appreciate our friendship."

"Yeah, of course."

"I didn't think we would be anything more than that. But I don't know, traveling together, fighting the good fight will do that to you."

"We are crew." I stuck a fist out for her to pound, but she shook her head instead. Her eyes glassed over with tears.

"I can't go with you. If it were up to me, you would come with us."

"What are you talking about?"

"We have the Aegis. I need to get it to Zeus as soon as possible. Even stopping here was a huge risk I didn't want to take. But I knew you wouldn't want to just abandon Alice, so I—"

Gharis put a friendly hand on my shoulder. "We decided it best to let you make your own choice."

I felt like she'd punched me in the gut. Bile filled my mouth and the world seemed to tilt on its side. "You guys are edging me?"

"We'll come back for you." Seneca took my hand in hers. "I just need to get the Aegis to Zeus so we can stop the Unseelie."

"So Alice doesn't mean anything to you?" I shouted.

"Of course she does, Zak! But we are talking about one child versus tens of thousands of people. Not to mention my home—and yours!"

My heart practically exploded. I stumbled backward, not believing what I was hearing. "You said it yourself. You said it was your fault they took her! You said it was to lure you out and you would help me make this right. So now you plan to shove off and leave me without the Aegis to at least protect myself?"

"You know we can't risk the Aegis, and even worse will happen if they capture me. They'll be able to raise Mob—that will be the end of everything." She kissed my hand and tried to plead her point.

I pulled away from her. "Right, then. I ditched Abby for you, you know. Do you remember that? Even before I knew they took Alice. I sided with you against my only *real* friend. Because I wanted to help you."

"This is part of helping me!"

"At the expense of my sister!"

Alana pushed us apart. "Listen. There's no point arguing this. Zak. I'm sorry, but I never had any intentions of stepping foot in the Seelie court. This is what Seneca wants. I'll take her to Olympus and be on my way. But I don't want to stay here any longer than I have to."

"Have some compassion," Gharis said.

Alana shot him a look. "My hands are tied."

I looked back and forth between the three of them, but I let my cold hard gaze linger on Seneca. "Yeah, it's all brass, we're crew right? You do your thing and I'll do mine. I've been running on my own for practically all my life just fine."

She looked up and sighed. "It's not like that."

"Rust happens." I palmed the handle of Jotunn at my side. "I can do this on my own."

"Listen," Alana said. "Your mother, she—"

"Is just another person in a long line of people who walked on me. Thanks for the ride. I'll be heading out."

"Zak," Seneca shouted. "Wait!"

I didn't. I headed toward the city without looking back. I wouldn't let Alice down.

19

Fey, man, and creatures of all shapes and sizes walked up and down the avenues in elegant clothes: long coats, top hats, walking sticks, bodices, sparkling shoes, and the finest dresses. The men and women looked perfect, white as pearl or sparkling bronze, blemish free faces held exaggerated smiles and blissful eyes. With every person I passed, they bowed or curtsied. Even the stranger creatures with their crooked eyes, pointed noses, and sharp teeth didn't look nearly as scary as they should. They too had a rather odd finery to them.

I felt strange walking amongst the Seelie. I feared at any moment, everyone would stop to point and stare, as if my imperfections would stand out like a sore thumb amongst the parade of perfection. I kept my head down low and cut through the crowds as fast as I could, using the Ivory Castle's peaks as my compass. The closer I got to the castle, the more I noticed a change in the crowd. At first, just dots of darker figures spread sparsely, but soon I noticed more and more beings that didn't fit in with the perfection of the Seelie. Trolls, goblins, and elves who wore matted clothes or fabrics mixed with leaves and branches. Some puffed wisps of dark smoke out of pipes. Most carried weapons, various blades and pistols. The Seelie gave them space as they snarled and made angry faces, walking around with a general ill ease.

I avoided the Unseelie as best I could, until I realized how much time I lost dodging around the city. They didn't know me. I was a nobody. I had nothing to fear. If I just walked amongst the crowd, there would be no way for them to know me as an enemy. With the castle portcullis coming into sight, I decided to just walk in like I belonged.

When I approached the gates, two armed Unseelie elves approached. They both looked practically identical, with gray skin, red eyes, and greasy hair. They each wore scowls that made me take a step back. Intricate war paint decorated their faces. Red splashes that still dripped... at least, I hoped it was paint.

"Where do you think you're going?" The closest one raised a barbed sword. On instinct, I reached for Jotunn, but when the other approached, I thought better of it.

I took a deep breath, making sure to stand up straight and make direct eye contact with the speaker. "I'm heading into the castle. I wanted to see if I could catch a glimpse of the prince..."

He looked at me questioningly before grunting an unintelligible response and stepping out of the way. "You won't get far without an invitation. If you hang around the castle grounds too long, you may end up troll food. But it's your choice."

The other sniffed the air. His gaze shot around with concern before falling on me.

"Okay, thanks for the advice." I tried to make my way around the two.

"Wait!" said the sniffer. "He doesn't smell right."

The first elf came close and sniffed at my hair. "Repugnant indeed, but all the Seelie smell funny."

"No, that's not a Seelie smell," the other said, sniffing at my clothes. "That's a different smell."

I took a step back and let my hand fall lightly to the hilt of my sword. "That's 'cause I ain't no rust Seelie."

The two regarded me with curious faces. "Oh, so what are you?"

I had no intentions of revealing where I came from. "Free Fey. I traveled from the southern forests."

"I have a cousin who's Free Fey, weird bunch they are. How can you not have an alliance?"

"Don't like being told what to do, is all."

"So, why the interest in seeing the prince?"

He had me there. "Well… because… because he's unifying both nations. Perhaps there's more to this loyalty. What I mean is, I never had much love for the Seelie… but I was never looking to go to war. If the Prince is taking over everything, might as well show some respect. You know?"

The first nodded, but the second still looked skeptical. I wanted to separate his head from his body. Knowing my luck, he'd still give me the stink eye. I nodded to both and tried to walk past them once more. I thought I made it until one drew his sword. "That's not Free Fey on you. That's Sky People stink!"

They grabbed me. One pulled Jotunn from my side, while the other had his blade at my neck.

"What are you rust heads doing?" I struggled against them, but they were a lot stronger than they looked. I couldn't believe I let them disarm me so easily.

"You want an audience with the prince, then?" one said.

"Sure, we'll take you to him, but you might not enjoy the meeting," the other added, before they both broke into cackling laughter.

They roughly bound my hands behind my back and shoved me to the castle entrance. Sloppily put together tents and sleeping rolls covered the grounds like a refugee camp. Unseelie moved about the lawns, smoking pipes, fighting, yelling at each other, and eating. Complete chaos. Some heads turned as we approached the wide arching entrance of the Ivory Castle. Some laughed, others pointed, and I tried my best to glare at each and every one of them in the eyes. I wouldn't show fear. These gangly creatures seemed like commoners who followed the court all the way from Unseelie territory.

A large beast lumbering at the castle entrance drew my attention. It could easily be over ten feet tall and looked like a mix between a steam engine and an elephant standing on its hind legs. Black steam puffed from its copper tusks, a steel cage glowed orange where its stomach should be, with the heat of spinning cogs and pistons. Its trunk held a cudgel the size of a small child. The closer we got, the stronger its heat felt. The two guards didn't seem to mind, but my skin baked from the intense heat of the monster's internal furnace.

The three of us had to look up at the beast; he hunkered down so his eyes could scan our faces. A strange static sound buzzed from its mouth, then music, then static, then the sound of someone clearing his throat.

"You hear me now?" It said before the static came again.

"Hello?" one of my captors said into the beast's giant ear.

Static.

"This thing is so useless, a big hunk of junk if you ask me."

"I can hear you!" The voice finally came in loud and clear. "Ah, there you go. Who is that, Jarek and Mace?" The elephant like head turned back and forth between the two and then stopped at me. Its huge eyes focused, but at the same time didn't seem alive. "And who is this?"

"It doesn't have a name," Jarek said.

"It?" the voice from the beast repeated.

"It's a sky thing," Mace added.

"Oh, how very interesting. I'd love to examine it," the elephant said.

I struggled against the two guards. "No one's examining me. Rust brain!"

The beast stood. "It can talk!"

"I think most of them can," Jarek said.

"I must have it." The elephant stomped its foot with excitement.

Jarek shook his head. "You know the protocol; we have to take him to the prince."

"Ah, but the prince has been sent to Olympus," the elephant said. "The queen demanded he start the invasion at once."

"The queen?" I struggled against the guards. "What are you talking about?"

"I didn't know… well then, we'll take him to see the queen," Mace said.

"Perhaps I'll speak to her myself on this matter!" The elephant said.

"Right, then. Do your thing. But as for now, you going to let us pass?" Jarek asked.

"Oh! Of course, of course. Please do be mindful of my specimen." The beast moved alongside the door. "Although it might be just as useful dead… I guess it doesn't really matter as long as I get to examine it. I wonder." He leaned in close to me. "Do you have hollow bones?"

"I have to insist," Jarek said. "You discuss it with the queen." They pushed me into the castle and out of his reach.

"What queen? Do you mean Mob? But how?"

They ignored me and kept prodding me forward. We walked through a hall decorated with tapestries featuring regal looking elves and fairies in various poses, all trying very hard to show off their wealth. One portrait stood out the most to me: a picture of a family, what I assumed a mother, father, and daughter. The girl with her long beautiful golden hair and a crooked smile. Even though she looked younger and incredibly different, I recognized Seneca. I looked away from her endless ocean-blue eyes. The guards shoved me on.

The castle felt desolate and abandoned. I could almost feel the dust and cobwebs brushing my skin. Wilted flowers decorated the dreadful halls, and the air smelled thick with mold and dust. I couldn't imagine Seneca growing up in a place like this. The Unseelie took over and poisoned it, creating a shadow of what once was. We walked down a corridor lined with antique coils, cogs, and pipes set on display. The walls shined with copper and tin that reflected a light with no source. My escorts brought me before massive arching doors. Two elven guards stood at either side. Neither looked at us. They stared straight ahead and stood deathly still.

"We found a sky person," Jarek said. "The Puck said he wants all sky people reported immediately."

The guard on the left held a staff. Without a word, he banged the steel bottom on the marble floor, making a loud *clank* that echoed all the way down the hall. I stepped back as the grinding of gears turning and mechanics humming to life filled the room. The doors opened outward and the strong smell of roses came through. The soldiers dragged me past the doors before they finished opening, into a grand hall. Mirrors covered all the surrounding walls, giving off the illusion that endless halls and rooms filled the space beyond. Two simple thrones of wood and cushion waited at the far end. The woman sitting in one made my heart thunder with fear.

Long stringy hair of silver shimmered with life over her shoulders, encasing a sickly pale face and black lips. Pointed ears jutted out from under a crown that tilted to the side and sparkled with black onyx and silver. She wore a black suit that looked like liquid, fitting form to her frail body. Long fingers like spider legs tapped impatiently on her armrest. She leaned forward and smiled, flashing thin needles of teeth that kept a serpent tongue at bay.

"It smells," she said, with a condescending tone. "Why did you bring it here?"

Jarek hesitated. "Umm… my queen, I was only following orders—"

"Which were to bring smelly creatures before me?"

"A sky creature… that's what you are… umm, smelling."

She looked me over, this time with more interest. Her eyes burned with red fire. As much as I wanted to stand tall, I couldn't help but feel my knees shake under her gaze.

"A sky creature?" Her tongue slithered out and playfully tempted the outer edges of her lips. "How delightful! Bring it closer."

Jarek pushed me forward. My legs gave out under me, and I fell before her.

"Well at least it has manners," she said. "What is your name, thing from the sky?"

I looked up at her and took a breath to steady my nerves. "Zak… Zak Walker."

"Zak Walker?" She tapped her long creepy finger at her chin. "I know that name… you wouldn't have any relations with Alice Walker would you? Tiny little thing, barely speaks a word. Most delightful really. Often, creatures tend to speak more than they should."

"She's my sister," I said. The mention of her brought me strength. "I've come for her! Is she here?"

"Yes, yes, of course she's here. She's my pet. Such a beautiful creature. So sweet and tender…" Her tongue made an appearance again, and I wanted to rip it out of her head.

"If you've hurt her—"

"You'll what?" She leaned closer, so close I could smell the stench of decay seeping from her skin. "Will you rise up and fight me? Silly thing. Now what to do with you?"

I stood. "Listen. I know why you took her. You needed her to lure Seneca out—"

"The Rose girl?" Her leering smile faded. "Where is she? She's turned into quite the headache. Do you know where she is?" She looked at her guards. "Does anyone know where she is? Where do we stand on that, did everyone just stop searching for her? Such incompetence."

"She's gone!" I shouted. "How were you freed without her?"

"Freed without her?" The smile that crept across the queen's face creeped me out. She clapped her hands together and seemed to gleam. "Excellent! How delightful. Was it one of mine that killed her? Jarek, quickly find out who slew the Rose girl so I can reward them."

"She's not dead," I said. "She's just gone, she left…" I was confused and frustrated. "I was told Puck needed the blood of a Rose to raise you, how is it you're here?"

Her cackle felt like a smack to the face. "I have my ways. As for the Rose girl, I just wanted her dead. A thorn in my side." To the guards, she yelled. "Why isn't she dead?"

"You got what you wanted," I whimpered. "Please give me my sister back."

"Oh, but she's having so much fun," Mob said. She waved her hand at a nearby mirror and the glass fogged over. The reflection shifted, and through the haze, a clear image of Alice sitting in a lush garden with flowers in her hair appeared. A creature sat next to her, the same creature I saw outside my house. A giant with skin like bark and limbs made of tree branches. Leaves grew from his head instead of hair, and crooked bark teeth overlapped his mouth. My heart nearly stopped as his huge hands reached for her. She laughed and leaped into his reaching arms. The beast hugged her tight while Alice giggled. A different kind of sensation weighed on me as the glee sparkled in her eyes, a happiness I'd never seen before.

"Where is she?" I asked.

"In my garden with her friend, another pet of mine. Dryad… that's his name, I think. Never got around to naming him something proper. Couldn't be bothered really. Anyway, no need to worry. She is in good hands."

"Seneca is gone and you're awake! Just let us go," I begged.

"Seneca was a nuisance. An effort that took up too much of my son's time. She may have been the original plan. Until he realized there would be a more convenient method."

"What are you talking about?"

"We found Alice, and I need her for one more thing."

20

She gave me no other explanation before demanding I be carted off to the dungeon. I spent hours sitting alone in a cell that must have been meant to cage dogs. I tried to close my eyes and save my strength, but I couldn't stop thinking of how happy Alice looked, and what Mob said about her. *Why did she want her?* My back ached with pain, and my bones stiffened within the cramped space. I tried to sit up, but the low ceiling meant I had to be in a constant hunch. I couldn't lay down either because the length of the cage barely gave me enough room to spread my legs. Similar prisons lined the walls on either side. Even though other prisoners whispered in hushed tones and cried out in pain, all the nearest cages were empty. I spent the first couple of hours trying to force the door open. I knew it was impossible, but out of sheer stubbornness, I tried to pry the bars open with my bare hands, hoping maybe I could summon some emergency strength from the depths of my soul.

I don't know how much time passed until someone came to see me. A woman approached, her motions fluid and graceful. She wore a cloak around her shoulders, hood pulled low over her face. Soft brown hair fell out from underneath. I caught glimpses of her tan skin as she scanned the dungeon. The sight of the food she had with her made my stomach rumble. Once she made eye contact, she hurried over to me.

A soft whisper escaped her lips. "By the gods… you must eat and gather your strength." She pushed the plate of bread and cheese into the cell.

"Since when do Fey care about my health?" I wanted to hate the woman, just because. But the food made it hard. I bit into a piece of bread.

"I'm no Fey," she said.

I stopped eating and looked at her questioningly. She pulled back her hood and let it fall to her shoulders. I dropped the bread and cheese. I'm certain my mouth hung open as I looked into those eyes. The same pained eyes she had when she walked away six years ago.

"Mom?" The word felt alien to my lips. I never thought I would use that word again.

Her eyes welled up with water as she rushed toward the cage and reached for my hands. I let her take them, more out of shock than anything else, but I relished the feel of her skin against mine.

"Zak. I've missed you so much. I can't believe this—I thought I'd never see you again."

"Because you left, you left us… you left me. Why did you leave?"

"I had to; I never wanted to leave you and Alice. But it was for her own good."

"What are you talking about?" I pulled away. "What is going on? Why are you here?"

"There is so much to explain." She thought for a moment. "We don't have time though."

"Way I see it is we have all the time in the world, unless you have a key to this cage. Even if you did, I'm not going anywhere until you tell me what's going on. Rust, Mom, you can't just show up without any explanation."

"Okay, okay. Just listen and don't ask any questions until I'm done. I have a lot to say and not much time."

"So stop wasting it and get on with it."

"You were so young when I left, but do you know what I used to do?"

"Scavenge."

"Right, I was a scavenger. I was a damn good one too. I made a lot of money and had quite the reputation. Olympians sought me out for plenty of expeditions. I was very committed to the job. I had ambition and a passion for it... I feel horrible saying it, but my job came before my family way more than it should have. Your father didn't take well to that. He felt like he should be able to support us on his own while I should have been home taking care of the house and family. I just didn't have that in me. I wasn't that type of person. I needed excitement and adventure."

"So you chose adventure over me?"

"No! Not at all. I love you so much it hurts, Zak. You were the world to me, and the only thing that kept me coming back. It reached a point with your father where we had nothing left, no love, no desire. But I refused to leave you. So I always came home. On one of my last expeditions, I led a group of scavengers to the outskirts of the Seelie Court. On that day, Oberon was out hunting wild Redcaps. We stumbled upon each other by mere luck. I was taken aback by his charm and looks, and oddly enough, he seemed to be just as smitten with me."

"He glamoured you?" I asked hopefully.

"No. I was intrigued. We spent a lot of time together him and I. We were friends at first. I visited him more and more on my expeditions. Soon I would go even when there wasn't a job. By the time we became... lovers... I decided that I needed to make a choice: either stay in the Seelie Court or go back to Olympus for good. The choice was already made. I was pregnant."

"Alice..."

"She's not your father's."

The world came tumbling down.

"I knew what it would mean for my baby to be a bastard child of Oberon. It was nothing good. Especially if Queen Titanya were to find out. She would no doubt torment my child to no end."

"Weren't you the least bit worried what the queen would do when she found out you were messing with her husband?"

My mother smiled. "Like I said, at that time, I had an unquenchable thirst for adventure. I never thought sensibly. It might have been my nature or the call of the Fey. I didn't once fear for my safety. But when I knew my child was at risk, my whole perspective changed. I needed to get away and never return. So I went back home... to your father. I told him I was pregnant and would quit the business for good. He was surprised at first; he acted like he wanted me to think about it. But I knew he was really pleased with my decision. I feared, though, that he would always suspect Alice was not his. The timing just didn't work out. She looks nothing like him either. If he knew, he never let on. So we lived in a house of lies.

"Soon after Alice was born, I received a message from Oberon. He knew of his daughter and he wanted her, for what purpose I dread to even consider. I couldn't let her be taken, so I made a choice. I walked away from my family and came back here. I begged Oberon to leave Alice alone. I promised myself to him in exchange for her. His anger was so great he claimed to no longer love me. But a bastard child had no place in his court, so he agreed to my terms, if only to see me suffer. I was made a personal servant to the queen. By then, she had already learned of our indiscretions. She did not make my life easy."

"All this because you wanted a little adventure?" I didn't know if I was angry or hurt, most of all, I didn't know if I should hate her or feel so incredibly sorry for her.

She looked away, trying to avoid my eyes, her hands squeezed around the bars of my cell. "Yes. I've made too many mistakes, mistakes that have put you all in danger... you will never know how sorry I am. How much I think about what I should have done. Not a day goes by that I don't regret losing you."

It all seemed so sincere, the child in me wanted to believe everything she said, but I just wasn't ready to accept her apology. "That's what Mob meant when she said that she used Seneca to find Alice. Alice has Rose blood in her. They used Alice to raise Mob! We were always too late."

"All it took was a prick of her finger, a drop of blood to unlock the seals that kept Mob bound in her prison."

"What will she do?"

"Next she'll awaken the Iron Dragon. We have to stop them or Mob will crush Olympus."

"Can you get me out of here?"

"Yes, I think so. I can't risk it until later tonight. I have an ally close to Mob. I just had to see you and make sure you were okay… to tell you to hold on…"

I took a deep breath and made a choice of my own. I put my hands on hers, and the warmth of my touch seemed to give her strength. She looked up into my eyes and let a smile spread across her lips. I gave her a smile in return. It felt so good to be with her again. I would have to let everything else be a problem for later. "Okay, I'll wait for you. We are all going home tonight. Even if I have to rip this piece of rust place apart piece by piece."

When she left, I cried. My sobs added to the echoes of the dungeon, probably lost amongst the sounds of so many others suffering. I didn't know if I cried tears of joy for finding my mother again, or because everything that's happened in our lives made me so sad and angry. Alice and I suffered because of our parents. Issues they had, and they couldn't get their rust together. We were the victims. Alice didn't even know who her father truly was!

I punched the wall, letting the sting of pain run its course through my body. I punched until my knuckles swelled raw and tender, throbbing as blood trickled down my hand, Olympian blood made up of far different things than Alice's. I thought back to the things she would see, her imagination that drove her crazy and one day made her stop talking. She could see the Fey. For so many years, she saw creatures that no one believed her about, creatures that horrified her into silence. All because my mother didn't stick around to explain things. Even I had refused to believe her stories. She must have felt so utterly cogged.

I felt like I should have hated my mother. I couldn't. Just thinking about seeing her again filled me with excitement. I have to admit I couldn't stop thinking how things would change when we got home. With Mom and Alice in tow, we would go about rebuilding our lives. Surely, Mom would singlehandedly slap some sense into my father and make things right. Then we would move somewhere, somewhere far from The Fringe and start over. Somewhere safe from the Fey... I felt stupid and naïve like a little child. A happy ending seemed impossible. But I would try my hardest to find one, if not for me, for Alice.

———

My mother came back later that night with someone else. Dryad crouched down behind her. He smelled of grass and flowers, probably from playing with my sister. He looked fiercely dangerous, but something about him seemed soft and loving, maybe because of the way my sister smiled in his arms made me feel I could trust him. But that same image also made me very jealous of him.

"What's that thing doing here?" I asked.

"Zak, Dryad isn't a thing, he's a forest spirit... and he's been protecting Alice for me. He used to be Mob's personal pet." She reached up and scratched behind Dryad's ear. "But all he needed was a little love and tender care."

"Right, kind of like your kids?" I felt bad about the jab as soon as I'd said it. The hurt in my mom's eyes made me feel horrible. But she didn't give me time to apologize.

"Dryad, open the cell door please." She took a step back. Dryad grabbed the bars with his giant hands, and with no effort at all, ripped the door from its hinges.

"Umm... thanks." I crawled out. My legs gave out under me, and I would have been lying on the ground if Dryad hadn't caught me. He supported my weight as I tried shaking circulation into my legs.

"I managed to get my hands on these." Mom handed me a bundle of cloth, I unrolled it and found Jotunn. *Way to go Mom!*

The bundle had a sword for her too, which made me worry. "Can you use that?" To answer my question, she spun her sword around in a series of complex arcs and spins. "Brass."

"We have to move quickly. Will you be able to keep up?" she asked.

I couldn't help feeling offended. What did she think I was, the same little boy she left behind? I pushed off Dryad and stood tall on my own two feet. "Of course I can keep up. I made it this far on my own."

She responded with a proud smile.

My mother led us through the dungeon into a maze of corridors. I couldn't tell one hallway from the other. They all seemed to blend together with the same decorations and designs. She moved like she knew these tunnels, so I had to put my faith in her. We gradually descended into the bowels of the Ivory Castle. She led us to a spiral staircase that dropped deeper into the underground. Thick and moist air greeted us that smelled of rust and metal. The farther we went, the more nervous I got. I felt myself falling further and further from the sky, I ached to see the clouds that soared over my home. I swore I would get back to the sky soon with my family beside me.

The stairs ended at another tunnel. The walls felt rocky and sharp, as if dwarves had used their crudest of tools to dig out the guts of the Earth. Light flickered up ahead, and with it came the sound of voices. We sped up and followed the lights to an opening. Mom held me back, pointing a cautious finger. I peeked around the entrance corner and saw Mob. Standing, she looked ten times creepier than before. Her spidery limbs twitched with such erratic motions I could barely tell what she was doing.

Ten guards flanked her, and most importantly, at her side, holding her hideously long finger, stood Alice. Candles poorly lit the room, but it was enough for me to see the mound of dirt that stood before them and the head of a ferocious dragon, its eyes closed and its mouth open wide. Ivory teeth gleamed in the candlelight, and its hide was made of flaky rusting iron.

"My dear pet, I have awoken," Mob shouted. "But I have yet to regain my full strength. I need you to lend me your power and aid me on my quest in restoring this world. We must rid it of the sickness that threatens to destroy it all. With you by my side, my armies shall rise. The time has come for the Iron Dragon to scorch the skies and shake the ground. We will watch our enemies perish and take the world for our own. I will not be content with just this world; I will rule the Earth, skies, seas, and the netherworld! We were both merely weapons to the family Rose. But no longer. The blood of a Rose shall wake you from your slumber like it has me. I, Queen Mob, will restore all of existence to its splendor, before the taint of man!"

"We have to do something," I whispered.

"I know… but we're outnumbered," Mom said.

"So what, we wait and do nothing?"

"I'm thinking…"

Mob continued. "Once the dragon has carved out a path for us, the Unseelie shall be many, the Unseelie shall go far, and the Unseelie shall reign supreme!"

I felt the shimmering cold of Jotunn at my side; the sword hungered for blood. I have to admit I did too. Mob took my sister. I didn't give a damn if she was only my half-sister. I just knew I had to get her back and make Mob pay. I stood and drew my sword.

"What are you doing?" Mom tried her best to grab my arm, but I wiggled away from her.

"The Unseelie can kiss my cogs." I ran out into the open with my sword raised. The first guard noticed me and came at me with shocking speed. I barely had time to swing. He deflected it, but his steel frosted over. The guard staggered back in surprise; I drove the sword into his chest and pulled at my blade as his skin turned ice blue.

"Zak!" Mom screamed.

Another guard swung a sword at my head, I ducked the blade, which sailed over me and shattered the first guard into a million tiny pieces of ice. With Jotunn free, I sliced it across my attacker's leg. As tendrils of frost vines crawled up his thigh, I rammed my shoulder into his stomach, knocking him to the ground. I tried to get back to my feet, but he grabbed a hold of my shirt and pulled me in close while the other guards converged. They piled onto me, squeezing the air from my lungs; the weight of a mountain seemed to be on top of me. My ears filled with countless voices of guards yelling and cursing. Darkness crept into the corner of my vision.

A roar like the sound of trees falling shook me to life. One by one, the guards went flying off. When I could breathe again, enough space opened for me to see light. Dryad tossed guards around like rag dolls, my mother at his side, fighting off others like a master swordswoman. I rolled out of the way before another guard brought a heavy axe down on my head. I let Jotunn's cold embrace me; I swung at the guard's chest with a ferocity I didn't know I had, slicing through armor that froze on contact. With a final gurgling wheeze, he fell, and his body shattered.

"Get Alice!" Mom fought two guards of her own. Through all the chaos, I lost sight of my sister and Mob. I found them at the dragon's head, Alice struggling, kicking and screaming in her effort to get away. The queen clutched her wrist and pricked her finger on the dragon's tooth. The cavern rumbled and dust fell from the ceiling. No one else seemed to notice at first, not until the ground shook and a crack opened up, belching heat.

Everyone fell to their knees, except Mob who laughed hysterically and finally let Alice go.

I crawled over to my sister and picked her up. She wrapped her small arms around my neck, still crying in pain. I tried to back away, but couldn't keep my balance. The ceiling caved in and I had to dodge falling debris while trying to leap over the newly formed chasm.

The cavern fell into chaos. Mom fended off an attack, searching for a chance to go on the offensive. Mob raised her hands toward the dragon and chanted something in a language I couldn't understand, and the ground split wider. I ran a few steps more before I lost my footing and tumbled down as a fissure erupted right under me.

For a second, I thought I'd comeall this way for nothing, but my fall jerked to a stop; my arm practically pulled out of its socket. I stared past my feet at clods of dirt falling to oblivion for a second before peering up at Dryad's branchy fingers tight around my arm. He peered down at us with a comforting smile. Ignoring a guard slashing at him, he pulled us up.

Another guard joined the attack, hacking away pieces of bark with his sword. Dryad didn't seem to register pain; his eyes remained locked on Alice's. He wanted so badly to protect her. He lifted us up over the lip of the chasm to safety. Another guard came storming in, tackling him over the edge. Dryad whipped around, lashing his three attackers with a tendril of roots, and dragging them with him into the darkness without as much as a scream.

"Zak, we have to get out of here!" Mom shouted from the cavern entrance, a trail of dead guards leading up to her feet.

Alice cried hysterically. I carried her across to our mother. Even though Alice tried to fight against it, Mom took her from me so I could catch my breath as the entire room came apart. The dragon's head jerked to life, its long neck, shoulders, and wings appeared as rock fell away. The rest of its body must have been buried underneath the cavern.

Mom pulled at my arm. "You'll have enough time to see it later; we have to go now!" She took off running.

I went after her as the world crumbled around us. I could barely keep up with the panic of being buried alive taking me. I'd never get to see the sky again. I wouldn't die with the clouds. The temperature rose so quickly sweat covered my body.

"Why is it so hot?" I asked.

"The Iron Dragon is waking; its belly is a huge furnace. It'll bring down the whole Ivory Castle."

"Why would they bury it under the castle; didn't they know it would be destroyed if it ever woke?"

"They never meant for it to be woken. After the fall of Mob, Oberon built the castle over it as a sign of commitment to protecting the dragon and making sure it was never used again."

"Lot of good it did them..."

"We'll worry about that later."

"This isn't the same way we came!"

"We are taking a different route. This tunnel leads throughout the city. We are getting as far away from the Ivory Castle as possible. Up ahead, there's a light. We're almost out."

When we reached the outside, a mechanical roar pierced the sky. I sat on the ground to catch my breath. Mom sat next to me. Alice pushed away from her and wrapped her arms around me, crying on my shoulder.

"It's okay," I said. "You're safe now. I'm going to take you home."

I ran my hand through her hair and rubbed her back reassuringly.

Mom looked at Alice with hurt eyes. She tried to hide it, but I could see right through her wall.

"We need to warn Olympus," I said. "We have to get back. They need to prepare."

"For a war they can't win?" Mom asked. "We'd be safer here. I know a place where we can go far from the Unseelie, amongst the Free Fey."

"I won't turn my back on my home," I said. "Besides, Zeus and Seneca have a plan."

Laughter rocked us both from our rest. Mob stepped out as if she were casually walking through a garden. Her gaze fell on me with such delight, I felt like a fly caught in a spider's web. "Reunions are so special. Just the other day, I was reunited with my son. We planned such glorious things. Zak Walker, and family, you do understand that I am Queen of the Unseelie. You cannot defeat me. So I offer you this chance to live amongst the Fey, all you have to do is tell me where Seneca Rose is and what she and Zeus are plotting."

"If you can't be defeated, why are you so worried about Seneca?" I asked, handing Alice over to Mom.

"Don't try my patience, child. Tell me where she is and I will give your family asylum."

"Mom, take Alice and run far away from here." I got up and held Jotunn before me, the temperature in my body dropping. My limbs froze over, but it felt good. The sword hungered for more.

"Really?" Mob rolled her eyes. "How boring."

She waved her hand and my chest felt like it exploded. I fell to one knee but refused to give up. I was the only thing standing between Mob and Mom. I used the sword to help me stand. The ground froze at my feet.

Mob raised an eyebrow. "Seems I have yet to reach full strength.

Let's try this." She waved her hand again, with a lot more force. The invisible impact threw me to the ground.

"Zak!" Mom yelled.

"Stay… back!" I struggled to speak, let alone stand. Mob waved her hand in a downward sweep. My spine felt on the verge of snapping. The taste of warm, metallic blood filled my mouth. After the pressure subsided, I fought my way to my knees, staggering, trying to get my feet back under me.

"I'm impressed. I wonder if your mother is as strong. What do you say we test it out?" She turned to my mom and Alice. Her hand extended, slender fingers seemingly reaching out for their life force.

Shadows converged over us, blanketing the forest in darkness. At first I thought I was dying, and mourned my sister's fate, until I heard the familiar voice of Seneca shouting from above. "Zak, look out!"

I looked up at the bottom of the Highwind's hull. Seneca fell toward me at incredible speed. I feared she would crash to her death until wings deployed from her pack and she righted herself just in time to land at my side.

"I didn't like the way we ended things," she said. "So I figured it was more important we do this together, being crew and all."

"Seneca Rose," Mob shouted. "How nice of you to join us."

"Mob, as hideous as ever." Seneca helped me up and handed me the Aegis. "You would think all those years of sleep would do something about those wrinkles."

Mob thrust her hands forward; I pushed Seneca clear and used the Aegis to shield us both. An explosion of lightning thundered over the forest. When the smoke cleared, Seneca and I stood surrounded by burnt grass, sizzling with smoke.

"This was your plan?" Mob asked Seneca. "Do you think the Aegis is enough to defeat me?"

Energy still crackled around the shield, it radiated and warmed one arm, while Jotunn sent waves of cold through my other. The two opposing forces seemed to meet in my stomach and fuel my chest with a cold fire. The pain from Mob's earlier attacks faded, as strength swelled in my muscles and power surged in my blood.

Mob tried to strike me with another one of her energy blasts. I brushed it aside with the Aegis, and countered with an attack. She was not prepared for me to come in swinging. Her hand shot up trying to stop Jotunn's downward arc. She screamed in pain as her fingers fell to the ground encased in bits of ice. Mob stumbled back, holding her injured hand to her chest. She snarled and tried to run, but I smashed the face of the Aegis into her back, sending her crashing to the ground.

She stumbled around on all fours, coughing up black tar-like blood. Before she could pull it together, I stuck my blade deep into her back. Her screams cut short as her body froze over. Once I pulled Jotunn free, the wound it left behind frosted over in seconds. The power was overwhelming. I wanted her to get up and continue fighting. Something in me begged to inflict more pain. The sword needed me to. Before I could, Seneca touched my arm. It took me a moment to calm down.

"We have to go," she said.

The Ivory Castle fell in a heap of smoke. From the ashes, the Iron Dragon's hulking figure emerged. It's howls threatened to shake the Earth apart. My head felt clouded over. I couldn't focus.

"Zak, let's go." Mom pulled my arm.

"We have to get back to Olympus." Seneca's voice sounded far.

"It's hopeless!" Mom said.

Why? Mob was dead. My mother and Seneca pulled me along leading me somewhere without question.

"Climb the ladder," Seneca said.

Someone tried to take Jotunn from me, but I pushed them off. The cold chill of the blade made me feel whole.

"It's okay," Seneca said a million miles away. "You can hold onto it. But you have to climb the ladder."

"Please, Zak!" Mom's shout shook me from my stupor. I sheathed the sword and my head cleared. She climbed the ladder up to the Highwind with Alice clinging to her neck. Seneca urged me to go next.

"But she's dead," I whispered.

Seneca shook her head. "She's too powerful. You only slowed her down. We have to get back."

I put my hand on the first rung, and then looked back. Already, Mob's color was returning as ice liquefied around her. I looked up at Seneca. "You came back."

"Yeah, we're crew right? I was dumb to think otherwise." She pushed me on and climbed up after me.

21

"You idiot!" Mom yelled at Alana. "You let my son go up against the Unseelie alone?"

Alana helped my mom and Alice get on board. "Well rust and bones... Helena Walker... I didn't think I'd see you again."

I climbed over the railing as the dragon shot up into the sky. Seneca pushed in behind me.

"Zak bought us some time," Seneca said. "But we have to get moving!"

Alana and Gharis were all that remained of the Highwind crew. Having taken an active role against the Unseelie court, the captain gave her crew the chance to disembark. Only Gharis, ever the loyal one, stayed at her side. So Alana took the helm while Gharis checked on supplies below deck. Seneca kept to her bunk from the moment we left the Seelie Court. She was hurting and cut herself off from everyone. I decided to give her space and stayed with Mom on deck. I explained to Alice who Mom was and why she'd had to live on Earth in order to protect us. Alice, of course, was more excited to be on the Highwind.

Alice laughed whenever Alana turned the wheel and we felt the ship shift. Mom practically glowed with cheer, her hands resting on

Alice's shoulders, whispering encouragement into her ears. The sails picked up and propelled the ship at a steady pace. *We were finally going home.* I'd spent most of my life wanting to get off Olympus, but now I couldn't wait to return.

The world below drowned beneath the clouds. *How long before the Unseelie came for my home?* I would do what I could to protect it. All my life, I was just a passenger, a background character in everyone else's lives. Another cog in the gears of fate. All my life, I'd been trying to escape my fate, but perhaps I should just accept it and do what I was meant to do.

We reached Olympus after the sun had set, using the stars as our guide. An eerie quiet greeted us in the city. The torches and lanterns that usually lit up the night were off. Alana steered while Mom and I watched from the deck as she softly put the ship down in the empty harbor.

"This doesn't feel right," I said.

"Unless things have changed that much since I left, the harbor is usually a hub of activity," Mom said. "What are you thinking?"

"Too soon to tell. The only thing we can do is have a look." The excitement I had about coming home faded to apprehension.

Alana docked the Highwind and I led the way to the Fringe. Empty streets spread everywhere, a creepy silence in the air. Mom thought it best we stick to the alleyways and out of sight just in case Puck's goons were still around. Sneaking from building to building, we stayed to the shadows and back streets when possible. I stopped near the Doc's office; I needed to see Abby and make sure she was all right.

"I'll be right back," I said. "Wait out here while I check it out."

"Be careful," Mom said.

I snuck around toward the front entrance. Someone was moving about, I put my ear to the cracked opening in the door, rustling and muffled curses came from inside. I slipped in, making sure to be extra light on my feet. Even though I stood in the dark, I could tell the noise came from the back room where the Doc kept medical supplies. I followed the sound to the storage room and found a mess of medicine and potions thrown about, shelves turned over and papers scattered around. In the corner, a shadowy figure hunched over, searching a cabinet. I stepped forward and the figure stopped moving.

"Who are you?" I asked.

He spun around and I barely had time to catch the flash of metal as he slashed at me with a blade. I easily deflected it with a jab to the arm, knocking the weapon harmlessly to the ground.

"Zak?" Mason's voice yelled just in time for me to stop another strike.

My muscles loosened up. "Rust! Mason, what the hell are you doing?"

"Looking for supplies, cog head. Where have you been? Abby said you went to Earth. What the Hades kind of rust is that?"

"Where is she? Why are you robbing, Doc? He's crew."

"I'm doing it *for* him, man. You haven't been here. Things have gone off the handle. Cogging Fey, they came out of everywhere. No one saw it coming. We were well up rust creek before we knew what was happening. It's like a veil lifted and they were there all along."

"Calm it! I don't know what you're talking about."

"This Fairy… Puck's his name; he's bossed up. He came straight out and told everyone they had to bow down before him. The Money Men tried to put him in his place, but he edged them. Then all these Fey showed up out of thin air like, poof. They took over in a day. Set a curfew, said if anyone disobeyed, they'd get edged too."

I didn't realize how tightly I'd balled my hands into fists until they started to hurt. "It gets worse. Queen Mob is on her way here with an army—and a dragon!"

"You're full of rust. There's no dragon. What the hell does she need an army for, we're already done."

"She wants to edge Olympus, all the humans and gods with it."

"You should have stayed on Earth."

"Nah man, I fight with my crew." I put my hand on his shoulder.

He nodded and shoved me off in a friendly way. "We have to get to the Crow's Nest. Doc needs these meds right away. Got ourselves a gang going there, trying to create anarchy around the city. But he got hurt bad. After Abby…"

"Where is she?" I pushed.

"Let's get back, I'll fill you in."

I led Mason back outside where the others waited. His jaw practically fell to the floor when my mother greeted him, but his shock wore off as soon as he saw Alana. He sidled up next to her real quick and kept asking her stupid questions the whole way back to the Crow's Nest.

The bar's boarded up windows seemed all wrong, with no light shining through the cracks. The Crow's Nest usually stayed open all night, and seeing it shut down worried me. Once we reached the entrance, Mason tapped with a series of knocks and pauses. After a tense couple of minutes, the door opened and Fray peeked out.

"Zak Walker? By the gods! We thought you were dead." She opened the door and rushed us all in, all but Gharis who she halted at the door with a commanding hand. "What's he doing here?"

"Him and Alana are with us," I said. "I wouldn't have got back without them. He's crew. I swear on it."

She looked him up and down with skepticism in her eyes. "He's neither Olympian nor Fey..."

Gharis bowed down slightly. "Trust me. I'm no threat to you or your kind."

"I'll be keeping my eye on you." She cautiously let him pass.

She led us into the back where she opened a trapdoor and climbed down a ladder into a well-lit area. Barrels of alcohol lined the walls, tables with supplies, and cots with injured people. At the center of the room, a handful of people argued around a table cluttered with maps. My father the loudest amongst them.

"Dad!" I don't know what took over my body, but I found myself running to him and hugging him. I expected him to shove me off and say something with breath smelling of alcohol, but instead he hugged me back with strong arms.

"I thought you were lost for good," he said. "I'd nearly given up hope. After reading your letter, I thought you'd never come back, between that and Alice... I didn't know what to do."

Alice crept over, cautiously eyeing him up. I pulled back from our embrace and held my hand out to her. She came over and hugged our… my dad. He looked nervous at first, with his bandaged up hand and arm, but I gave him a reassuring nod. He lifted her up and swung her around. Before he could put her down, Mom came over. His eyes went wide.

"Helena?"

"John… it's been a while." She almost blushed.

"By the gods, you look as beautiful as the day you left. You brought my children back to me."

"We have a lot to talk about."

A loud bang on the table made us jump. Gunnar—Odin—slammed his mug down hard to get our attention. "As heartwarming as this reunion is, we have matters to finish discussing."

"You old bastard," Dad shouted. "I thought I was all alone, and now I find my whole family returned. Give me a moment."

Odin looked displeased, but bit his tongue; he looked around the table seeking support. This couldn't be the rebellion Mason told me about. Odin, Fray, a couple of Crow's Nest regulars, some Rats, and my dad.

"We got the Aegis!" Seneca pointed to the shield on my back. "How about you raise the dead now and we'll sort Zeus later?"

Odin shook his head. "I will not put my people in harm's way again. Unless Zeus is standing by my side, I will not make a move. Besides, only Loki can steer the dead back to life."

"Great," Seneca moaned. "Good talk."

"Did you at least get the medication?" Odin asked Mason, who seemed to have forgotten all about it.

"I got it right here. Where's the old man?"

"Out by the back. Take Zak with you, he's going to want to see him."

We both ran to the back of the basement to find the Doc laid up on a cot. It pained me to see his chest wrapped in blood stained bandages, and his eye swollen shut. I felt the pull of Jotunn at my side, almost as if the sword sensed my rising anger and begged me to embrace it.

"Doc," Mason said. "I got them meds you asked for."

The Doc turned his head toward us with a nod. It seemed to take his one good eye a while to notice me and he tried to sit up. "Zak? Oh, gods I thought you were dead…"

I walked over to him and took his hand in mine. "I'm back, Doc. You're going to be okay. Mason got meds and everything. They did a number on you. Why would they do this?"

"Because they took her… I tried to stop them, but I was outnumbered. Puck took my little girl!" His eyes filled with tears and he sobbed. A feeling of dread filled my stomach. The call of Jotunn grew stronger.

"What happened? How could you let them take Abby?" I shouted, grabbing the Doc's arm a lot rougher then I meant.

"Ease off, Zak," Mason said. "Doc damn near fought off an army of Fey on his own trying to keep her safe."

The Doc grabbed my arm and pulled me toward his bed. "You have to get her back. Please! They took her because of you!" He coughed violently. I wanted to calm him down, but I was scared I'd only make it worse. Fray came over and shooed us away while she tended to the Doc.

I was about to question Mason when Odin called me over. "Zak, I need you to remember why you came here."

"Why did Puck take Abby?" I stormed over to the table. The power of Jotunn and the Aegis burned in my belly. "Was it because of me?"

"We have something he wants," Seneca said. "The Unseelie know we can easily change the tide of things. Puck knows your weakness.

"Abby…"

"If you want to save her, you have to get the Aegis to Zeus," Odin said.

But with the power of the shield and the sword I could edge Puck myself. A chill ran up my side and a storm brewed in my head. "No, no that doesn't make sense. If Puck wants to fight me, I'll give him a fight!"

"That's not the answer," Seneca said. "And you know it. He thinks he can stop you from delivering the Aegis to Zeus. It's a trap. Rushing after Abby is what he wants, what he expects. Don't you get it?"

All eyes were on me but the thunder drowned out their words. "I can get Abby back and take out Puck on my own. I sorted Mob just fine."

"Zak, what's wrong with you?" Seneca shook my shoulders. "Remember when I thought the right choice was leaving you behind? I was wrong and I came back for you because I trusted you. I trusted you with the Aegis and the lives of everyone. We're crew right? So trust me. I'll go after Abby; I have a bone to pick with Puck. You… you get to Zeus."

The tension eased off. Seneca's eyes burned with the light of a beacon in the fog. I fought back my pride and presented the shield to Odin. "We just need to get it to Zeus so he can free Loki… that's when you make with your part of the deal right… Odin?"

His eyes bore no surprise. He looked around the room and focused on the injured. "That's going to be a problem. The Fey are patrolling the streets. Worse still, Puck knows Zeus is somewhere in Empyrean. He just doesn't know where, so he damn near has an army camped at the gates. No one gets in or out."

"Aren't you a god? Why don't you just blast your way in."

"All the Olympians working together lost the first Fey war. I may be a god, but I know my limitations. I won't make a move until Loki is free and Zeus is restored. I won't risk myself or Fra—Freya."

I didn't want to turn my back on Abby, but I was the only one who could get to Zeus. They depended on me to do the right thing. "So it's settled then. I have to get Zeus geared up." I held my fist out to Seneca. "And you… find my girl."

She gave me a pound on the arm. "I won't let you down."

Mom and Dad both shouted, "No!"

"I won't let you do that," Mom said. "I only just found you."

"It's suicide," Dad added.

All eyes were on me, waiting to hear what I had to say. I felt a bit of pride. I liked the attention; I liked people thinking I was high rank.

"Look here." I pointed to my ink. "Everyone knows I got rank when it comes to ratting. I could be in and out and no one will know. I know this city like the back of my hand."

Alana stepped forward. "I'll come with you."

"No. This isn't Earth. Here I got all the skills. It'll be easier alone. I can watch my own back."

"I don't know…" Mom took my hand and looked at me pleadingly.

"I know you're worried, but I've become a man since you walked. I can take care of myself. I need to do this. Everyone is depending on me."

"He can do it," said Seneca, surprising me. "I believe in him."

I nodded my thanks. "I'll just need some wings." I looked at Odin and thought about what the fortune teller said. "Like the kind you keep on display?"

I left the bar sometime during the middle of the night. It felt good to be a lot closer to the stars and red moon again. I made my way to the edge, armed with Jotunn at my side, lugging Odin's wings and the Aegis on my back. The wings were like nothing I'd used before, but I would make do. Twice, I had to duck into an alley while elven guards traipsed on by. Every guard I saw had a weapon drawn and alert eyes, ready for a fight or an excuse to kill. I wanted to put them all in their place, but I couldn't risk messing up, not while Abby and so many others depended on me.

Every time my anger and pride tried to get the best of me, I thought about Abby. The farther I got into the Fringe, the fewer guards I saw. They underestimated the Fringe Rats. I made a run for the edge, feeling the hairs on the back of my neck tingle like I could be caught any minute. I peeked over; far below, bits and pieces of the Earth tried to make an appearance though the thick clouds building under us. I doubted I would ever miss it.

I took a breath and leaped off. Free falling felt good, the wind rushing past me, the weightlessness of my body, the feeling of being free. That familiar feeling came over me again. *Maybe today is the day I don't pull the cord.* I pulled it before I could think for too long. The wings fluttered to life and a motor buzzed in my ear. Plumes of steam propelled me back up toward Olympus. The underside felt more like home to me than topside. I finally felt like I'd returned. The pipes, steam, and gears that kept my city afloat welcomed me with their clockwork perfection. I maneuvered closer and got a bearing of the different sections of the city. Luckily, I was going to Empyrean; the wealthy had all the best parts and machinery, which would be easy for me to get into.

Once I reached the underbelly, I hooked myself in with a harness and cut off the wings' motor. The wings folded back neatly into the pack, allowing me to squeeze into the knot of pipes. I enjoyed seeing the craftsmanship of the mechs that went into this section. The maintenance shafts were what made it so brass. Rats weren't allowed to work on them here, so they had to have fancy shafts for their workers to get underneath all safe and sound. So I planned to make my way there as soon as possible.

I hung upside down from the piping and pulled myself across the underside. Every now and then, I had to detach my harness and hook it up to another pipe. My hands suffered, but I couldn't turn back now. If I messed up, my life was literally on the line. I tried not thinking about the numbing pain shooting up my wrists or the sweat pooling into my eyes. I stopped to catch my breath, and hung from my harness to give my hands a rest. While hanging upside down, I looked up and watched the clouds clear, giving me an amazing view. I knew Mob would be here soon. I had to keep moving; I couldn't let exhaustion get to me. *Keep putting one hand in front of the other.*

Finally, I made it to the shaft with a sigh of relief. A simple padlock sealed the steel grate, almost too easy. I muscled my way closer and inspected the lock. I could crack it even *with* the blood rushing to my head. I pulled my pins out, careful not to drop them. It took some patient tinkering, but the light snap sent a thrill up my spine. I took the lock off and let it fall. *Maybe it would shatter Mob's skull on the way down.* I unhooked my harness and crawled into the narrow opening. It smelled like sweet pine, and clean air bathed my face. They kept the hatch clean and neat for their workers. Meanwhile, we worked on pipes that could barely hold our weight. The wealthy cared little for me and mine, while I risked my neck to help them.

I forced myself through the small space, crawling higher into the bowels of the city. Soon, I would be right below street level. Unfortunately, with the enforced curfew and silence up top, I couldn't tell what part of the city I was under. I had to trust my instinct and skill; the farther I went, the closer I would be to Elysium, and by then I had to have passed the city gates. At the end of the shaft, I came upon a rain grate, simple steel bars that separated me from freedom. I stared out into the town square, scanning for any signs of the enemy. From there, it would be easy to get to Elysium unseen. I found the lock along the edge of the grating and went to work.

After opening the hatch, I peeked outside and found two elven guards in deep conversation, walking down the opposite avenue. I pulled myself out of the tunnel and ran to the nearest building. Leaning up against the wall, I waited for my eyes to adjust. I had to cross two blocks out in the open to reach Elysium. I knew I could make it easily without getting caught.

Once the guards walked out of sight, I ran. The sound of my feet clapping against the ground seemed so loud I worried it would bring a whole army on down my head, yet no one stirred. Odin said they had the outside of Empyrean fortified and relied heavily on the gates to keep them in. They thought the gods were imprisoned.

I held my breath and ran the rest of the way. The Elysium gates were closed with no guard on duty to open them. I looked up and down the block for any signs of life, but spotted nothing. The lights in the building were on and I could see people moving about inside. The gates had no lock to pick, so instead, I touched the tip of Jotunn to the bars. The steel iced over with a satisfying crackling. I kicked at the frozen bars until they shattered.

The Aegis lightly hummed and vibrated against my back. I took it off to examine it. A light yellow color resonated from its edges, thunder and lightning echoed in my head. Something in me begged to be found. I held the shield out before me and stepped through the broken bars. As I approached Elysium, the sounds grew louder and the vibrations became so strong it felt like being shocked. I tried to drop it, but my fingers wouldn't obey. The Aegis wanted to find Zeus, and I would not be able to stop until it did.

"Stop," someone yelled from behind.

I couldn't turn around. The Aegis pulled me toward Elysium, begging me not to stop.

The front doors opened and a figure stepped out, cascaded in light. Bang!

My thigh exploded in pain, and I fell to my knees.

"Anna? Is that my Anna?" A hollow voice echoed in my head. "It's been so long since I've seen my beautiful Anna."

I tried to focus past the pain and discomfort. My vision blurred, but I managed to see a bewildered Zeus shuffling toward me. He wore raggedy pajamas, a robe that half fell from his shoulders, and one slipper. Behind him, Hera took slow steps forward holding her hands up in case he should fall. My muscles froze, I couldn't move.

Zeus' eyes seemed wild and I wondered if mine looked the same. But for all his erratic movement, he kept coming toward me. "Anna, where have you been?" As soon as he drew near, the uncertainty in his voice cleared up. "My beautiful Ann—Aegis..." He reached for the shield. I held it out with weak arms and prayed he would take the burden. Guards shouted something I couldn't discern.

When Zeus' frail fingers touched the shield, a blinding white light erupted. I gasped for air and felt as if I were falling. I rolled back and a sharp blow rocked the back of my head as I hit solid ground, far, far away from where the white light encapsulated Zeus. Thunder raged and lightning cracked across the sky, bolt after bolt hit the funnel of light that circled the god. My skin charged with static and the smell of ozone wafted through the air.

When the light finally cleared, Zeus stood before me, his white beard perfect and his eyes intense. He radiated power. I tried to speak, but found no words. So instead, I fell into darkness as the world slipped away.

22

I woke up on a cot. My whole body felt like it'd been ripped to shreds and put back together wrong. I stared up at the ceiling, mesmerized by a flickering lightbulb. Bandages dressed my thigh, covering a dull ache that made me wonder why it didn't hurt as bad as it should. I tried to ignore a soft buzzing and figure out what happened. I needed to know if Seneca found Abby.

"You're awake," Mom said, her face coming into focus over me. "How do you feel?"

I tried to sit up, but gave up as soon as the pain shot through my spine. "I feel brass. Where are we?"

"You're back at the Crow's Nest. You've been out of it for a whole day."

"What? How did I get here?" I fought through the pain and forced myself to sit.

I felt a strong force approach.

"My savior has awoken." Zeus' voice thundered like a coming storm. His eyes sparked with lightning and focused all their power on me. "I have yet to think of a proper way to thank you my boy. You've done me a great service. I did my best with your wounds, but I dare not give you too much ambrosia. You'll still feel pain for some time."

"Thanks." I rubbed at my thigh. "So… you're all godlike now?"

"Yes and not a moment too soon. Even now, the forces of Mob are converging on us. My son's pride and joy will soon fall if we do not act soon."

"Your son, he's…"

"Hephaestus, creator of this metropolis, though he seems to have long since disappeared."

"No… Ares, I had to—he's dead. I had to kill him in order to get your Aegis back. He wanted me to tell you he was sorry," I lied.

Zeus took a deep breath and the air crackled around him. "I will not blame you for the death of my son. Truly, he died the moment he betrayed us. Yet still, he was my son and I cannot fault his nature. What had to be done was done."

I wasn't zapped into ash, so the day was definitely starting good. "So what now?"

"I would release Loki from his bonds, and raise the dead to fight off the Fey threat. But I owe you a debt, so I chose not to act."

"Why? What does this have to do with me?"

"Puck. He holds your friend hostage. He wants to speak to you. I will not make a move until I have the okay from you."

I got up and out of bed. The buzz slowly cleared up. Jotunn sat at my side, begging to be picked up. Shouting, screaming, clanking of steel against steel rang from outside. A war raged outside while I was in bed. I pushed past Mom who tried to steady me, and ran out into the main room. I looked out between the planks on the window at chaos. Bodies were laid out on the streets. Fey and Olympians fought, and casualties from both sides fell. The sky ran red like an ocean of blood and in the distance, the Iron Dragon make loops around the city, blowing billows of fire.

I turned to Zeus. "You have to stop this! Why aren't you fighting?"

"Zak, they have Abby and Seneca," Mom said. "Puck said they would be given to the dragon if the gods interfere. He wants you to come alone."

"Where are they?" I shouted.

"He's waiting for you at the cabin," Mom whispered. "But Zak, it's obviously a trap. I only just got you back."

Alice took my hand and looked at me with horror in her eyes, as if she felt sorry for me. I turned back to the window and watched as my world fell to chaos. Alice hugged me tightly and smiled. She believed in me.

"I have to stop this." I pushed my pain aside and went to the room where I awoke to gather my things. I put the wings on my back and embraced the call of Jotunn. Without the Aegis, the sword's chill took over my body. I would end this right now. I marched out. I turned to Zeus. "I'm going to get my girls back. Just be ready to unleash Hades on these rust heads."

"I'm coming with you," Mom said.

"No. He wants to talk to me. I should do it alone. I don't know why, but I feel like I have to."

"When the time is right," Zeus said, "just call my name."

I walked out into the street. Even though the fighting surrounded me, my peripheral seemed to blur. I ran straight for home. Nothing else mattered in those moments, Jotunn wanted Puck's blood and so did I. I pushed people out of the way and the Fey seemed to avoid me. Every step I took echoed in my ears, somewhere deep inside, I thought that perhaps this would be my last stand.

I will die tonight.

I ran through the streets to the Fringe edge. The Iron Dragon circled around as if taunting me, like a vulture waiting for its meal, ceasing its barrage of fire attacks. When I finally reached my cabin at the end of the world, the dragon dived over the side.

Three elves stood guard over Seneca. She sat on the road leading to my house, her hands tied behind her back. Two elves had their weapons drawn, and one held a leash with a raging Redcap pulling at the other end. I slowed my run down to a confident stride.

Seneca was the first to see me. "This is so awkward."

"Are you okay?" I asked.

"Yeah, perfectly fine. I was just about to overpower these guys and single handedly save Abby... but since you're here I guess I should be the bigger person and let you have your moment of glory. Get the girl and all that good stuff."

The elves looked back and forth from me to her. They tensed, ready for a fight.

Jotunn practically sang in my ears. "Thanks. I appreciate you putting me first."

"Do you think you will finally kiss? You have to kiss her after a daring rescue." Seneca made mock kissing sounds, then threw herself sideways into the closest elf, knocking him to the ground. I lunged at the second elf, he brought his sword up quicker than mine, but I ducked into a roll and came up on the other side of him. I slashed my blade across his back and kicked the newly formed ice patch into the Redcap. To my surprise, the Redcap didn't seem to care they were on the same team and went to quick work chomping on the elf's face, while the beast's handler tried to get it under control.

Seneca sat straddled across her fallen guard, head-butting him repeatedly in the face. I ran up behind her and cut her bindings. She expertly knocked the rust out of the elf, leaving him unconscious.

When she stood, she wavered, and her eyes spun. "Oh, dizzy."

Something slammed into me from behind, throwing me head first to the ground. Wild hands tore at my back. If it wasn't for Odin's pack, I'm almost certain the Redcap would have ripped its way to my stomach.

"The sword," Seneca shouted.

I hesitated. I didn't want to share Jotunn with anyone else. It was mine. The power was mine. The Redcap took a hold of my hair and pulled. I tried to angle the blade behind me but couldn't get a good position.

"Zak!" Seneca insisted.

I tossed her the blade. She caught it in midair and brought it down behind me. The satisfying squish of ice cutting flesh, and the crackling of the creature icing over filled me with a rush of satisfaction. I shoved the iced Redcap off my back and scrambled to my feet. The remaining guard took a nervous step back.

"The sword." I held my hand out to Seneca, fearing she wouldn't want to return it.

She gave it back without argument. "That sword makes me feel weird. Be careful with it, will you?"

I pointed it at the elf. "Just one more!"

He dropped his weapon and ran off.

"Where's Puck?" I asked Seneca.

"Out back, this way." She led me to the side of the cabin to a clearing overlooking the world below. My gaze went straight to my beautiful Abby, way too close to the edge. Puck stood beside her, a blade to her back. Ice-cold rage filled my heart.

"You've caused quite the stir, boy," he said. "It's not often someone can hurt my mother."

"Ugh," Seneca moaned. "Those two have such an unhealthy relationship."

Puck laughed. "Oh, Seneca Rose, always quick with the wit. Yet, Mob is awake, your kingdom has fallen, and the Iron Dragon and the armies of the Unseelie are marching. Soon, Olympus will be no more."

"Right. If everything is brass, why are you hiding behind a girl?" I asked.

"I may be arrogant, but I'm not stupid. Zeus and his kin can't stop us. But they can be incredibly annoying. I'd rather the destruction of the human race go down without a hitch so we can begin the process of healing this world. I'm sure you can appreciate that. And my mother thinks you are a problem that needs to be dealt with. It seems you and that sword have overstepped your boundaries."

"All I have to do is give Zeus the word."

"But you won't, because I have insurance." He shoved Abby closer to the edge. She looked defiant and struggled against her restraints.

"Are you okay?" I asked.

She nodded. "Zak. Tell this rust bucket to hop off!"

My heart kicked up a beat at the sound of her voice, making the chill of Jotunn ease off. When I heard her, I knew I would let the world burn just for her.

You will fall saving the one you love.

Puck still talked, but I wasn't hearing anything he said. I focused on Abby. I swear I could hear her every breath. I could feel her heart beating, and it beat in time with mine. She took a tiny step backward, toward the edge. I held my breath, paralyzed as she took another.

She nodded at me and I knew what she planned to do. "I trust you, Zak."

"Puck," I said. "I'm not a boy. My name is Zak Walker. If you don't know what that means, ask around. They'll tell you I'm rank true and true. I'm a Fringe Rat. The Money Men might not give a rust about me, but I've spent my whole life crawling around the guts of this city, making sure she runs brass, keeping her alive. This is my city, and I'm not letting a cog head destroy it. So I'll defend it to the end. And even though I got rank, I learned that sometimes I can use a little help. Zeus, now!"

Lightning and thunder circled in the sky like a vortex of chaos. A steady beam of electricity erupted and headed straight toward Earth. Before Puck could react, Abby leaped off the side. Time seemed to slow to a crawl.

If this was the story of my life and I died today, what would the story-tellers say about me? They'd say I was a hero.

I ran to the edge and jumped off headfirst. I knifed it, straightened my arms against my sides, and kept my legs pointed straight. Abby didn't scream or flail; she looked up at me with complete and utter trust. She held up her bound hands. I reached for them, inching closer and closer, feeling the pull of the Earth's gravity. I barely noticed the dragon swoop down behind us. Our fingers could barely touch.

A second more, and I grabbed a hold of her wrist. But the hold wasn't good enough. I needed both hands. Jotunn sang in my head. I still had the sword out. I couldn't let it go; I needed it. It made me more than I was. I looked to Abby, our eyes met for a moment—I swear she smiled. I let go of Jotunn and grabbed a hold of her with my free hand. I pulled until her body pressed against mine. She wrapped her arms around my neck.

The dragon flew up toward us, its mouth open wide. I pulled the ripcord on my wings and they burst out in a flutter of life, slowing our descent, but not quick enough. The dragon swooped in fast. Sparks of flame ignited in its throat. I pulled the other ripcord and the motor sputtered to life, straining against our weight, but soon we flew back toward Olympus with the dragon hot on our tail.

Years of being a Fringe Rat taught me skills. Skills I thanked the gods for at that moment. I flew us all around, swerving left and right, barely staying out of the dragon's path. Luckily for us, it was big. Even though it had a huge advantage in speed, it couldn't maneuver well. I flew circles around its head while heading for the city. I kept my distance, but couldn't get it off my back.

A horn blew so incredibly loud I thought it impossible. I feared my ears would explode. Abby screamed and I tried my best to cover hers. It sounded like the heavens themselves cried. I lost control; spun wrong, and clipped one of my wings on a building. We crashed and I tried my best to take the brunt of it so Abby would have my body as a cushion.

Feeling dazed and broken, I struggled to help Abby up, but I already knew we wouldn't escape. A ship of bone rose in the sky behind the dragon, as if crafted from the remains of a giant. Loki stood at the wheel; behind him, warriors shouted and clapped their swords to shields, Freya amongst them, wearing a glimmering suit of armor with wings.

Odin kept his promise.

They would never make it in time.

Abby looked up at me and I got lost in her eyes. "Zak, I'm glad you're here with me." That lavender scent came off her hair.

"…me too. I'm sorry I couldn't save you."

"It's okay," she said, "I love you."

As soon as she kissed me, all our memories together came flooding back like a tidal wave. When we were little, I stole some meds from her dad. As punishment, I had to work weekends at his office. She would order me around and I hated her for it. After that, she would always hang around me and the guys, even when I tried to get rid of her. She had a tendency of kicking our butts. Soon we were insepara- ble. When we became teenagers, something happened. She started to look and act different and I started to feel strangely toward her. Always too scared to say anything. I didn't want to look like a complete cog. I kept my feelings to myself, bottled up tight, even though everyone swore they knew. The last time I saw her, we fought. It wasn't our first serious fight, we said things and yet through it all, she still trusted me with her life.

"I love you too." I held her tight and kissed her harder.

2 3

The dragon opened its mouth and took a deep breath in. I waited for the inevitable end. The oily-fuel stink of its breath washed over us; the fire would soon follow. Abby pulled away from me and looked at the dragon. She would bravely stare death in the face. I did the same. Before the flames came, a shadow swooped in and grabbed us by the collars of our shirts. We held onto each other tight as we flew away from an explosion of fire, the world burning at our backs.

I looked up to Seneca struggling to hold our weight, veins popping from her neck, her face blood red. Yet she still wore a mischievous grin. She flew us to safety, smoke cascading from the tips of her copper and brass wings.

She choked out a laugh. "Told you you'd get a kiss!" She winked at me. The weight finally being too much for her, she dropped us close to the ground.

"You saved our lives!" Abby shouted.

She spun around in the air and curtseyed. "Yeah it happens. Sorry. Can't talk now. Revenge and stuff." She drew a sword and flew straight at the Iron Dragon. It launched at her, spewing flames of fire; she easily dodged and circled around its head, swinging her sword in wide arcs, attacking it at inhuman speed.

I untied Abby and held her hand as we ran through the streets, dodging fights as best we could. I wanted to get back into it, but I had to get her to safety. In my rush, I caught glimpses of battles. Alana ran after a horde of trolls, shooting them down one by one. She nearly had the last one when a shimmering pixie light attacked her. She waved her pistol wildly at her face trying to shoo the creature away. It distracted her enough for a troll to get the upper hand. He tackled her from the side and raised a fist. She maneuvered her legs under the monster and pushed him back, jamming her pistol under his chin. We already crossed the street by the time I heard the bang and splatter.

Gharis fought off two elves with his sword not too far from her. Watching his complicated legwork and the way he swung his sword with ease made me realize I had a lot to learn.

I couldn't find Zeus, but every time an Unseelie came into our path, a bolt of lightning vaporized them, followed by a rumble of thunder that sounded a lot like laughter. He was somewhere watching over me and helping to clear the path for my escape.

An explosion close by knocked Abby and me to the ground. I looked in the direction of the blast, up at a ship made of wood, flesh, and piping. Its balloon seemed to be made of living tissue while the mast breathed out steaming black smoke. Mob stood at the helm, shouting orders while her men fired cannons at the ship of bones. I finally caught sight of Zeus aboard Loki's ship, knocking cannonballs from the sky with quick bolts of lightning that sent them careening into surrounding buildings. A school of crows swarmed the Fey on deck and chased them overboard.

I stopped running and pointed at the ship. "The gods are fighting back!"

Abby followed my gaze as the flock of crows fused into a dark shadow. It marched toward Mob who appeared startled for only an instant. The shadow shook off the darkness, and in its place stood Odin. He wore leather armor and had a heavy two-handed sword at his side, both hands on the hilt ready for action. Mob lunged at Odin, but he managed to deflect her clawed hands with his blade. Lightning exploded next to her, nearly throwing her from the ship.

Zeus landed next to Odin, standing proud and tall. Both gods seemed like the best of friends while Mob struggled to her feet. A second mass of crows appeared out of thin air, cawing wildly and landing all around the deck. One by one, they struck at Mob, pecking at her skin and pulling at her hair. She fought them off savagely, but every time she destroyed one, another took its place.

Lightning crackled overhead. Zeus' hand shot up, catching the beam of electricity, and an explosion of blinding light erupted in the sky. We covered our eyes, cringing at the harshness of Mob's shrill cry.

"Zak," Abby said. "We have to go!" She dragged me toward the Empyrean.

I pulled her in the other direction. "No, wait. Your dad and everyone are at the Crow's Nest."

"That's at the Fringe; that's the most dangerous place to be during an attack!"

"No one had access to Empyrean."

She ran ahead. I barely made it two steps before an explosion of fire threw me to the ground. I rolled over onto my stomach in a daze, and Abby yelled something from beyond a wall of flames, but the ringing in my ears drowned out her voice. Puck aimed one of the cannons on Mob's ship at me, while the dragon and Seneca played a game of cat and mouse right above me.

"Abby, go! I'll meet you there." I hoped she could hear me over all the noise.

But I didn't have time to think about it, I focused on Seneca's battle. All her blows deflected harmlessly off the beast, and she moved too fast for it to land a strike. They could have fought forever, except Seneca slowed down. Whenever she got close to a tall building, she tried to land and catch her breath. The dragon wouldn't relent; it didn't breathe or tire. It couldn't be controlled… except… except it could be. I had an idea.

I fought my way to unsteady legs and ran across the street to the closest high building I could find. I shouldered my way past the door and ran inside. A scared family huddled around their young children.

"It's okay," I said. "Just stay inside."

The back stairs led me to the second floor and a long hallway of rooms. A small hatch in the ceiling was my best bet at getting to the roof. I pulled the cord that released the door, climbed the ladder into the attic, and went straight for the window. Even with my body sore and my limbs screaming in pain, I managed to climb out the window and reach for the roof edge. It gave me the perfect view of the beast inhaling air and getting ready for another shower of fire.

"Get out of here, Zak!" Seneca gasped on the roof of a building across the street. She waved me away. "I don't know if I can keep this up for much longer…"

"Use your blood," I shouted.

The explosion threw me from the building. Once again, death reached for me and I almost welcomed its embrace, except Seneca caught me. She could barely carry me, but she flew us away from the crumbling destruction. Mob's ship headed straight for us while Puck continued to fire.

"Seneca use your blood. Mob said her and the dragon were weapons of the family Rose. If the blood of a Rose can wake it, it can control it."

"Rust!" She flew me over to the ground and dropped me gently. "Might as well stay here and enjoy the show. If this doesn't work, we're all dead anyway." She bit into her finger; blood trickled down her hand and coated her lips. She turned back toward the dragon and flew straight for it. She yelled, "I am Seneca Rose, Heir to the family Rose, and you will bow down before me!" She flicked her hand at the dragon, letting drops of blood splash its face. The mechanical beast roared and snapped its teeth at her.

Seneca pulled a small knife from her belt and ran the blade across the palm of her hand. She flicked more blood at the beast, but this time held her bloody hand out toward it and let it see the crimson liquid. "I said, I am Seneca Rose of the family Rose and you will bow before me, rust brain!"

The dragon closed its mouth and bowed lower than Seneca. She reached out and placed her hand on its forehead. Seneca hopped onto its neck and used its horns as handholds.

"I think me and Gas Breath have a bone to pick with Puck." She patted the dragon on the side of the neck and yelled, "Hiya!"

The dragon flew off straight for Mob's ship, breathing fire like an endless hose of destruction. The masts and hull went up like dry tinder. Whoever was steering tried their best to turn the ship. *Bad move.* The dragon straightened like an arrow and flew clean into the ship's exposed side, shattering it into toothpicks. The stern flew in toward the city while the bow hurtled with a screaming Puck to the awaiting surface below.

With the dragon having switched sides, the Unseelie on the ground seemed a bit hesitant, but still they came. Loki docked his ship and let loose his warriors. Men and gods alike rushed into the battle with their weapons held high, shouting for Olympus. A man and woman with bronze skin and golden hair led the fighters; they looked so similar, they could have been twins. They shot arrows left and right without hesitation and all their arrows found their mark. The Unseelie who made it past their arrows fell to the swords and axes of all the fallen warriors Loki brought back. Meanwhile, Loki stood upon the deck of his ship with his arms crossed, bellowing with laughter.

I limped back toward the Crow's Nest, exhausted and ready to sleep for an eternity. Even though the war raged on, cheers of triumph already started to spread. Puck was gone, I'm pretty sure Mob had been sorted, and we had control of the Iron Dragon.

Abby, Mom, Dad, and Alice waited outside the Crow's Nest. As much as I wanted to run to them, I could barely walk. I took slow steady steps as the world around me burned. They waved. I smiled and tried to wave back. But my arm didn't want to work with me. They kept waving, wildly... almost panicked. Mom screamed. A searing pain buried itself deep into my back. I looked down and found a gleaming blade sticking out of my stomach.

I fell to my knees and then onto my back. Mob stood over me with an evil smile; even with badly burnt skin, fried hair, and festering blisters in a number of places, she still managed that sickening smile. She lifted her weapon up and inspected the blade before licking my blood off. She stewed in my defeat, almost gloating. "You've made an enemy of me boy; you'd be wise to die now."

"Zak!" Mom jumped over my body and swung a blade at Mob's neck. But the blade didn't connect with anything. Mob turned into thousands of little spiders, roaches, and crickets, which escaped into the city cracks.

Everything started to get cold. It reminded me of Jotunn. I could barely focus. Sounds and sights mixed and meshed into the wrong thing. I lay on my mother's lap, this I knew for sure. She said something. Her eyes lost in defeat. Abby sat at her side. I could barely feel the warmth of her hand. My dad stood in the background, crying openly. Everyone needed to calm down. It didn't hurt anymore; I would be fine. I just needed rest. So I decided to rest my eyes. I closed them, and the darkness engulfed me. I felt so light. Like soaring without wings. I wanted to soar forever, into the deepest darkest reaches of the empty void, without the shackles of my body. I could do that.

But a voice anchored me. A tiny voice, weak and frail, but at that moment the most important voice in all of existence.

"Zak," Alice said. "Please wake up, Zak… wake up…"

EPILOGUE

I know what you're thinking. Freya! She'll bring him back. Unfortunately, she could only bring back Demigods or Fey, which I wasn't. So there's that. I have to admit, if I died, it would have been a brass ending. I could have been remembered as a hero. If it were the end of my story, maybe. No, my story only just began. I couldn't die, not yet.

I woke up three days later. It didn't look good for a while; at least that was what they told me. Nevertheless, the Doc, along with the help of Zeus and my stubborn nature, managed to pull it together and bring me back from death's door. Everything hurt like a world of pain. I wouldn't let anyone else know that. Everyone looked at me like some sort of hero. It felt good. My recovery melded together as I lost track of when I dreamed and when I remained awake. The days Abby sat at my bedside, I felt great. I remember watching her sleep, her hand in mine. *This is paradise.*

The time I spent with Mom, Dad, and Alice felt strange. Dad practically changed into a different person; he gave up drinking. He and Mom were trying to give it a second shot, and if it didn't work out, Alice would still be well cared for. By the way, she started talking a lot, sometimes too much! We weren't a perfect family, but we had to try and that'd was what counted. A family tries.

Seneca went off with the Iron Dragon. She planned to hide it somewhere on Earth. She wasn't looking to deal with that sort of responsibility and wanted to get rid of it as soon as she could. As much as Oberon protested.

Yup, Freya did her thing and brought back Seneca's parents too. The Seelie Court started rebuilding and pushing the remnants of Unseelie back into their territories. Oberon and Zeus had also been in talks, getting a treaty together where humans and Fey could coexist. The political rust went over my head. I just felt brass everyone started crewing up, because of things I set in motion.

On my first night home, back in our cabin at the end of the world, I had a visitor. I sat on the porch watching the stars when he appeared next to me.

"You look well," Zeus said.

"Not nearly as well as you," I said.

"I will forever be in your favor," he said.

I gave him the most arrogant of smiles.

He took in my home with an unimpressed stare. "Do you plan on living out the rest of your life here?"

"Not sure I have much choice," I said. "It's the life I was given."

"Well, I present you with the opportunity to decide where your life goes from here, by arranging for you to attend school in Empyrean."

"What?" I choked. Facing Iron Dragons and evil Fey was one thing. But going to school in Empyrean was a whole other horror.

"Don't be so delighted," he said. "However, be warned, I have only offered you the chance to attend. It's up to you to prove that you belong there."

"I'm grateful, it's brass of you and all… but I just can't. I—"

"You what? Plan to rot here in this cabin forever? Will you be content slowly withering away as the world goes on without you? Always remembering that one time you were more than just a cog in the gears of fate…"

"I…" I didn't know what to say. "I need time to think."

The cabin door opened, and Alice ran out to my side. She hugged me tightly and looked up at Zeus with wide eyes. I looked down at her and ran my hand through her hair.

Zeus knelt down close to Alice. "Your brother is quite the hero isn't he?"

She slowly nodded.

"Do you believe he's meant to do great things?" Zeus asked.

Alice looked at me and smiled her big beautiful heart-melting smile. "Zak is the bestest!"

That's when I knew my decision. "Okay, I'll go… I just don't know what you expect."

Zeus waved me off. "I expect you to become the man I know you were meant to be."

"Right, then," I said, holding out my fist. "We're crew, true and true."

Zeus looked at my hand with a raised eyebrow.

I took his hand and brushed his knuckles against mine. "You're right. I wasn't meant to rot here. This will always be my home, but there's so much more for me to do. I've already mastered being a Fringe Rat, now it's time for the next challenge." I looked at Alice, who smiled in return. "It's time the world knew my name."

Fin.

ABOUT THE AUTHOR

WILBERT STANTON IS AN AUTHOR, SCREENWRITER, AND DREAMER...

Wilbert Stanton is a YA, SF, and Fantasy author. While he has a love for these genres, he has authored a variety of short stories that branch out into others.

Wilbert is also a screenwriter with a passion for horror and drama. He has worked on both short and feature films, while perfecting his pilot Born Entertainers.

Born and raised in New York City, Wilbert learned to embrace the diversity and beauty of the world from a young age. He's studied Psychology, Computer Science, and is now completing his English degree at Hunter College. Using life experiences, and his love of 80s SF/Fantasy as inspiration, he's created magical worlds that are both exciting and nostalgic.

He's also an avid gamer and loves all things geek!

LOOKING FOR MORE?

Visit www.immortalworks.press for more about this author and other enthralling books.